To

Carol

What Becomes of the

Brokenhearted?

Rachel Crawford

with thanks

'e Best wishes

Rachel Crawford

Crediton 24/10/15

i

Dedicated to Lance Corporal Jamie Fleming,
his parents, Alison and Stewart and his brother, Rory.

Prologue
2353 hours, 26 September 2012

Dinger cautiously unlocked the tin box then placed his suicide letter over his stash of tablets. He tried to block out the sight of the tin's other inhabitant, Suzanne's red knickers. Fortunately, his goodbye letter had been much easier to pen than the stupid farewell ones he had been forced to write before his deployment.

His suspicions might be unsubstantiated but Dinger was convinced the bullet that had taken Bradley's life had been meant for him. As his actions had deprived Suzanne's child of a father, forging new memories, when his friend could not, was inconceivable.

Once the evidence of his future plans was secured, Dinger stared at the round silver disc next to the key. Gently lifting it towards his lips, Dinger kissed Bradley's dog tag then ran his finger over best friend's name. "See you soon mate," he told his friend whilst returning his key chain around his neck.

Chapter 1

1132 hours, 27 September 2012

Ella being struck dumb suited Nicky. After all she wished to vent not chat. It was too late to voice her opinion regarding her own banishment but that wasn't going to stop her letting Ella know how she felt about Suzanne abandonment.

"Can you tell me what gives you the right to turn up after all these years, fuck up my daughter's life and then piss off again?" Nicky raged. Ella remained silent. "My lass is in tatters thanks to you. First the paperwork for the DNA test turns up, then that stuck up bitch tells Susie she's not allowed to see you anymore. I thought you said your bosses wouldn't remove you?" When Ella failed to respond Nicky continued, "Oh I get it, you removed yourself. Couldn't give my lass a day or two to get over saying goodbye to the love of her life before you did your fucking disappearing act again?" Silence. "Well? Answer me you selfish bitch, I know you're there. I can hear you breathing."

Afraid of Larry's reaction if she revealed the caller's identity, Ella desperately tried to string a sentence together that would not alarm her husband. "I didn't... I mean it wasn't me who..."

"If not you then who? Oh wait a minute, I get it. Limp Dick's still calling the shots?"

Nicky's reference to Larry infuriated Ella enough to let down her guard. "If you are referring to my husband your description is as inaccurate as your assumptions. Neither I, nor Larry, asked for my removal. As for fucking up lives, can I point out that your arrival back in mine nearly cost me my marriage and may well have cost me my career?"

Larry quickly jumped to his feet and attempted to snatch the phone from his wife. Swinging around Ella place her palm over the receiver and shook her head. "No, Babes, she needs to hear this from me." Before he could answer Ella returned the phone to her ear just in time to catch something about DNA. She cut Nicky short. "For God's sake I know it's not ideal but she shouldn't let Paul goad her. He knows Bradley's the father. Once she's had the test she can take the results and tell the annoying little fart to shove them."

"And what if they prove Bradley's not the father? What then?"

"Don't be daft of course the baby's Bradley's!" Ella yelled.

"Well I'm glad you're sure," Nicky snapped sarcastically.

"But…" Ella stumbled; Nicky's insinuation had knocked the wind out of her.

"Oh for fuck's sake, why did you have to keep harping on about the money?" Nicky raged. "Susie needs to believe she's having Brad's baby more than she needs cash. There's no way she'll take that test. Tell the little shit he's won. He and his tramp of a wife can piss every penny up against the wall."

When tears sprang to his wife's eyes Larry successfully grabbed the phone, hit the red button then removed the SIM card.

2224 hours, 27 September 2012

Curled up in Larry's arms, Captain Ella Harris pleaded with her brain to switch off. Last night her husband's absence and her constant evaluation of her behaviour over the past thirteen days had made sleep impossible. Tonight he was home and, although she was mortified to find out the reasons for her removal from CVO duties, she no longer had to ponder them. Sadly, something else was now crippling her ability to slumber - she was desperate for news of Bradley's loved ones.

Ever since her Commanding Officer had ordered her to take a leave of absence, whilst he investigated her conduct regarding the care of those closest to Lance Corporal Bradley Craig, Ella had been in turmoil. Thoughts of how she had failed the brave young soldier and left a nasty stain on her previously unblemished career tortured her.

She had been aware that withholding information regarding her connection to Bradley's fiancée could land her in the poo. It was just the depth of the excrement she had failed to consider.

At first it had been easy to blame Bradley's runt of a stepfather for her predicament but now, staring at the ceiling, Ella accepted that the majority of Paul's accusations were justified. She had prayed for Suzanne, not Bradley's mother, Linda, to inherit the soldier's estate. She had planted the seed in Rick Pashley's head regarding his future grandchild's entitlement to Bradley's estate and she had failed to contact Paul when Linda had collapsed on the day of the funeral. Undeniably, she did prefer Bradley's fiancée's company to that of his mother's. In her defence, her preference had nothing to do with the girl being Nicky's daughter and everything to do with Linda's lack of concern over her eldest son's death. Unfortunately she couldn't see that explanation winning her any favour at a disciplinary hearing.

The only allegation Ella could completely refute was her reason for taking the appointment of Casualty Visiting Officer. Saying she had requested the assignment in order to secure Bradley's estate for her friend's daughter could not be further from the truth. If Ella had suspected that the soldier's fiancée had the slightest connection to the woman who had wrestled her to the ground nineteen years earlier, she would have crushed Usain Bolt's record in a bid to distance herself from the girl.

Paul sharing his accusations with the press might have put her career at risk but it had been her own cowardly behaviour that had jeopardised her marriage. The pain she'd felt from revisiting her old stomping ground and facing Nicky paled into insignificance when she thought of how she had nearly lost Larry. For over twenty years not only had he put her career ambitions before his own, he had nursed her through her eating disorders and failed IVF attempts then forgiven her when she took another lover. Even at that dark hour Larry had not headed for the door, yet within hours of hearing of Nicky's reappearance he had done just that.

Try as she might to convince herself that Larry's return was all that mattered, Ella couldn't stop thinking about Bradley's brood. Was Linda agoraphobic? Ella knew little of the condition but it would certainly explain Bradley's mother's inability to attend her son's funeral. Linda had definitely wanted to, she had spent all morning preparing for the event, and yet when the time to leave came, she had collapsed in the hallway. The memory of Linda ripping her hat from her head then attempting to remove her dress, whilst screaming out her son's name, made Ella shudder.

When had Linda last left Garvey Grove? To Ella's knowledge Paul ran all necessary errands and even bought his wife's clothes. If that was the case how could he be oblivious to her condition? But, if he did know, why encourage her to attend the funeral?

'*The money,*' Ella's inner voice offered.

Surely Paul didn't believe the twelve thousand pounds his mother-in-law had offered would miraculously enable his wife to step outside. Maybe she was mistaken about Linda's condition. There were plenty of other possible explanations. The thought of bidding her son farewell or her recent acquaintance with sobriety could have caused her breakdown. Maybe the drugs she was taking for her alcoholism had caused some chemical imbalance in the woman's brain.

'*Stop thinking about Linda and get some sleep.*' Her inner voice pleaded.

Ella ignored it. If Linda did have agoraphobia, what next? Given how difficult Paul had found it to cope with his wife's battle against alcohol addiction, would he ignore this new ailment? Carry on as they had for the last God knows how many years?

How would Linda's parents, Joyce and Charlie, be affected by what they had witnessed yesterday? Seeing their daughter in such a state must have been heartbreaking. Joyce had reluctantly left her daughter in Charlie's care while she attended Bradley's funeral. What had she found on her return? Ella's feelings of hopelessness increased when she realised Bradley's grandmother would never be able tell her. In the last thirteen days she had grown extremely close to the lad's grandparents, especially Joyce. Never speaking to her or her lovable husband again was unthinkable.

As for Suzanne, Ella's mind was racing with possible scenarios that might explain the question mark regarding her child's genealogy. Earlier, Larry had quickly dismissed her theory that the girl must have been raped. He was not in the least bit surprised Nicky's daughter had been unfaithful. What did Ella expect when the girl's mother was a self-centered tart who had left Suzanne in the care of her stepfather so she could run back to a man who used to rearrange her face more than Ella did the furniture?

5

Larry concluded it had been the girl's destiny to end up in such a predicament. With a mother like Nicky and being raised on an estate mainly populated by single mothers it was the obvious outcome. Maybe Bradley's demise was God's way of punishing her for trying to saddle a decent lad with another man's child. Her husband's harsh words pained Ella. Not only because they were so callous but they were totally out of character. Nicky really did bring out the worst in him. Although Larry loved to chastise her for only seeing the good in people she knew it was also his preferred option.

Even though infuriated by Larry's lecture, Ella allowed him to berate her without reproach. She was grateful for his return so bit her tongue whilst he listed her many failings. She was too trusting, too forgiving and too willing to put others before herself and her family. She needed to accept, no matter how much she willed it, she could not make bad people good. His lesson endeth by pointing out her insistence to see the best in people would inevitably end up with her feeling foolish and let down. Given the revelation regarding Suzanne's unborn child, Ella felt both.

When Paul had originally alluded to Suzanne's unfaithfulness, Ella had struggled not to render him unconscious. The discovery his accusations were not unfounded brought bile to her throat. On first meeting Paul and Linda, Ella had been tempted to give credence to Larry's belief that some people did bad things for sheer enjoyment. Still, even after Nicky's disclosure, Ella found it hard to believe that Suzanne would willingly betray Bradley. She chose not to convey these doubts to Larry.

Once he'd said his piece, Ella made a conscious effort not to mention any of the inhabitants of her childhood stomping ground. Instead, she grovelled profusely, begging Larry's forgiveness for not informing him sooner that Nicky had resurfaced. He, in turn, apologised for leaving her alone to deal with the trauma of Bradley's funeral.

By means of recompense, Larry cooked up a sumptuous meal. Later, when Ella complained of overeating, Larry's suggested way to work off the calories resulted in her running upstairs whilst discarding her clothing. Given the energy she had used in an effort to keep her slim figure surely sleep would embrace her soon.

6

Chapter 2

Entering the kitchen Ella was greeted by the smell of bacon and the sound of her husband's laughter.

Recognising DJ, Christian O'Connel's voice on the radio, Ella giggled, "What's Richie done this time?" She asked.

The phone ringing dissuaded Larry from enlightening his wife as to why Christian was lampooning his sidekick yet again.

Ella felt a mixture of euphoria and nausea when she heard Jess's voice. She desperately wanted to discover what damage she had done to her career but not of the punishment it would generate.

"Is there something wrong with your mobile? I've been trying you all morning." Jess asked.

"Yes, sorry about that. Thought it best to remove the SIM card as most of the people I am prohibited from speaking to have that number," Ella replied sulkily.

"I think temporarily suspended, would be a more fitting description."

"Meaning?"

"That Bradley's grandmother can be quite formidable. She has refused to deal with anyone until you are reinstated. So has his father. Even better, Paul is no longer in the equation. Charlie's thrown him out."

"Oh my God. Where has he gone?"

"Why would you care? This whole mess is down to him. If he hadn't gone running to the tabloids you'd be visiting his wife instead of me."

"How is Linda?"

"Joyce is looking after her but insists she needs your help. She called Mrs Horton-Smythe and told her Linda was too ill to cope with a new CVO. Apparently she's a bit shy and doesn't like strangers," Jess sniggered.

"Well that's partly true. She can't stand anyone, including strangers. I bet the General was furious when he found out Joyce had involved his wife."

"According to Bradley's father General Horton-Smythe was very sympathetic."

"Rick spoke to the General?" Ella gasped in disbelief.

"Yes, he informed him that Paul's allegations were unjust and malicious. He insisted that he alone had secure legal representation for Suzanne's baby so if you were disciplined in any way, because of his actions, he would have no option but to go to the newspapers himself."

"Really? I can't believe it."

"And I can't believe you didn't warn me how drop dead gorgeous he is. I went all unnecessary when I met him."

"I take it you're talking about Rick, not the General."

"I'll ignore that. Anyway, maybe I should get to the point. The CO wants to see you. Do you think you could pop in around eleven?"

0858 hours, 28 September 2012

For once Larry was the one pushing his breakfast around his plate. The prospect of his wife's reinstatement as CVO for the Douglas's troubled him. "Did Jess say anything about Nicky and Suzanne?" He asked.

"No. If Susie is blaming me for the DNA thing she probably won't want me around. Anyway, as the reason I was ordered not to contact her remains, I doubt I'll be reassigned to her."

"What reason?"

"I've got history with her mother."

"Haven't you just? Let's hope it remains 'History'. Last thing we need is that cow hanging around." Larry pushed his half eaten breakfast to one side and picked up his coffee. "I'm pleased Joyce and Rick have spoken up for you but if you are reinstated I think you should insist someone else looks after Suzanne."

"I don't think I'm in a position to barter but I'll make it clear that would be my preferred option. I doubt it will come to that. My previous connection to Suzanne's family will be seen as a conflict of interest. Plus, if it turns out the child isn't Bradley's, I'm not sure she would be entitled to a CVO." Ella hoped she would. Suzanne definitely needed support. Deep down she dearly wished she could be the one to administer it but could not risk Larry leaving again if she voiced this.

1100 hours, 28 September 2012

Ella's meeting with the Commanding Officer was a total contrast to her last. Instead of listening to all her shortcomings as a CVO she was commended on the bond she had managed to forge with Bradley's family.

The CO was satisfied the majority of Paul's accusations were nothing more than sour grapes. With Joyce's guidance, Linda had stated that, even though neither of them had behaved in a manner deserving of such consideration, Ella had been patient and compassionate when dealing with her and her husband. Bradley's mother had also rejected Paul's claims that Ella had attempted to sabotage their chances of inheriting Bradley's estate. To support this statement, Linda pointed out that Ella had drafted a letter to enable her to receive the ADT money.

Ignoring that during their last conversation, Ella had openly admitted she would rather Suzanne inherit Bradley's estate, the CO informed her, given the lack of evidence regarding Mr Douglas' allegations, she was to be reinstated as CVO for Bradley's family. Due to Ella's connection to Suzanne's mother, the girl would remain in Jess' care. Although it was the result Larry had hoped for Ella couldn't help feeling a pang of disappointment. "What if I bump into Suzanne or her family whilst I'm visiting Mrs Douglas?" She asked.

"No one is saying you have to ignore the girl. If you should cross paths there is nothing wrong with enquiring about her or the baby's wellbeing just steer clear of anything to do with Bradley's estate or family." Ella's smile caused the CO to scowl. "That does not mean you can actively seek her out. Jess is her CVO so you have no reason to visit. If you choose to there will be consequences," he warned. "There is likely to be a legal battle between Suzanne's unborn child and Mrs Douglas and you cannot get caught in the middle."

"Is that still ongoing? I thought Suzanne had changed her mind about pursuing Bradley's estate."

"What makes you say that?" The CO asked suspiciously.

9

Although fearful of the repercussions Ella decided to be truthful. "Her mother rang me yesterday." Sensing the CO's anger, Ella quickly continued, "I made it clear I was no longer her point of contact however before she accepted that, she confessed the baby might not be Bradley's after all."

"Oh." was the only response the CO could muster but his disappointment was evident.

"I think Suzanne would rather go through life penniless than to discover her child isn't Bradley's. There is no way she will agree to a DNA test."

"I see," the CO answered despondently. "The problem is Mr Pashley engaged the lawyers, not Suzanne. Does he know the baby might not be his grandchild?"

"I doubt it." Ella shook her head. "If only the bloody will would turn up. One of Bradley's colleagues is adamant they signed each others."

Her words flicked the CO's tilt switch. "Ella, I hope you are not going to start will chasing again. Maybe Bradley discovered Miss Jarvis was sleeping around and recalled his will, have you thought of that?"

"I suppose, but according to his unit it was sent to Glasgow so how come they never logged it as received?"

"Stop right there." The CO took a deep breath. "I take it you want to remain CVO for Bradley's family?"

"Yes, sir."

"Then I am ordering you to forget about the will. Your fixation with the document has caused enough grief. Leave it to the lawyers. Assist Lance Corporal Craig's family in any way possible but if they have any questions regarding their inheritance put them in touch with the relevant agencies then desist from assisting further. Understood?"

"Yes, sir" Ella replied meekly.

"Good. Now, why don't you visit Lance Corporal Craig's grandmother and see if there is anything you can do for her or her daughter. You might also want to thank her and the boy's father for intervening on your behalf. The General was touched by their loyalty. Believe it or not, he was the one who recommended your reassignment. He still thinks you were highly unprofessional but, as he knows first hand how important support is when you lose a loved one, he's prepared to overlook your deficiencies on this occasion. Be careful though, he has given you just enough rope to hang yourself so make sure you don't kick over the stool."

1132 hours, 28 September 2012

Jess was eagerly awaiting Ella's departure from the CO's office. "Well, can I give you these back?" She asked holding out two envelopes.

"I guess so," Ella replied taking Bradley's farewell letters to each of his parents. "Do you still have Suzanne's and the one for the baby?"

"Yes and Father O'Sullivan has his brother's and grandparents'. He didn't want to deliver them until Rick and Linda got theirs. As they were both refusing to deal with me we decided to see how your interview went."

"Best we get Father O on the phone to synchronize our watches then," Ella suggested. "Rick flies back to Australia on Wednesday so we need to get a move on."

Due to Linda's current battle with the booze, open spaces and her husband, it was decided Joyce should be present when her daughter received her letter. This meant she would need to receive her correspondence first so Father O suggested he escort Joyce home after Sunday mass and ask her to ensure Charlie was there. At the same time Ella and Jess would hand Rick and Suzanne their correspondence. Once Joyce had recovered from the shock of hearing from Bradley, she would be asked to deliver the two remaining letters to her daughter and grandson. Ella and Father O would offer their assistance if Joyce thought the task too burdensome.

Holding up Suzanne's letter Jess looked awkward. "I'm not sure how she's going to react. She held herself together for the funeral but now she won't dress or speak, well not to me. She just sits and stares at the floor. Apart from the occasional sob, she's practically catatonic."

The subsequent tears that trickled down Ella's cheek did not fall for Suzanne but for another young girl. Although it had been over three years since the officer had met Julie Dunn their one encounter was always lurking, ready to trigger such emotion.

28 June 2009

It was six years since she had knocked on Marjorie Grant's door to break the news of her husband's death but the memory of the woman's reaction still haunted her. Learning her second Casualty Notifying Officer duty did not involve a fatality eased the tightness in Ella's stomach.

Reading the details of Rifleman Dunn's injuries Ella considered her reprieve a minor one. Hours earlier the young soldier had heard the sickening click as his foot landed on an improvised explosive device. He was now in a military hospital in Afghanistan fighting for his life. Sadly he'd already lost the battle to save his legs and left hand.

At nineteen years old, Jack Dunn was still a boy; a boy who now faced a life of challenges and suffering. As for his eighteen years old wife, she hadn't signed up for this when they, and their three month old baby, had happily left the registry office two weeks prior to his deployment.

Captain Lewis, the Unit Families Officer, greeted Ella and Staff Sergeant Melanie Hamilton then quickly informed them of the young family's background. The story grew sadder by the minute. Julie Dunn had grown up in care and had no family support nearby. As she had only been in her married quarter a few months she had not cemented any meaningful friendships with the other wives. The only person Julie spoke to regularly was her neighbour, Lizzy. Being a seasoned army wife, Lizzy had endeavoured to guide Julie through the highs and lows of marrying a man in green.

Captain Lewis addressed Melanie, "I know you've probably been brought along to hold the baby but as Lizzy's looked after Julie since young Dunn was deployed I think the girl will find it easier handing the child over to her." Captain Lewis turned his attention to Ella. "My Colour-Sergeants round at Lizzy's now getting her prepared."

"Is Julie aware there has been an incident?" Ella asked cautiously. In the past well-intentioned soldiers had phoned their wives to reassure them they were not the casualty currently being

12

reported on Sky news. Unfortunately, this had resulted in the true identity of the injured party escalating around camp, thus making notification a race against the gossips.

"No, the poor girl's oblivious. Our lads know better than to phone home when something goes down and the press haven't reported anything yet."

Opening the door Julie Dunn put her finger to her lips and whispered, "I've just got him down for a nap." Assessing her visitors, Julie's smile faded. She had no idea who the two women were. Seeing Lizzy hovering about behind added to her confusion. Something was definitely troubling her neighbour.

Ella spoke first. "Mrs Dunn, I'm Captain Harris, I need to speak to you about your husband. Do you think we could come in?"

Most wives tried to mentally prepare themselves for the knock on the door but it seemed Jack becoming a casualty had not occurred to the young girl. Confused, Julie looked toward Lizzy who stepped forward, took her hand and led her away from the door. "Come on pet, let's go in the front room." Ella and Mel gratefully followed.

Lifting the baby's carrycot, Lizzy assured Julie she was only taking the child into the kitchen whilst the officer explained the reason for her visit. After reluctantly watching her friend leave, the girl swung around and eyed up Ella suspiciously.

Once the words, "I'm afraid I have some bad news. Your husband has been injured," were spoken, Julie shut down. As Ella explained that it was too early to judge the extent of Jack's injuries the girl failed to react to any of the information being offered. Worried her carefully prepared speech was falling on deaf ears, Ella joined Julie on the couch then gently touched the young mother's wrist. The girl was rigid. Taking hold of her hand, Ella repeated that once Jack was well enough to return to the UK, the girl would be taken to him. Her reassurances failed to provoke a response. Ella looked to Mel who shrugged then mouthed 'Shall I get the neighbour?' Ella nodded.

"And call out the unit's doctor," she whispered.

The next forty five minutes were excruciating. Even when her child started to cry, Julie remained stoic. The doctor said he

13

had heard of cases where individuals blocked out 'negative' language to allow them the pretence that the event had never occurred. He suspected Julie was currently in self preservation mode so they would need to coax her back to reality. Once his examination was complete, Lizzy placed her arm around the girl's shoulders and attempted to fill the awkward silence with promises of help when Jack came home. Although Julie did turn to face her neighbour it soon became obvious by her vacant stare that none of Lizzy's words were breaking down the wall erected in her mind.

Watching, Ella wondered how the girl would react when she finally allowed her brain to process the news she had just heard and what the future would hold for the young family when Jack did return. There would be years of rehabilitation for his mind as well as his body. Would Julie be strong enough to pull him through? The baby was a blessing. He would give Jack something to focus on other than his horrific injuries. Then again, realising you would never play football with your son or teach him to ride a bike must be soul destroying.

Ella tried to recall the more uplifting stories she had heard; the ones of injured soldiers achieving incredible things; climbing mountains, running marathons, becoming para Olympians. She prayed Jack Dunn would set himself similar goals.

The Casualty Visiting Officer's arrival meant Ella was free to go. Ashamedly, she was grateful to escape the hopelessness of the Dunn's living room. Her inability to assist crippled her. Julie Dunn's short-lived happiness as an army wife was well and truly over. With that sad thought Ella headed for the door.

Within minutes of driving away the officer had to pull over. Her vision was too impaired to see the road ahead. As Mel was also failing to keep her emotions in check, she quickly passed her boss a tissue then wept openly.

1146 hours, 28 September 2012

Jess was unconvinced that Ella's reinstatement as CVO had caused her current emotional state but, as her colleague seemed determined not to offer an honest explanation, she allowed Ella to retreat to her office to fetch her CVO Log book.

Once at her desk, Ella quickly logged on to the Human Resources system, typed in Private Howard Jackson's service number then nervously scanned for details of his will. The CO had only warned her not to chase Bradley's will but she was pretty sure if he found out she was investigating his friend, Beetle's, he would be equally perturbed. Jess was expecting her back in her office so they could compare CVO notes. The last thing she needed was the CO's right hand woman to come looking for her and catching her in the act so she would have to move fast.

Chapter 3

1357 hours, 28 September 2012

Walking on to the Haddington, Ella felt the same apprehension she'd had on the day of Bradley's death. That time she was fearful of confronting someone she hadn't seen for nineteen years, now she was fearful of engaging people she had know for less than nineteen days.

Rushing up the stairs to number thirty-three, Ella was relieved to arrive at Linda's door. Joyce quickly ushered her into the hallway then opened her arms. "I don't know if this is allowed but I think you deserve a hug young lady. Is that okay?"

"I think I'm the one that should be hugging you," Ella said accepting the show of affection. "I can't thank you enough for speaking up for me."

"Nonsense love. You didn't deserve any of the bullshit Paul spouted, I'm just sorry we got you into bother," Joyce said releasing her grip. "Lucky Mrs Horton-Smythe gave me her number after the funeral. Not so sure her husband'll be too chuffed though. After our little chat I had the feeling he was in for an earful."

"And then Rick called him!" Ella grimaced.

"I know, that was my idea," Joyce grinned. "Rick was happy to help. He did feel a bit rotten threatening to go to the newspapers though. Especially after the General had been so nice at the service."

"Who is it, mum?" A groggy Linda out.

"It's Ella love, she's come to see how you are," Joyce replied.

"How are you feeling today?" Ella asked brightly as she entered the living room.

"I'm a single, alcoholic, agoraphobic who missed her son's funeral. How do you think I feel?" Linda whined.

"Come on love, enough of that. Thought we'd agreed no more pity parties. Onwards and upwards." Joyce said with forced enthusiasm. "Take a seat Ella, I'll put the kettle on."

On the officer's first visit to number thirty-three she had met Linda, the drunken, foul-mouthed hag. Less than a week later she had been greeted by sober, manic Linda and two days ago she had left hysterical, frightened Linda laying on the couch being soothed by her father. The Linda that stared vacantly at her now disturbed her the most. Once again, her thoughts returned to Julie Dunn.

She had replayed the words she had used to notify the girl over and over again in her head. What could she have said differently to better prepare Julie? Had she blurted out the news too quickly? Should she have let Lizzy and the child remain in the room?

According to the pyschaiatrist, Jack's injuries had caused memories of Julie's childhood traumas to resurface. Sadly her unfortunate past had left her terrified of facing an uncertain future. Thankfully, before jumping in front of the train, she had pushed the baby's pushchair towards her mother-in-law.

1423 hours, 28 September 2012

The fear that she might have somehow contributed to Julie Dunn's suicide always reduced Ella to tears.

"Are you okay love?" Joyce asked.

Looking up Ella took the proffered mug, smiled weakly then blinked away the evidence of her distress. "Oh my God. I'm so sorry Joyce, my mind was elsewhere."

"Anything I can help with? Last couple of days must've been hard on you."

"Believe me it's nothing to do with that." Ella look quizzically at Joyce, "When memories pop into your head, do you ever feel the same emotions you did at the time they happened?'

"Often, but normally I just want to thump somebody, not cry." Joyce laughed, "Mind you, that somebody's usually my Charlie."

Ella smiled. "I can't imagine him doing anything that would warrant such violence."

Joyce looked towards her daughter, hoping Linda would relish the chance to castigate her father but she seemed oblivious to their conversation. Turning her attention back to Ella, Joyce shrugged. "I'll not burst your bubble lass, if you want to think my husband's perfect you crack on. I know the feeling's mutual. If you were twenty years older I'd be worried."

"And I might give you cause to be," Ella teased.

Linda slowly rose from her seat. "I'm gonna go up for a lie down mum."

"Okay, lovey. I'll give you a shout when dinner's ready." Once Linda had left the room, Joyce lowered her voice. "It's the medication that's making her like that. Doctor says once they sort the dosage out she'll be back to normal. Charlie asked him not to bother; says he prefers her this way, less gobby."

Joyce held up a plate of mini rolls, when Ella declined she held the plate higher. Defeated, the officer took the cake and unwrapped it.

Patting Ella's hand, Joyce smiled ruefully, "I wanted to thank you for practically carrying me out of here the other day. I don't think I would've made it to the church without you."

Although it had only been two days ago, Joyce's near collapse after seeing the crowd waiting to pay their respects on the day of Bradley's funeral, seemed like eons ago to Ella.

"I must admit the whole thing is a bit of a blur," Joyce continued. "Can hardly remember anything after Linda's funny turn." Joyce stopped speaking for a moment whilst both women recalled Linda trying to rip her clothes off whilst hitting her head with a lit cigarette.

"I'm glad Charlie pushed me outta the door. If he hadn't I would never have met the General's wife and that little posh lass would still be sat here looking like a rabbit caught in the headlights." Joyce grinned. "Don't get me wrong Jess's nice enough, she's just not one of us, if you know what I mean. Doubt she's ever set foot on a council estate, let alone chatted with the locals. She can't understand half of what Charlie says. Just as well really 'cos he keeps harping on about her not having enough life experience to deal with the likes of us. My Charlie was adamant it was you or nobody. Of course I felt the same."

Jess was one of the most educated people Ella knew. At twenty-six she seemed to have degrees in degrees, and a bucket full of A-Levels, two of which were in languages. Inwardly Ella chuckled, even after living in Sheffield for nine months, Jess was still to master the 'de da' language of Yorkshire.

"I'm really touched you both stood up for me," Ella told Joyce. "If you hadn't my bosses might have believed Paul's accusations."

"Please don't mention that idiot. He only turned up here with a bag full of booze after the funeral. I thought Charlie was going to kill him."

"I heard he'd thrown him out."

"Yes, he did and then insisted we stay with Linda in case the runt comes back."

"So you're both living here?"

"For the time being. Can't say it's ideal but at least Linda's getting on better with her dad. He's been brilliant with her. He's the one sussed out the agro-whatsit."

"Agoraphobia?"

"That's it. He saw summat on the box. Quizzed her for ages about it. Seems she hasn't set foot out of this place for years," Joyce said shaking her head. "I just thought the lazy mare was happy for Paul to fetch and carry for her. She's not exactly sociable so her not going to the pub or attending family get togethers didn't ring alarm bells. I used to get so angry with her for not going to parents' evenings though. Then there was Bradley's Pass Out Parade. She wouldn't entertain it, I guess I know why now."

"Someone must have noticed."

"The boys were hardly here and I only ever dropped by to pick up or return them. For all we knew she could've been out all day. Paul must've known but it probably suited him to keep her locked up."

"Surely Linda knew something wasn't right?"

"I think she used the booze to block it out."

"So what now? Will she get treatment?"

"According to the doc, agora-whatsit is a form of depression. She's already on anti-depressants for the booze so he's going to send round a counsellor who deals with the other stuff. It'll be tricky treating her for alcoholism and depression but apparently the two tend to go hand in hand so she won't be the first."

"I suppose if she falls off the wagon it'll be even more difficult."

"When are things owt but with our Linda?" Joyce laughed. "You're right though, we need to keep her off the ale. That's why we've moved in. The only person stupid enough to fetch her it is her pillock of a husband. As long as we can keep him away we're in with a chance."

At the top of the stairs Linda struggled to hear everything her mum was blabbing to the nosey cow. How far back would Joyce go? To when Linda was naive enough to believe she deserved a better life? No doubt that would give Miss Fucking Perfect a good giggle.

June 1991

At fourteen, Linda had her future mapped out. Cockily, she announced she would own a successful chain of hairdressing establishments by the time she was thirty.

Unlike her mother, Linda was damned if she was going to end up as some posh trout's lackey. Joyce's kowtowing to an over indulged bitch like Mrs P, infuriated her. The woman was completely out of touch with the real world. Who, in their right mind, goes for a shampoo and set and leaves having bought the hairdressing salon?

Two years before Linda's birth, Mrs P's usual hairdresser had had the audacity to catch a virus on the day of an important fund raising event. Desperation and her friend's insistence that, although on the wrong side of town, Hair Perfection employed the best stylist in Sheffield, had led her ladyship to Joyce's chair.

At twenty-two years old, Joyce was totally in awe of her new customer. Everything about Mrs P oozed class; her clothes, make up, nails and that voice, Joyce had only ever heard accents like that on television.

Nervously applying lacquer, Joyce was both relieved and astonished when Mrs P announced that she would never let another touch her hair, then made the current owner an offer she couldn't refuse. Once the salon was under new ownership, Joyce was appointed as its manageress.

Whenever Joyce proudly told the story of her rapid promotion, Linda would snort. She could not remember a single day that her mother wasn't at Mrs P's beck and call.

Not only was Joyce treated like a skivvy in the salon, she was expected to assist with Mrs P's 'work'. Linda's blood boiled when the snotty bitch referred to throwing tea parties and charging an inordinate amount for a buttered scone as work. What was more contemptuous was that Mrs P didn't even provide the food for her charitable activities. Instead she convinced suckers like Joyce to donate. Hearing her victoria sponges were much sought after might be enough of a reward for her mother, but not Linda.

What also boiled Linda's piss was the stuck up bitch expecting her mother to drop everything and rush over to the mansion whenever she held an evening fundraiser. Not that Joyce was allowed to mingle with the guests; her purpose was solely to ensure Mrs P did not have a hair out of place. What Linda failed to comprehend was that her mother looked forward to such occasions. An evening in Mrs P's company was certainly more agreeable than her stroppy teenage daughter's. Joyce enjoyed hearing about the trials and tribulations of being a surgeon's wife and Mrs P was always supportive of Joyce's constant struggle to bring up her daughter alone whilst her husband was unavoidably detained.

Joyce and her boss had an unusual friendship, in the main because neither of them recognised it as such. The bond they shared had been cemented fifteen years earlier when both women were surprised to find themselves with child. As with their lifestyles, the circumstances regarding the pregnancies were miles apart. Linda's conception, by her unmarried catholic mother, was not as joyously received as Richard Junior's.

At thirty-nine, Mrs P had given up on conceiving naturally so she considered her child to be a much awaited miracle. No one was more pleased than Joyce when her boss announced her impending motherhood and no one more sympathetic than Mrs P when her distraught employee made a similar, less vocal, declaration.

Less than six weeks after tearfully alerting her mother to her predicament, Joyce strategically placed her bouquet over her tiny bump and walked towards a beaming Charlie. Later, at the wedding reception, her new husband's reaction to Mrs P's generous gift caused much hilarity. 'If the coppers catch sight of that I'll be banged up again' he'd protested and immediately banned the item from crossing their threshold. Convincing the Pawn Broker Charlie had not illegally liberated the ostentatious candelabra had not been an easy task.

Joyce's waters had broken as she was putting the finishing touches to her boss' hair. In contrast to the child's devout grandmother, who was praying the child would be two months late, Mrs P was elated by Linda's timely appearance. Rushing from the salon she had instructed her staff to deliver all Richard Junior's unworn neutral coloured clothing and the spare Silver Cross pram to Joyce's home. Once again Charlie was bricking it. Never mind his lass being donned out from top to tail in John Lewis gear, her being pushed around in a pram like Princess Anne's kid was bound to bring the filth to the door.

Fourteen years later, as her daughter twittered on about her plans for world domination, Joyce considered the posh pram and expensive clothing might have been the catalyst to Linda's ideas of grandeur.

Chapter 4

1533 hours, 28 September 2012

Promising to call back the following day, Ella left number thirty-three. Once on the veranda she couldn't avert her gaze from Suzanne's front door. Since being reinstated she had imagined possible encounters with each of Suzanne's clan. Some were inordinately less appealing than others. The thought of facing Suzanne's sister, Louise, and stepfather, Dave, was just about bearable. Imagining bumping into the girl's mother or biological father, Sid, made her tremble. As for an encounter with Suzanne, that was too painful to contemplate.

Spotting Louise in the carpark, Ella worried that her daydreams were going too far.

"Thank God you're here," Louise snapped. "I'm bloody freezing. I've been waiting here since I noticed your car."

"I'm sorry, I thought you'd been told, I'm no longer looking after Suzanne. If it's urgent you need to contact Jess."

"I'm more than aware you're not looking after my sister," Louise spat venomously. "That's why I'm here."

"Sorry?"

"And so you bloody well should be. Lying to us all. Making Susie trust you, just to let her down. Hasn't she had enough of that in the past?"

"Believe me Louise, the last thing I wanted to do was hurt Suzanne. If it were up to me I'd be with her right now," Ella admitted.

"Isn't it up to you? You're a grown woman for God sake."

"It's not that easy."

"Because of our bloody mother. Everything that goes tits up in our life is down to her." Louise looked uncomfortable. "With the exception of losing Bradley I suppose."

"It's not your mother's fault, it's mine. As soon as I realised who she was, I should have said something."

"So why didn't you?"

"Ironically, I was worried they wouldn't let me look after Susie."

Louise sighed then leaned against the wall. "She's in tatters. Mum telling you the baby might not be Brad's hasn't helped. Now she's convinced you'll think she's a slapper who didn't really love him."

Ella was surprised. "Your mum told you she'd called me?"

"She told us everything. Think she was trying to get a reaction from Susie but it didn't work."

"Everything?"

"I think so. We know you were best mates for years and we know why you aren't anymore. She also told us you knew our bastard of a father better than you let on," Louise accused.

Ella did not want to get onto the subject of Sid so reverted to Louise's earlier statement. "I don't think Susie's a slapper and I'm sure she loved Bradley. Please tell her that." Ella looked around the car park. "I know this is going to sound lame but I really have to go. If I'm seen talking to you it could end badly."

"What if we go somewhere we won't be seen?" Louise suggested pointing at Ella's car.

"I… Well really, I should…"

"Surely your god-daughter's entitled to ten minutes of your precious time," Louise sneered. "You've never been there for me in the last twenty years so how about being there for Susie?"

That knocked the wind out of Ella's sails. When she had rejected the devil, renounced evil and promised to set a good example to the child in her arms, she'd no reason to doubt her words. She had been proud to stand in front of Nicky's friends and family and vow to be a guiding light for Louise yet within a few years of making her oath she turned her back on the girl's mother and, by virtue, the child.

Louise did not wait for a response. Instead she walked to the passenger door of Ella's car and stood expectantly. As with the girl's mother, Ella found it impossible to challenge her so obediently unlocked the car.

Paul Douglas cursed when he saw the two women enter the car. He had also been waiting for Ella, but as his presence on the estate was not welcome, he'd chosen to hide behind an adjacent car. Maybe all was not lost. Louise might have put the mockers on his current plan but he might be able to use their liaison to his advantage. Standing upright he sauntered to Ella's car and tapped on the window. He had to stifle his laughter when she looked up in horror then locked her car door with a shaky hand.

His signal to roll down the window ignored, Paul moved to the front of the car and placed an envelope under the windscreen wiper. "Make sure Linda gets that without those two interfering old twats seeing it. If not I might have to tell your bosses whose company you've been keeping!" he yelled, pointing at Louise.

Once Paul departed, Louise retrieved the envelope and placed it in Ella's lap. "It's nowt to do with me but if I was you I'd burn the bloody thing." Louise turned to Ella, "Well, shall we get off now before any other nutters bother us?"

"Sorry. Yes. Of course. It's just… Shit. He's the last person I wanted to see. If he tells my bosses."

"What? Everyone knows he's full of shit. If he tells anyone he saw us I'll say I pressured you into giving me a lift because I was late for work. Now can we get out of here or I will be?"

"Okay. Right. Yes. Let's go."

"And calm down. Last thing we need is another death in the family."

"Why who's dying?" Ella squealed.

Louise laughed, "No one, but if you don't settle down, you'll probably wrap us around a tree."

1617 hours, 28 September 2012

They opted to stop at a back street café. Once seated, Louise began, "I need you to get in touch with Dinger."

"I'm sure Jess can do that for you." Ella replied.

"No she can't. She tried and apparently he's not fit to speak to anyone yet."

"Well then, maybe when he's better?"

"He got shot in the shoulder not the throat. There's no reason he can't talk to Susie."

"Is she able to travel?"

"What is wrong with you people? She managed to get to Brize so a trip to Birmingham's hardly going to kill her."

"I thought she wasn't feeling very sociable at the moment, that's all."

"If you mean she hasn't washed, dressed or eaten without assistance since the funeral you're right. I'm hoping giving her something to get dressed for might snap her out of it. The day before the funeral she was desperate to see Dinger so maybe the chance of talking to him will encourage her to get a wash."

"Did Jess say why he wasn't fit enough for visitors?"

"No. I don't mean to be rude but she's not much of a go-getter is she? I ask her to organise a visit, she says she can't and then moves on to the next thing. When I pushed her, she more or less said she wasn't there for me. Told me, as the request hadn't come from Susie she wasn't about to start badgering busy people on my behalf. Snobby cow."

Ella felt the need to defend her colleague. "She has a point. If the doctors don't think Dinger's well enough for visitors it's not really our place to question it."

Louise looked contrite. "Fair enough, but could you find out why? Susie's got it into her head that he doesn't want to speak to her because of the baby. If you were to tell her that wasn't true I'm sure she'd listen."

Ella was horrified. "Louise, I can't speak to Susie. Anyway she's not thinking straight. Why would Dinger be angry with her because of the baby?"

"She's worried Bradley told him about her sleeping with someone else."

"So Bradley knew?"

"Of course he knew. She wouldn't keep that from him."

"And he stood by her?"

Louise looked angry. "Yes, he stood by her. It was his bloody fault she did what she did in the first place. And Dinger's. Of course, she couldn't see that but fortunately Brad could. He managed to convince her one little mistake shouldn't ruin the rest of their lives."

"I'd hardly call a child a little mistake."

"Not the child, the other bloke."

"I'm sorry, but I'm confused. How can Bradley be responsible for Suzanne being unfaithful or Dinger for that matter?"

"She wasn't unfaithful."

"Really is there another term for sleeping with someone other than your boyfriend?"

"Have you ever seen 'Friends'?" Louise snapped.

"The TV show?"

"Yes. Bradley and Susie were on a break like Ross and Rachel in Friends." Louise said smugly. "Only at the time Susie didn't know it was a break she thought he'd dumped her permanently, thanks to bloody Dinger."

Ella's heart sunk. "What has Dinger got against Suzanne?"

"Nothing. In fact they get on great. I'm the only one that thinks he's a womanising tosser, the rest of our lot think he's walks on water, including Susie." Louise looked at her watch. "I need to get off now or I really will be late for work."

Ella was disappointed her curiosity needed sating. For a start, who was the other candiate for the father of Suzanne's baby? *'Dinger?'* her inner voice suggested.

Pulling away from the café, Ella quizzed Louise, "If Dinger was partly responsible for this mess why would Suzanne want to see him?"

"Because she doesn't know. Brad didn't want her to find out Dinger was involved. He only told me because I kept giving him shit about it. Not that I stopped once he did. I was still being evil to him when he left." Louise drew her fingers over her eyes to stop her emotions physically showing. "Other than Dave, Brad's

27

the only decent guy I've known. It hit me as hard as Susie when he hurt her. Wish I'd cut him some slack now."

"I'm sure he understood. He was probably pleased she had someone like you fighting her corner."

Louise smiled. "Which is what I'm doing now. My gut tells me the chance of seeing Dinger could get her off that couch and out of her PJs. Please, can you find out when she'll be able to visit him?"

"Let me see what I can do? I won't be able to speak to Jess until Monday though. By the time I get back to the office, she'll have left for the weekend." There was no reason Ella couldn't phone her colleague but she wanted a couple of days to establish a plausible excuse for questioning her about Dinger.

Louise was unimpressed by the postponement. "Make sure you speak to her first thing Monday then," she ordered. Once again Ella marvelled at the similarities between mother and daughter.

Still smarting as she left the car, Louise stroppily asked Ella if she had used her fall out with Nicky as an excuse to run off with her rich hubby and abandon her friends. Suspecting her mother had not told her the whole story, Ella pointed out Nicky had physically attacked her. When the girl replied, "Not without good reason," Ella was flummoxed.

1837 hours, 28 September 2012

Once home, Ella sat in her study staring at the three letters she was yet to deliver and wondered how Linda would react to Paul's. These days the only constant about Bradley's mother was her unpredictability. Linda had not mentioned Paul during Ella's visit. Did that mean the prospect of never setting eyes on the odious little man appealed to Linda? It certainly appealed to Ella but as Charlie had been the one to send Paul packing there was a possibility his wife would want him home. If so, what right did she have to keep the couple apart?

Then again was it her place to enable a reconciliation? Even if it was, she couldn't do it. Joyce and Charlie would regret their staunch defence of her if she had a hand in Paul's return. The last thing she wanted to do was upset them.

Her mind was about to implode. Deliver or not deliver? If she didn't, Paul might see it as an act of revenge for the allegations he had made against her and run to the newspapers claiming she was keeping him from his wife's side when she needed him most. Worse still, he could tell the CO he'd caught her conspiring with Louise on the day she had been ordered to stay away from Suzanne's family.

If she did deliver, Charlie and Joyce could complain that marital guidance was not within her remit. They might repay her disloyalty by going to the newspapers themselves. Telling the story of how she had stabbed them in the back after they had fought so hard to save her career.

Though Ella couldn't imagine Linda's parents being as vindictive as their son-in-law hurting them was unthinkable. Rightly or wrongly she could not put Linda's possible happiness above her mother's.

That morning she had promised her CO no more secrets. She was already courting disaster with her investigations into Beetle's will; not keeping her superiors in the loop regarding the letter could be the equivalent of career suicide. It would certainly give the General more ammunition to question her professionalism.

Calling Pete Waller was the perfect solution. She knew her obsession with the will and failure to divulge her connection to Suzanne had vexed him, maybe including the Casualty Procedure guru in this decision could go some way to appease him and give her a 'Get out of Jail Free' card. If Pete ordered her to hand over the letter, she might be able to convince Joyce she had done so against her will.

Initially, Pete's stance was that Ella had no right to withhold correspondence between a man and his wife. He reconsidered when she highlighted that delivering the letter might disrupt Linda's recovery and would definitely alienate her parents.

Pete's next instruction was to to return the letter to Paul Douglas and advise him to invest in a stamp. This suggestion originally appealed to Ella until it occurred to her that by doing so she would guarantee its non-receipt.

"Linda avoids going anywhere near the front door so there's no way she'll get to the letter before her parents. Once they see it they are bound to destroy it," Ella explained.

"That's not our problem. Which I will happily tell the newspapers, Mr Douglas or anyone else who questions our decision."

"There's one more thing you should know." Ella bit her lip. She was not looking forward to Pete's response. "I was with Suzanne's sister when Paul handed me the letter. In fact we were in my car."

"Why?" Pete's ability to fill one word with so much rage dissuaded Ella from her planned honesty; instead she decided to go with Louise's version of events. "The CO said if I bumped into Suzanne or her family I should be polite but point out I was no longer able to assist them with CVO matters. Louise cornered me in the car park. Her friend was supposed to give her a lift to work but hadn't turned up so she asked me to drop her off. As I was driving past where she works I couldn't think of an excuse not to."

"Did you discuss anything to do with wills, inheritances or paternity tests?"

"No." *At least that wasn't a lie.*

"Then no harm done. Thankfully, I know you've made me aware this time so if Mr Douglas does start spouting his poison I'll be ready. As I told you before, transparency is the best policy. That way I'll always have your back."

"Thanks Pete. I just hope he doesn't go running to the newpapers again," Ella replied.

"So do I," Pete paused as if considering the possibility. "Is there any chance his wife wants him back?" he asked.

"I honestly don't know."

"Well then hold on to the letter until you've spoken to her. If you think she might we'll revisit this. If not, return the letter to Mr Douglas."

After agreeing to wait, Ella bid Pete farewell then placed Paul's letter in her desk drawer.

Could Linda be missing Paul? Surely not. It was nigh on impossible for Ella to conceive a viable reason why anyone would voluntarily spend time in his company. His body wasn't the only thing that emanated an offensive odour; his personality stank too. Still who was Linda to be choosy? Bradley's mother would have to accept her relegation to the Conference League. Gone were the heady days when she had attracted the attention of the Premier League in the guise of Rick Pashley. The thought of Bradley's father distracted her from her dilemma. She really should call him. '*A booty call*' he inner voice suggested. 'Very happily married,' Ella subconsciously replied.

1859 hours, 28 September 2012

Rick answered after two rings, "Ella, good to hear from you. Do I take it our campaign to bring back the Haddington One was successful?"

"Yes, thanks to your efforts."

"Don't thank me I was merely a foot soldier, Field Marshal Joyce led the campaign."

"So I gather, but I still wanted to thank you. I also wanted to check if you're still flying back to Australia on Wednesday?"

"Afraid so, I need to get my house in order so I can spend some time with my grandson when he decides to make an appearance."

The reference to his grandchild unsettled Ella. He obviously wasn't aware of Suzanne's indiscretion. "So you're sure it's a boy too?"

"Susie seems to thinks so."

"Have you spoken to her lately?"

"No. I'd like to but she won't come to the phone and I'm a little wary of setting foot on the Haddington."

"Because of Linda?"

"Yes," Rick laughed, "Still scared of her after all these years. Pathetic I know."

"Please don't let her put you off. From what I gather Susie's a little lost at the moment so a visit might do her good. Now the funeral's over losing Bradley has hit her hard."

"I thought she was handling it a bit too well. I'll try again. I'm doing the dutiful nephew bit today. Getting around all my mother's siblings while I'm in town but I'll try and get over to see her at the weekend."

"Can you pencil me in for Sunday morning, I've some paperwork I need to give you." Ella realised it wasn't a very accurate description but it didn't feel right telling Rick over the phone about his son's farewell letter.

"Of course, name the time and place and I'm all yours."

'*If only...*' 'Happily married woman!' Ella inwardly giggled. How many times would she have that conversation with herself before Rick Pashley departed for Oz?

"Let me check my diary and get back to you," Ella replied before saying goodbye.

1917 hours, 28 September 2012

Larry's announcement that dinner was about to be served was a welcome diversion. Pouring herself a perfectly cooled glass of Prosecco, Ella appreciated the wonderful aroma coming from the kitchen. Tonight, Larry deserved her undivided attention. She would concentrate on him and forget all about letters, wills and illegitimate children.

Larry had a similar thought. He would use his tried and tested method to unburden his wife; make her laugh then make her squeal. Ella pretended to choke on her drink when Larry entered the room. Wearing an apron with the logo 'Does my sausage look big in this?' and nothing else. After placing a plate of salmon en croûte in front of his wife, Larry turned to reveal a badly drawn heart with I and U at either side, on his right bum cheek.

"What sausage?" Ella giggled.

Larry winked, "If you eat all your dinner, I'll show you."

Dinger was still smarting from the humiliating dressing down the ward sister had administered. Bollocks to the old dragon, what did she know? He didn't tell his mother to fuck off back to Preston because he was in pain or feeling sorry for himself. He told her to fuck off because he couldn't cope with her constantly thanking God for not taking her son. In Dinger's mind she was thanking the almighty for a monumental fuck up. "You got the wrong guy, moron." Dinger muttered under his breath.

The doctor's reassurance that, as his wounds were healing nicely, he should be able to recuperate at home soon added fuel to his fury. How was being trapped with three clucking women going to aid his recovery? His sister's reaction to his injuries equalled his mother's in the drama stakes. Plus, as his eldest sibling had recently left her arsehole of a boyfriend and ran back to mummy, his nephews were currently residing in his bedroom. Where the hell was he going sleep?

The only upside to going home was that the counsellor wouldn't be constantly harassing him. When was he going to get it through his thick skull Dinger didn't want his feelings examined or to discuss the effect losing his best friend had on him? The thought of the mealy mouthed, loafer wearing, prat feigning empathy brought about a rage Dinger found hard to repress. He didn't want pity or to have his guilt eased. He deserved to suffer.

For his family's sake he wished he could bypass his necessary visit home and be taken straight to the morgue. As much as the women in his life irritated him, he didn't relish the thought of them having to find him once the deed was done. A picture of Bradley's lifeless body flashed through his mind.

Chapter 5

0945 hours, 29 September 2012

Larry was letting his wife have a lie in. She'd had an awful week and him leaving her to cope alone hadn't helped. Still his gamble had paid off. Ella's visits to the Haddington would become less frequent now the funeral was over, as would Nicky's, so Larry felt he could finally relax. The chances of the two women speaking were slim, especially as Ella had sworn never to converse with her old friend again.

Although he had promised otherwise, he saw no benefit confessing he had purposely held back information to ensure Nicky's exile from his wife's life. What good would it do Ella to discover Nicky had only attacked her because Sid was wielding a knife? Not that that was necessarily true. He only had Nicky's word her crazed boyfriend intended to stab his wife, it was just as plausible she had beaten Ella up for the sheer pleasure of the act then made up the story about Sid to cover her tracks. Why should he risk his wife's wrath when there was no evidence of a blade's existence?

He knew Ann and Hazel would be annoyed by his decision but was confident he could convince them to stay silent. Ella's oldest army buddies had managed to keep his secret for nearly twenty years so surely they were capable of doing so for another twenty.

"That was just what I needed," Ella announced entering the kitchen and stretching her arms above her head. "I haven't slept that well in ages."

"Morning sexpot," Larry said kissing his wife hard on the lips. "Did our little bout of bedroom aerobics tire you out last night?"

Ella grabbed her husband around the waist. "You underestimate my stamina, sir, I think I could easily manage another session," she teased.

"If that's the case we better increase your carb intake. What can I get madam for breakfast? Bagels, pancakes, fruit salad, full English…"

"Pancakes would be lovely," Ella replied. "Can I have strawberries and natural yoghurt with them?"

Larry poured a cup of coffee and placed it on the breakfast bar." Of course my lady." He pulled out a stool. "Now sit and watch a master at work," he instructed as he strutted towards the Aga.

With his back turned, Ella allowed her smile to fade. She'd lied about having a good night's sleep. Fortunately, when she'd sneaked into her study at three am Larry had not stirred. It wasn't just Paul's letter that had kept her from her favourite pastime; she had been unable to stop herself speculating the possible location of Bradley's missing will. Last night's fantasy that it had accidentally been filed under Craig Bradley instead of Bradley Craig was totally plausible. Of course it didn't top her all time favourite resurfacing; the one in which Bradley had placed it in his farewell letter to Suzanne. What she wouldn't give to be there tomorrow when the girl opened it. Just as well she wouldn't, she'd be tempted to rip the envelope away and shake it until the writing fell off.

Her other theories went from the sublime to the ridiculous, culminating in the one about Paul blackmailing the lady from the Document Handling Centre. Stupid really, how could he possibly know that Margaret used to be Marvin and had an unpaid fine for fly-fishing without a licence? That possible scenario had reared its head around five am when all credible and a few incredible ones had been exhausted.

"What are your plans for today?" Larry asked.

'*Torturing Margaret/Marvin until she/he fesses up,*' Ella's inner voice suggested.

"Not a lot. I promised to pop around and see Charlie later and I need to touch base with Father O'Sullivan and Jess about the farewell letters. Other than that I'm all yours."

"How do you fancy doing something really radical like clearing the backlog on the Sky box? It's nearly at one hundred per cent and you know whose programmes will fail to be recommissioned if the need arises," Larry warned.

Ella's scowl did nothing to deter Larry's threats. "New season of Downton's started. You've two episodes to watch unless you want me to press the yellow button of death."

"You know who'll die if you do that and there's not a court in the land that would prosecute. Definite justifiable homicide." Ella shouted as she ran for the living room.

Placing her coffee beside her, Larry kissed Ella's head then handed her a plate of pancakes and a fork. "Now I'll be getting about my duties ma'am. If Branson's Irish lilt proves too much for you to bear you'll find me in the parlour. Feel free to sate your frustrations on a lowly footman at any time." Doffing an imaginary cap, Larry left his wife to her guilty pleasure in the hope she could forget her CVO duties. He'd chosen not to mention her three-hour visit to her study in the early hours. Her poor attempt at tiptoeing meant she didn't want him to know and he thought it best to allow her that misconception.

1305 hours, 29 September 2012

Opening the door, Charlie's face broke into a huge grin. "Now aren't you a sight for sore eyes?" he said ushering Ella inside. "Linda's a lot better today. I think they've finally got her meds right. Quick warning though, don't mention Bradley's funeral, her idiot hubby, Rick the Prick or the war," he whispered.

"The war?"

"Got that one off Basil Fawlty, thought it was a good line," Charlie winked.

Her impulsive reaction to playfully slap Linda's father surprised her more than Charlie who feigned pain as he rubbed his arm. "Careful there lass, you'll be doing our Joyce outta a job," he said opening the door to the living room.

Seeing Beetle sitting beside Linda, Ella wondered if she had been granted a direct line to God. Firstly, the Almighty had brought home Larry, now he'd given her the opportunity to speak to the young soldier whose Human Resources record she'd been scanning the previous day.

As she considered a quick prayer asking the almighty to magic up Bradley's will her inner voice reminded her of her pledge to make no further requests if her husband returned. 'Could be one of those three wishes things' Ella thought. '*You were pleading with a deity not a bleeding genie'* was the stroppy answer she received.

On seeing the officer enter, Beetle stood. "Afternoon ma'am. I just popped in to pay my respects to Mrs Douglas, I'll be off now."

The shout of "No" from both Linda and Ella startled Bradley's friend. Ella composed herself. "I mean, don't leave on my account, I won't be staying long."

This time it was Charlie's turn to object. "You'll at least stop for a cuppa?"

"She'd better, 'cos I've poured her one," Joyce said handing Ella a mug. "And you may as well sit back down," she told Beetle, "I've made you one too. Hope you like Battenberg."

"Looks like we've been captured," Ella told the young soldier. "Remember, number, rank and name only." Beetle gave a nervous laugh then returned to the couch.

Linda, the chameleon, had morphed again. Today she was the congenial hostess. Whilst fawning over Beetle, or Howard as she insisted on calling him, she produced photograph after photograph of her eldest son. Beetle was fixated.

Enjoying the male attention, Linda was unimpressed when Ella stepped into her limelight. "How long will you be staying at Suzanne's?" she asked Beetle.

"I'm heading off tonight. Susie's taken to sleeping on the couch which makes things awkward as that's usually my bed."

"Stay here." Linda's offer surprised everyone in the room. "Please, Phil's room's free." Seeing the boy's reluctance she continued. "Go on Howard, it'll be nice to have a bit of company, these two old farts are driving me mad and I don't want to think of you spending your Saturday night alone on camp."

Feeling unable to say no to Bradley's mother, Beetle turned to Charlie for assistance. Mistaking the soldier's look as a question instead of a plea, Charlie spoke, "It's okay with us son. Mind, our Linda's only got five channels and there's no boxes or play whatsits here so you might get bored."

"We could play cards," Linda suggested. "Gin Rummy. We haven't played that for years."

"Or ever," Charlie muttered. "I could take the lad to the Flying Horse for a pint."

"That's probably a better idea but don't think of sneaking there just yet," Joyce instructed. "I, I've a few bits I need to pick up at home." Joyce turned to Ella, "Would you mind running me up there, love?"

"Of course, but I'll need a quick chat with Private Jackson before we go."

Joyce turned her attention to the young soldier. "Now, make your mind up son, are you staying or going? I've a meat and potato pie in the oven that'll easily stretch to four."

"Now there's an offer you don't get every day," Charlie said then looked at the boy suspiciously. "I bet you've never had Henderson's Relish have you lad?" Beetle shook his head. "Well you're in for a treat. Now go and get your bags and let Susie know you're staying here."

Accepting the decision was no longer his to make, Beetle headed for the door. Ella caught him in the hallway. By the time she had gleaned the information she required Joyce was ready to leave.

Linda was too busy absorbing every detail of the photograph before her to acknowledge their departure. How had it ended up in her mother's box? Years ago, after she'd liberated it from Mrs P's handbag, she had committed every detail of the photograph to memory.

July 1991

Inspecting the picture, Linda surmised Richard Pashley was good looking enough but his wardrobe would require an overhaul before they stepped out in public.

From an early age she'd had designs on becoming the next Mrs P, the only stumbling block was that the current one kept scuppering her attempts to meet her future husband. Frustratingly, volunteering to assist at a number of her future mother-in-law's charitable events had not facilitated the rendezvous she had hoped for.

Suspicious of her daughter's newfound compassion for Sheffield's homeless, Joyce had questioned her motives. Linda's explanation that she hoped Richard Junior might also be commandeered to hand out soup and sympathy did not satisfy her mother's curiosity. Joyce required no further clarification when her daughter cockily added," He's an only child and his parents are loaded. You do the maths."

The circles the youngsters mixed in couldn't have been more disparate so orchestrating a meeting was not an easy task. Whenever the lady of the manor visited her salon she twittered on endlessly about her son, most of it was drivel but one day Linda overheard a snippet to aid her quest. Richard's swimming team had relocated to the new pool at Pond's Forge. "Well if it's good enough for the Student Games it's good enough for my Richard," Mrs P had prattled.

After donning her sexiest swimsuit three times to no avail, Linda asked an attentive pool attendant about the swimming team's timetable. She was gutted to discover they met at six thirty every weekday morning and during training only team members were allowed entry to the pool.

As joining the swimming team was not an option, Linda resumed her earwigging during Mrs P's visit. It paid off. Letting slip her husband couldn't understand why Richard Junior and his pals would want to spend Sunday afternoons at the pool when they were there every morning gave Linda her opportunity.

The following Sunday evening, Linda flauntered into Joyce's kitchen and smiled triumphantly. "He's now called Rick," she informed her flabbergasted mother. "My mates would take the piss if I went out with someone called Richard."

Narrating the day's events, Linda revelled in her mother's disapproval. Rick's friends had been very impressed by the sight of her in her swimsuit. When she'd called Richard's name from the poolside, three of the boys had struggled to hide their erections. When her mother attempted to chastise her for her vulgarity, Linda retorted it was them that had the 'hard-ons' not her.

Rick was soon tempted out of the pool and into a less buoyant activity. Returning home two weeks later Joyce was dumbstruck to find Richard Junior groping her daughter on her

39

couch. She decided against divulging her discovery to Mrs P. Even when Monica Pashley complained her son was being very secretive and her husband had smelled cheap perfume on the boy's clothing, Joyce kept shtum.

Although Joyce feared Richard Junior's passion for her daughter might result in her receiving her P45 she did acknowledge there were some benefits to their liaisons. For one, her daughter's mood had definitely improved. Lately Linda rarely flew of the handle and even gave Joyce the odd unrequested cuddle.

Rick also seemed happier. There was no requirement for him to play the role of the perfect son whilst in Joyce's home. He could openly laugh without reprisal and often did. The night Linda referred to Mrs P as Dorien from Birds of a Feather, Rick had tickled the girl mercilessly until she retracted the statement. Whilst sitting in the kitchen Joyce fought to stifle her own laughter. Both at the fuss her daughter was making and at her keen observation. Joyce had to admit Monica did have an air of Dorien Green about her, although her hair was much nicer.

Joyce was less enamoured with Rick's presence in the house during her absence. Linda had totally disregarded her mother's ban on unsupervised visits and Joyce had no notion as how to coerce her daughter into compliance. Linda was not the least bit perturbed by her mother's anger, nor did she respond to bribery or blackmail. Rick had more disposable income than Joyce and was happy to share it with her daughter. Her threat that Linda's chances of an apprenticeship at 'Hair Perfection' would be scuppered if Joyce told Monica what was going on was scoffed at. Even when it was made, mother and daughter knew she was too frightened to carry it out.

Feeling she had no choice but to accept the boy's visits to her house and, she suspected, her daughter's bed, Joyce bypassed the subject of the birds and bees and moved straight on to contraception. After pointing out her mother's own failings in that department, Linda assured Joyce she knew what she was doing. A few months later everyone found out exactly what that was - putting holes in Rick's condoms.

Chapter 6

Whilst grabbing a jar of jam from the pantry, Joyce tried to convince Ella to stay for dinner once they returned to number thirty-three. "If I put a few extra potatoes out the pie could easily stretch to five," she insisted.

Ella wondered how Charlie would feel about his portion sizes constantly being diminished by his well-meaning wife. Not wishing to offend, Ella claimed Larry was taking her out for a meal that night.

Joyce looked contrite. "Sorry, love I keep forgetting you've got a man to get home to. I shouldn't have dragged you over here. To be truthful I just wanted to get out of the house. I'm feeling a bit agro-whatsit myself. I've not left Linda's place since the funeral."

"It's okay, Larry isn't expecting me home any time soon. Still, if you'd rather be on your own..."

"Don't be daft, lass, I'm glad of your company, it's those two I needed a break from," Joyce replied as she flicked the kettle on. "Shall we have a quick brew before you take me back to the asylum?"

Placing Ella's tea in front of her, Joyce joined her at the kitchen table. "It'll do them good to spend a bit of time on their own. They've always been at loggerheads. Linda blamed her dad being locked up for her getting bullied. He blamed it on her lack of consideration for anyone but herself. Suppose they both had a point."

Joyce explained to Ella it wasn't the fact that Charlie was a thief that gave the other kids ammunition to belittle Linda, it was that he was an incompetent one. Unlike other career criminals in the area, Linda's dad always got caught. On the rare occasions he did successfully pull off a heist, the kids at school were quick to pounce. 'Check out Craig's new shoes 'eh. Guess her dad will be banged up again next week?' They would taunt.

It seemed whenever Charlie had money the police knew to search the house. They would inevitably find something incriminating that would result in his arrest.

"Poor Linda. Back then she wouldn't say boo to a goose. Just took all the crap they threw at her then came home and cried to me. I hated seeing her like that, Charlie wasn't my favourite person then I can tell you."

"What changed?"

Joyce pursed her lips. "Her bloody body, that's what. She got boobs."

Joyce explained Linda's confidence had grown at the same rate as her ample chest. Something else that increased at an alarming pace was her ability to manipulate boys.

It wasn't that she was particularly interested in the guys. The buzz she got was seeing the faces of her playground tormenters when she stole their boyfriends. The other girls were still at the ironing board stage of their development so the promise of a quick feel of Linda's assets was usually enough to coax away the most committed teenage heart.

At first, Linda's actions had the desired affect; the girls hated her. In time that changed, after witnessing her power over the opposite sex they started to emulate her. As the boys flocked around Linda, the girls vied to be her best friend. Linda's popularity went from the gutter to the rooftops in one-term and four cup sizes. Although this was great news for her it had been an awful time for Joyce. Her shy, loving, awkward daughter became a manipulative, arrogant, disrespectful little tart.

"I should never have asked Charlie to speak to her. The day I took her to see him at the nick was the end of them," Joyce told Ella sadly.

Linda had chosen her wardrobe in the hope of exacting the same embarrassment on her father as his behaviour caused her. What she hadn't considered was the humiliation she would feel being labelled a prostitute by him in earshot of a full visiting room.

"He warned me that day if I didn't keep an eye on her she'd end up with a belly full of arms and legs." The memory of Charlie's premonition coming to fruition in the January of 1992 was not one she was willing to share with Ella just yet.

January 1992

The evening the Pashley family appeared at her door, Joyce had been psyching herself up to arrive at theirs. Linda had dropped her bombshell an hour earlier, Joyce was still trying to absorb the implications.

Without waiting for an invitation Rick's father pushed past Linda and stormed into the kitchen to find Joyce nursing a cold cup of tea. His weeping wife and sullen son obediently followed. Looking into Monica's eyes Joyce accepted that a friendship she had, until that moment been unaware of, was over.

Before Joyce had the chance to speak, Mr Pashley ripped into her. Had his wife not been charitable enough to the jailbird's wife and daughter? Did the conniving pair really think they could get away with trapping his son? Seriously, did they believe he would roll over and let his boy marry a tramp like Linda?

Joyce was confused at the mention of marriage until Mr P apprised her of his son's announcement during their dinner that evening. As if news they were about to become grandparents wasn't alarming enough he had informed them they were also about to gain a daughter-in-law. As soon as Linda turned sixteen he intended to marry her.

The young man who had issued that statement with such bravado now stood childlike behind his father. For the first time since his arrival Mr Pashley acknowledged Linda's presence. "My son is withdrawing his proposal. There will be no marriage," he informed her. Rick then found his voice but his insistence he'd promised to standby Linda was not rewarded with the response the young couple hoped for.

Mr Pashley took his wife's arm and headed for the door whilst telling his son his belongings would be forwarded to the Craig household in due course. When Monica pleaded with her son to also leave, Linda stated she was willing to move in with them if that helped.

Joyce felt the sting of Mr Pashley's derisory laughter as much as her daughter. When the evil cackling ceased Richard Senior launched into another tirade of abuse. This time every word was aimed at Linda. Did she really think they were going to have anything to do with her or her bastard? If Rick decided to standby her, he would do so without any financial assistance from them. She needed to face reality. Her little scheme had not paid off. "I'm sorry, my son may be the wealthiest of your candidates but his parents are not as gullible as he is. If you are quick, you might be able to pin this on one of the other potential fathers or better still flush away the problem," he told Linda.

With that Joyce found her voice. How dare Mr Pashley accuse her daughter of sleeping around? Didn't he know it took two to tango? The child was Rick's and she would make sure that he supported it, if not physically then financially. When Mr Pashley declared Rick had no money of his own, Joyce pointed out that he would one day, then forcefully invited them to leave her house. Linda was mortified when Rick followed.

The argument that ensued on the path outside gave Linda a glimmer of hope: The sound of three car doors slamming extinguished it. Flinging open the door, Linda ran to the end of the path just in time to see their car exit the street.

Unable to attack the cause of her outrage, Linda turned on her mother." Why did you have to kick them out?" she yelled." Do you think I didn't want to tell the horrible bastard to fuck off? We needed to keep him sweet. Now what am I going to do? For fuck sake why couldn't you keep your fucking mouth shut?"

Convinced it was the tension of the situation, Joyce turned a blind eye to her daughter's bad language. Another thing she would regret in years to come.

Chapter 7

1442 hours, 29 September 2012

After helping Joyce carry her belongings up to number thirty-three, Ella made her excuses and headed for the carpark. Her pace slowed as she neared her vehicle.

Her initial distress at the sight of Bradley's stepfather leaning against her car dissipated when it dawned on her this could be the opportunity to kick him in the bollocks she had longed for since their first encounter. After all she was trained in unarmed combat.

Pulling herself to her full height, Ella smiled, "Mr Douglas, how are you?"

Anger blazed across Paul's face. "How the fuck do you think I am? Thanks to you I'm out on my arse and my wife is being guarded twenty-four seven by Ronnie Biggs and Mother fucking Teresa."

Not letting her smile fade, Ella signalled for Paul to move away from her car. "Well as nice as it is to catch up I really must dash."

Her reaction threw Paul who contorted his face into what he hoped was a menacing look. "You're not going anywhere until I say so," he growled.

Ella laughed, "Seriously? "Focusing on Paul's feet she slowly brought her head up to face him. "You honestly think you can stop me?" she challenged.

The confusion in her aggressor's eyes told Ella he was far from confident. Taking full advantage of his dithering she clicked her car key, pushed Paul out of her way then jumped in the driver's seat.

Paul pulled the door away from her hand as she attempted to close it. "Not so fucking quick. I need to see Linda and you need to help me."

'So how exactly are we gonna knee him in his tackle from here?' Ella's inner voice enquired.

"I can't." she informed an irate looking Paul. "I can't invite you into the house and I think you, of all people, know she can't leave it."

"What did she say when you gave her the letter?" Paul snarled.

Deciding it was wiser to face Paul before answering his question, Ella climbed out of the car. "I haven't given it to her."

"Why the fuck not?"

"Because it's a bit difficult with both of her parents in the room."

"They can't see it."

"Therein lies the problem. They're reluctant to leave her on her own."

"Then make them. Offer to sit with her yourself."

"I'm not sure…"

"Well I am. I'm going fucking stir crazy at our Cindy's. I need to get back." When she attempted to get back in her car Paul grabbed her wrist. "Do you hear me? If they want her away from me so fucking badly she can move in with them. Just hope I'm around to see them trying to get her out of the fucking house." Paul's laughter was forced.

"You wouldn't do that to her," Ella replied, peeling Paul's fingers from her wrist.

"Watch me."

Noticing that a number of Garvey Close residents had taken to their balconies, Ella's mind wandered back to the last time she had stood arguing in front of a similar audience. That time it had ended with her 'then' best friend raining punches down on her whilst the baying crowd voiced their disapproval. She had no intentions of giving them such a treat this time. "Okay, leave it with me and I'll see what I can do," Ella said in an even tone.

1523 hours, 29 September 2012

Her encounter with Paul Douglas had thrown Ella completely off kilter so it wasn't until she arrived home she remembered she'd planned to pop into her office. Oh well, Beetle's information

46

would have to wait. Her intention was to have a long soak in the bath, get into her pyjamas and spend a night in her hubby's arms watching naff television.

Climbing the stairs she remembered the letters. Damn, she was supposed to contact Rick to arrange delivery. She'd have to call Father O to confirm timings before luxuriating.

"I'm afraid we've a problem," the priest informed her. "Linda's ex husband has been hanging around so Charlie won't leave her on her own. I could go around to Linda's house to give them their letter or I could give it to Joyce at church. Neither option appeals. I'd rather Joyce have Charlie's support when she reads it but if Linda's there she's bound to ask where her's is."

"I suppose I could give deliver hers at the same time." Ella changed her mind before the priest could respond. "No, if we do that it will be all about her. Joyce and Charlie will not get a chance to read theirs. What about if I offer to stay with her while they meet you?

"That could work. Let me call Joyce. I'll get back to you."

"Okay, I'll call Jess to tell her there could be a delay."

Jess informed Ella she had decided against delivering Suzanne's letter. "She's in a bad place. I'm not sure it's the right time."

"No improvement then?" Ella asked despondently.

"No, she just lays on couch in her PJs all day staring at the television. The doctor's diagnosed acute depression so I don't want to risk pushing her over the edge."

'*Julie Dunn*' Ella's inner voice screamed. Her desperation to see Suzanne made her nauseous. If only they would let her visit, maybe she could... What? What could she do that the girl's family, doctor and Jess could not? Seeing Suzanne might make her feel better but it would do nothing for the girl. "You're right we don't want to do anything to make her worse. Will you tell Dave and Louise not to leave her alone at any time? Just in case she does something stupid."

"Calm down Ella. The girl's not going to risk harming Bradley's baby. As there's no history of depression the doctor thinks she will snap out of it once she's had time to grieve. Dave's taken time off work so he and Louise are keeping a watchful eye and making sure she drinks and eats often. She complains she's not hungry but for the sake of the baby she's trying to eat."

Ella knew all too well how emotions could affect ones appetite. After her failed IVF attempts even drinking water felt like swallowing razor blades. "You should speak to Pete Waller regarding the letter," she suggested. "He's probably come across similar cases. Even if he agrees to delaying Suzanne's letter, I don't think I can wait. Rick is going back to Australia on Wednesday and I really think hearing a few kind words from her son will help Linda."

Although Ella had never met Bradley she sensed his words would be gracious and believed each recipient would feel better for having read them.

As soon as she replaced the receiver the phone rang. "Are you sure you don't mind sitting with Linda tomorrow love?" Joyce asked. "I feel awful dragging you away from your hubby on a Sunday."

"Not at all. It'll give you a break and Linda and I can have some girlie time." As soon as the words left her mouth she realised how implausible they sounded.

"Don't think our Linda's ever done girlie," Joyce quipped. "Still if you're sure. Father O is really keen to speak with us. Charlie's a bit worried. The last time a priest requested his company was to 'prepare' us for our wedding. He knew the only aisle he'd get me down was a Catholic one so he promised to follow God's path more closely. As he failed to keep that promise he always gets twitchy around men of the cloth," Joyce laughed.

Father O's okay though?"

"He is, which is the only reason I've managed to get Charlie to agree. For the life of me, I can't think why he wants to see us both, can you?"

"I'm sure whatever it is it's important," Ella responded, avoiding the question.

Rick's answer machine promised to get back to her. She hoped that would be soon. Ideally she would have preferred him to be the first recipient of his son's correspondence. She believed his would be the least traumatic delivery. Another reason for her eagerness was if Bradley had any last request, like his father retrieving his will from a secret lawyer, Rick would have more time to carry out his wishes. She really needed to stop with the daydreams.

Reluctantly, Ella turned off the taps. Before she could relax in her bath she would need to ensure her letter deliveries would not interfere with anything Larry had planned for the following day.

Venturing downstairs, she was surprised to find their elderly neighbour in the hallway. "Oh, hello love," Ivy said heading towards the door. "Thanks for letting me borrow you man tonight, much appreciated," she yelled as she left the house.

Ella turned to Larry expectantly. Looking extremely uncomfortable he began, "The Bradfield Ladies Choir are performing at the Dinnington Community Centre tonight and they need someone on the door."

"To collect tickets?" Ella asked.

"No, for protection. Last time a couple of the local gentlemen got a bit fresh and Mrs Eccles released her pepper spray. The choir vowed never to return but when it was put to the vote ninety five per cent were in favour of performing again."

"So if everyone other than the devout Mrs Eccles enjoys a bit of groping why ask you to be their bodyguard?"

Larry squeezed his lips together. He really didn't want to impart his next sentence. "Mrs Eccles requested me personally."

Sensing there was more Ella toyed with the idea of going to the toilet before pressing her husband further. She decided to chance it. "Why?"

Larry covered his eyes too embarrassed to see his wife's reaction. "Because Ivy told them that I was Princess Anne's bodyguard when I was serving."

Ella just made it to the toilet in time.

1647 hours, 29 September 2012

Larry's gleeful announcement that Ella was meeting Hazel at All Bar One shattered her fantasy of an intimate night with the remote control. He said he would drop her off and if he wasn't required to put an amorous geriatric in a half nelson would pick her up after the show.

"So I take it I don't have a say in this?" Ella pouted.

"Come on, be a mate. Ann's Victorian dad still won't accept they're a couple. He's now refusing to have Hazel in the house. You know she'll only mope if she's left on her own. "

"Thanks, now I feel bad for asking. Best I find something to wear," Ella said heading for the stairs.

Larry's smart retort was fortunately interrupted by Rick's phone call.

Chapter 8

1822 hours, 29 September 2012

Walking into the lobby of Rick's hotel, Ella's stomach was doing cartwheels. Earlier, after a quick diary check, she decided with a little rescheduling she could kill two birds with one stone. Her business with Bradley's father should not exceed forty-five minutes so she had changed the venue of her liaison with Hazel. They were now meeting at Rick's hotel bar at seven fifteen.

As Ella entered the bar she questioned her decision to meet in such a public place. Handing over Bradley's last words to his father in a crowded bar was hardly ideal. Since Bradley's death her emotions were in turmoil. If Rick faltered when hearing of the letter she didn't trust herself to remain professional. Maybe she should have applied her mascara after their meeting.

Rick stood, blinked exaggeratedly and smiled. "Well I must say I'm flattered you went to all this trouble for me," he said appraising her bodycon dress and four inch heels.

Ella blushed. "I'm meeting a friend later. Sorry I thought I mentioned it."

"You did, I'm just teasing."

'*You don't realise how true that is.*' 'Surely a man that good-looking should not be allowed to smell so good too', Ella thought. '*Back in the room, Adonis is speaking.*'

Rick smiled, "*What can I get you? Please don't say a low cal tonic. You're not driving are you?*"

"No I'm not, but I'll abstain if you don't mind. Is there anywhere we can talk in private? The conference room maybe?"

Rick looked bemused by her request but led her to the front desk to enquire. They were out of luck. Whilst running her pencil slowly around her lips, the immaculate redhead informed them that unless reserved, the conference rooms were locked after 6pm. "I'll see if I can find the keys," Red offered, ensuring she kept eye contact with Rick as she left reception.

If Rick read the signs he chose to ignore them. Two minutes later and a couple of shirt buttons lighter, the girl returned.

Bad news, the key safe was locked and the only guy with access had just gone on his break. He wouldn't be back for an hour.

"We could go to my room," Rick suggested.

As the receptionist glared at her, Ella desperately wanted to protest her innocence. There was nothing untoward about her accompanying the delectable Rick Pashley to his room; was there? Would going to a hotel bedroom with a man, other than her husband, be an act of betrayal? She shook off the thought. No doubt Rick would want to be alone when reading Bradley's letter so the likelihood was she'd be out of the room within minutes.

"I suppose your room will have to do then," Ella told Rick then turned to the receptionist. "It will only take a moment," she told Red. Instantly her cheeks flushed. Why was she telling the girl that? Was she seriously thinking she might need her as a witness for the defence!

Rick looked disappointed. "What time are you meeting your..." Rick held up his hands to make a quotation marks sign "'friend'?"

The absurd gesture annoyed Ella, what was he trying to imply? "Seven-fifteen," she replied defensively.

"In that case do you mind if we have a drink in the bar first? I've no plans for the rest of the evening." Sensing Ella's reluctance, Rick pleaded, "Please. It would be nice to have a conversation with a non-octogenarian today."

The options of waiting for Hazel with the charismatic Mr P or sitting alone like a sad loser was a no brainer. "Okay, why not? My friend's bound to be late." Since leaving the army, Hazel had made a point of never being on time.

1849 hours, 29 September 2012

If Larry didn't get off the phone Hazel was going to be very late indeed. She understood what was required. She was to cheer his wife up, not to let her dwell on Bradley Craig's clan and keep shtum regarding Nicky's secret. He didn't need to keep repeating his demands.

"Larry, if you don't bugger off, Ella will have plenty of brooding time because she'll be sat alone in the restaurant. I'm more than ready for my mission. Make her laugh - check. Make her merry, not drunk – check. Don't tell her that Nicky only hit her so her crazy boyfriend didn't stab her – check. Now will you go and make sure Mrs Eccles isn't receiving any indecent proposals and leave me in peace?"

1857 hours, 29 September 2012

Drinking in the company of an attractive man, without her husband, although perfectly innocent, made Ella anxious. Due to this her first Bacardi hardly touched the sides.

Rick was pleasant company. Currently he was explaining why he wasn't referred to as Doctor Pashley. As a surgeon he had earned the right to revert back to Mister. That made no sense to Ella. Larry had never sliced much more than a tomato and he was a Mister surely top surgeons should have a more prestigious title.

The more Ella learned of Bradley's father, the less her brain could comprehend his liaison with the boy's mother. "How in hell did you and Linda get together?" She blurted out after knocking back the remnants of her second drink. "Sorry, that was rude. None of my business."

Rick laughed. "I'm surprised you waited this long. It was the second thing Suzanne asked me and Nicky didn't even wait to be introduced properly."

On seeing Ella's reaction to the mention of her old friend, Rick returned to their original subject. "In answer to your question, Linda planned my seduction and our subsequent lives together long before we met. To her credit she nearly pulled it off, unfortunately for her my father turned up."

Ella thought she should stop drinking, none of that made sense. She tried to break it down. "Why would she plan to spend her life with someone she'd never met?"

"Because the who wasn't important, it was the bank balance that mattered. She wanted a rich husband, a big house and a chain of hairdressing salons with her name above the door. I was her best shot at getting all three."

"Why?"

"My mother. She owned the salon Joyce managed and Linda worked in."

"Your mother was a hairdresser?" Ella said incredulously.

"No. My mother was an heiress who happened to be very particular about who styled her hair. For her no one compared to Joyce so she bought the salon she worked in."

"You're kidding me," Ella accused.

"I'm afraid not. For my mother it was the logical thing to do. Bless her, she never had a hair out of place." Rick's smile faded.

"She's no longer with us?"

"Died just before Brad's tenth birthday. Not being able to find a decent hairdresser finished her in the end." Realising his attempt at humour was crass, Rick became serious. "It was cancer. By the time she complained, even my uber talented father couldn't cut it away."

"Your father's a surgeon too?"

"Yes. He likes to get into people's heads and play with their mind. With or without a knife."

"He's a brain surgeon?"

"A highly regarded one. Couldn't help mum though for all his brilliance."

"I'm so sorry."

"Me too. She was such a character. You should ask Joyce. They became quite close in an upstairs downstairs type of way. I think my mother missed her friendship as much as her coiffeuring skills."

"Was it your father's work that took you to Australia?"

Rick slugged back his whiskey and signalled to the barman for another round. "It was my father's pride, arrogance and obstinance that took us there. He was determined Linda's plan to trap me wouldn't succeed. Of course he got what he wanted. Bradley was brought up by another man and never got to meet his beautiful, loving, ever so dippy granny Pashley."

"That's a shame."

"She never dared to admit it but it broke her heart. I never realised how much until she died."

"Well maybe she's met Bradley now," Ella said attempting to lighten the mood.

"That's a nice thought," Rick replied wistfully whilst looking at his watch. "It's ten past seven."

Ella grimaced. "I hate to do this but do you think we could go to your room now?"

"I've had worse propositions," Rick teased. "Okay" he said grabbing their drinks, "Let's do this."

'Do what?' Ella's inner voice squealed. *'I thought you were just giving him the letter.'* 'I am'. *'Then why did you just go all peculiar?'* 'Shut up,' were Ella's final words to herself.

1907 hours, 29 September 2012

Rick wasn't the only one reminiscing about his mother. After her earlier conversation with Ella, Joyce was wondering how things would have turned out had Linda accepted Monica's first offer.

February 1992

Finding a new hairdresser was the least of Monica's problems. She had a salon to offload. As her only reason for purchasing the establishment was securing Joyce's talent, keeping it seemed absurd. Surprisingly her husband disagreed.

The salon was only a minor headache compared with what they were going to do about their son's dalliance in the cheap seats. Although Richard Junior had been grounded for the foreseeable future, Monica was under no illusion he would come to heel once his shackles were loosened. She suspected he and Linda would elope once legally able to do so. The prospect horrified her. She had waited so long for her beloved son, she couldn't lose him now.

Whenever his father was out of earshot Richard Junior would beg her to see Linda. When she refused he would call her weak and threaten that she would never meet her grandchild. After that he would storm to his room and refuse her entry until his father's return. He knew better than to behave in such a way in front of the master of the house.

Earlier, Monica's husband and mother-in-law had explained why she was not permitted to sell the salon then dispatched her to Joyce's home.

Now squirming in the seat besides her ex employee, Monica started to explain the reason for her visit. Firstly she stated that, although she beleived her husband's refusal to allow Richard Junior and Linda to marry had been delivered harshly, she supported the decision. It was obvious Linda had decided to wait until the problem could not be medically removed before making Richard Junior aware of his impending fatherhood. By doing so she might have ruined her own future but did she have to take their son down with her? Richard was to go to university, he would be a surgeon one day, maybe even enter politics. Having an illegitimate child hanging around was not acceptable so it was imperative her son's name did not appear on the birth certificate. The disbelief on Joyce's face was similar to that of Monica's when her mother-in-law had made the same statement two hours earlier.

Georgina Pashley had ordered her daughter-in-law to toughen up. For her son's sake she must make Joyce understand refusing their proposal would have grave consequences for the Craigs. The Pashley's lawyers were capable of stretching any legal battle over many years. How would the family survive without Joyce's income until then? Monica cleared her throat then explained the terms she hoped would mean her grandchild would not be raised on handouts.

If Linda agreed not to name Rick as the father, Joyce would remain as the manageress of the salon, Linda would have guaranteed employment after the child was born and, if she promised never to see Rick again, an extra two hundred pounds a month would be placed in her bank account.

Before enlightening Linda about the veiled bribe Monica had offered, Joyce sat her daughter down and assured Linda of her support. It might take a while for Joyce to find another salon but when she did she'd convince them to take Linda on as an apprentice. There was nothing to stop her becoming a top stylist. Joyce and Charlie, once he was released from prison, would help with the childcare. It would be a struggle but they would get through it as a family.

Once Joyce had finished, Linda insisted on hearing every detail of Monica's proposal again. Satisfied she had all the relevant information, Linda stood. "Sounds like they're pretty desperate to get rid of me," she chortled. "I'll give their offer serious consideration."

The fact that her daughter was prepared to give it any consideration saddened Joyce. What kind of monster had she created? She'd believed Linda's insistence that her love for Rick was genuine, now she was prepared to give him up for a few hundred quid and a job?

Two hours later, Linda assured her mother she'd no intention of selling herself that short. She wanted to own the salon. If Mrs P signed it over to her she would agree to all of their demands.

"And what about Rick. I thought you loved him?" Joyce replied disgustedly.

Chapter 9

1912 hours, 29 September 2012

The two women in the private booth looked on enviously as Rick led Ella from the bar. Ella desperately wanted to run over and tell them she was only going to his room to give him a letter. *'French letter?'* her inner voice enquired. 'I thought I told you to shut up.' Ella replied.

As they vacated the lift Ella's phone pinged. She was not surprised to learn that Hazel was running late. For a woman who didn't do make up and had had the same no-nonsense hairstyle for as long as Ella could remember, her friend took a surprisingly long time to get ready. Still, today Ella was grateful for Hazel's tardiness.

Entering his room Rick passed Ella her drink then took a long swig of his whiskey. "So what's so important that you need to get me alone?" Sensing Ella's discomfort Rick sighed, "Sorry, too soon?"

'Too soon for what?' Ella thought. *'Think Mr Hotstuff might have had one whiskey too many'* Ella's inner voice offered. 'Or I've had too many Barcardis' Ella thought.

Placing his whiskey on the table he motioned for Ella to take the only chair in the room as he sat on the bed.

Lifting the envelope from her bag Ella sighed, "I can think of no easy way to prepare you for this so I am just going to come out with it. Bradley wrote you a goodbye letter."

Had Ella punched Rick in the stomach he wouldn't have deflated so quickly. Trying, but failing, to regain his composure, "Okay" was the only response he could muster.

Ella stood and held out the letter. "Obviously you will want to be alone. If there is anything you want to discuss later please give me a call. I really hope it helps."

Rick looked up but made no attempt to take the proffered envelope. "I didn't... I wasn't..." he stuttered. "Oh my god that hurts," he said before curling up on the bed, holding his stomach and releasing a torrent of tears.

Ella stood rigid. This was the last reaction she had expected. Placing Bradley's letter on the bedside table she sat to the right of Rick. Pulling him into a sitting position, Ella placed his head on her shoulder and wrapped her arms around him. Sobbing uncontrollably, Rick allowed Ella to gently rock him. The ferocity of the sobs equalled the pressure of the hugs she received. Every time the volume increased his grip tightened. While Rick bawled, Ella stared into the dressing table mirror at her mascara stained face. Once again she had took her empathy too far.

When his tears stopped, Rick tore away from Ella, wandered aimlessly around the room then sat in the chair and placed his head in his hands. "My boy, my beautiful boy. I should've stayed. No, I should've taken him with me. He wouldn't have been there if I'd had the guts to do that. I came back for him. I swear I did." Rick's body convulsed and his tears started again. "I let him down so much."

Ella stood and walked over to where Bradley's father was seated. "It wasn't your fault. There's nothing you could have done. He had a good life. He had Suzanne and he loved the army. Please don't blame yourself."

Rick did not respond. As he gently sobbed, Ella contemplated leaving but how could she? He looked so helpless. When his tears again subsided Ella spoke, "Would you rather be on your own? I don't want to leave you like this…"

Rick looked up. "You're right, you're meeting your friend. You should go." When Ella shook her head, Rick held up his hand then stood and gently wiped mascara from her cheek. "I'm sorry, you shouldn't have to put up with this," he said uncomfortably. "I don't know where that came from."

"I think the heart would be a good guess," Ella suggested. "Is that the first time you've let it all go?"

"I don't think I let it, more I couldn't stop it but, yes, that's the first time I've cried properly. I think with all the talk of my mother and then realising that Bradley thought enough of me…" Rick's words caught, as if trying to free them he rubbed his throat then continued, "Thought enough of me to write me a letter." This time Rick managed to control his tears fairly quickly. "Look at me, I'm being a right girl," he laughed falsely.

"Sometimes a good cry is just what the doctor ordered or in your case, the mister."

Rick smiled weakly and signalled to the door. "I think I'll be okay now. You should go and meet your friend."

"Do you think I could freshen up first?" Ella asked pointing at the black streaks on her cheeks.

"Yes, of course, please use the bathroom. There's a hairdryer in there to, so you can dry your dress," he said pointing at the large damp patch on her shoulder.

Ten minutes later Ella vacated the ensuite, fresh faced and dry. Rick was sitting at the desk his whiskey in one hand, Bradley's unopened letter in the other. "I'm guessing I am not the only one. I hope the others took it better than I did," Rick cringed.

"They haven't received theirs yet."

"Oh, thought you'd get the easy one out of the way first?"

Ella shrugged. "We wanted to deliver them as close together as possible. Joyce and Charlie will get theirs after mass tomorrow then Linda and Phil will get theirs."

"What about Susie?"

"The plan was for Jess to deliver it at the same time but Susie's not too good at the moment so that's under consideration."

Rick nodded. "Well I better not keep you. Your friend will be wondering where you are."

"If you need anyone to talk to once you've…" She pointed to the letter, "I'll be downstairs, just give me a call."

"That's kind of you but I'll be okay." Showing his guest out, Rick gently grabbed Ella's arm then pecked her on the cheek, "Thank you."

Aware of how flushed her cheeks were and of their lack of blusher, Ella rushed to the lift.

Hazel threw Ella a puzzled looked when she joined her at the bar. "I've heard of posh frock, no knickers but posh frock, no slap that's a first for you," she said circling her finger in front of Ella's face.

"Bit of a mascara malfunction," she explained as she hugged her friend. Once released, Hazel grabbed Ella's cheeks then kissed her hard on the lips.

"What the bloody hell was that for?" asked a shocked Ella.

"For the benefit of those two nosy bitches," Hazel said signaling towards the two women in the private booth who had been watching Ella with Rick earlier. Ella smiled knowingly then cupped Hazel's bottom cheek and led her to a free table.

Her friend achieved the impossible. She managed to make Ella laugh, forget Bradley Craig and even put his gorgeous father to the back of her mind. There was however one casualty of her earlier promise to Larry; the one to get Ella merry not drunk. In Hazel's defence, her friend had been well oiled by the time they met.

The booth by the door became vacant shortly after Larry's arrival. It seemed the sight of his wife and her friend licking Larry's cheeks and nibbling his ears in unison was too much for the nebby ladies.

2257 hours, 29 September 2012

The pills caught in his throat but he forced himself to swallow. He hated what he had to do but what choice did he have? Dinger couldn't spend another night screaming out for a friend who wouldn't answer.

2258 hours, 29 September 2012

Swallowing the paracetamol, Joyce wondered how much longer she would be forced to sleep on Linda's lumpy bed. Even though she had brought her own bedding the thought of laying where Paul Douglas had before her made her skin crawl. That and Linda's earlier temper tantrum had triggered the headache she was hoping medication would disperse.

Joyce suspected Linda's outburst about being 'fucking babysat by Captain fucking Darling' was triggered as much by her need for alcohol as it was her dislike of Ella. Tonight's rant had started as an attack on the officer, swiftly moved onto what a useless mother Joyce was then escalated into her father being a complete loser and concluded with a full scale attack on the

Pashleys. Thankfully, Charlie's arrival with a chippy supper halted the abuse.

Joyce wondered had her husband not intervened who would have been next in line for an acid bath care of Linda's tongue. Probably Rick. Since learning her son and his absent father had been in regular contact, Linda was even more venomous when berating her first love.

Joyce remembered, all too well, the first time Linda called him a spineless fucking mummy's boy. It had been a few weeks after the girl had claimed undying love and enlightened her mother how she and Rick were going to be together despite his parents' objections.

March 1992

When Joyce had accused her daughter of being a money-grabbing little tart, Linda had taken great pleasure in informing her mother she was nothing of the sort. Yes, she'd offered to give up Rick if she was gifted the salon but that didn't mean she would.

After she'd moved into the flat above the shop, Rick would be able to secretly visit until it was financially viable to stick two fingers up at his parents. After that they would raise their child together. "Hopefully, when they see how serious we are and meet their grandchild they will let us marry." Linda snorted, "In the meantime I get to be your boss," she told a horrified Joyce.

Two weeks later, the arrival of Rick's letter sent Linda's temper off the Richter scale. He was an idiot; he was a spineless coward; he was staying in fucking Australia!

After her anger came disbelief, then despair as she realised how badly their foolproof plan had backfired. She'd never dreamed Monica could be so conniving.

Rick's mother's suggestion that visiting Aunt Emily might help their cause had led Linda to believe she was warming to the prospect of being a grandmother. According to Monica, Rick's liberal Aunt was one of the few people his father listened to. If anyone could persuade Richard Senior to allow the young couple to marry it was Emily. When his mother intimated his Aunt was definitely on side and Richard Senior had agreed to fly over to Australia to visit her, Rick's fate was sealed.

In his short letter, Rick explained his passport had been confiscated as soon as he'd cleared customs. Shortly after, he'd been informed he would take his A-Levels in Australia, then study medicine at the ANU. Once a qualified doctor he could either stay in Oz or go home and marry his beloved Linda. If he chose the latter they would pay his airfare and wish him well.

Mr Pashley had applied to emigrate. Given his expertise in neurosurgery and his brother-in-law's sponsorship his success was guaranteed. Until approved he was granted a temporary works visa at Canberra Hospital. He was due to start at the end of the month, giving him time to return to Sheffield to tie up a few loose ends.

Linda was inconsolable as she swore to have the Pashley's charged with kidnapping. They would not get away with it. She wasn't going to be left holding the baby. Once she had vented her frustration she fell into her mother's open arms and sobbed. Joyce recoiled when Linda admitted losing Rick was not the only cause of her distress. The fact that it was too late to abort was also a major contributor to her tears.

When Mr Pashley arrived at their house two days later, Linda flew at him. He was not going to win, she yelled. Rick's name was going on the birth certificate. She would ruin the Pashley's reputation. All their cronies would soon learn how they how they had kidnapped their son so he couldn't marry his true love and bring up his child. She was going to tell newspapers.

Mr Pashley had scoffed. Did she realise how ridiculous she sounded accusing parents of kidnapping their own child? The police had said something similar when she had tried to report it. He invited her to go to the papers but warned his lawyers would gag any reporter gullible enough to believe her lies.

As Linda's resolve faded, Mr Pashley's increased. It was time for her to admit defeat. Her little plan to leech off his son had failed. If she signed today he would still allow mother and daughter to keep their jobs and honour the two hundred pounds maintenance money originally offered. If she didn't she would have to chase Rick half way around the world to get a percentage of his pocket money whilst looking for another job. It was her choice.

Linda tried to barter with Mr P. Three hundred pounds and they had a deal. Mr Pashley immediately dropped his offer by fifty pounds. When Linda failed to respond he headed for the door.

Now aware this was one man she couldn't charm Linda chased after him.

Three plates and a chair were the victims of Linda's rage when she returned. "You can take it out of my hundred and fifty measly quid!" she yelled at her mother.

After educating Joyce regarding her failures as a parent and future grandmother, Linda moved on to her next victim: Rick. He was useless, in bed and out. She was glad to see the back of him. Not that he was going to get away with it. Once he started to earn his big doctor wages she'd have her cut.

A week later, Rick's letter swearing undying love and begging her to wait until he was financially independent lifted her spirits. She might have to wait a little longer than planned but the mansion wasn't completely out of reach.

As his parents had banned all contact with Linda, Rick provided her with the address of a friend, who had agreed to act as a go between. She quickly drafted her reply. There was no other man for her. She would wait as long as necessary to be in his arms again. Until then she would work hard to provide a good life for their son until he returned to provide a better one.

Linda remained in a buoyant mood until Bradley's arrival four months later. Cuddling her son for the first time she kissed his cheek. She had thought herself incapable of feeling such love. "Your daddy doesn't know what he's missing," she told the tiny bundle.

Chapter 10
0755 hours, 30 September 2012

After meeting up with Hazel, Ella's Bacardi consumption had not lost momentum so the bacon roll with lashings of brown sauce was just what the doctor ordered.

Last night, whilst carrying his wife to bed, Larry had assured her he also loved her to the moon and back but had no intentions of doing any of the obscene things she was suggesting in her current state. Before she was allowed to lay her head, she was forced to take two paracetamols and drink a pint of water. Having done so, Ella released a loud belch.

Larry recoiled, "Who had the fajitas?" he said wafting his hand in front of his nose.

"Not me," Ella replied defensively, "I had the Bacardi."

Now nursing her cup of coffee, Ella was disputing Larry's version of events. Not that she had an alternative to offer. "I've got to be at Linda's in forty minutes," she complained. "Why did you let me drink so much?"

"By the time I joined you the damage was already done. I think it's best I drive you over to the Haddington."

"So do I Mr H. Can we go via Maccy D's?"

0838 hours, 30 September 2012

Charlie opened the door to find Ella holding a strawberry milkshake whilst chomping on an extra strong mint. "Good night?" he laughed.

"Oh no, can you tell. I'm so sorry. I met up with a friend and…"

"Enough lass, everyone's entitled to a blow out once in a while."

Joyce and Beetle joined them in the hall. "Morning, love, Beetle's going to drop us off at home," Joyce said brightly. "Linda's still in her pit. If you can, will you get her to eat summat when she decides to make an appearance? There's a fresh pot of tea in the kitchen and some homemade scones Dave brought over last night. Help yourself." Taking in Ella's appearance Joyce looked concerned. "Are you alright love, you look a bit peaky?"

Charlie butted in, "Lass's fine, don't fuss. We need to get off. If you're not at church on time, Father O can't be late," he chuckled opening the front door.

"We'll get back as soon as we can," Joyce told Ella. "Thanks for this love, you're a life saver."

Beetle shuffled out behind Joyce, nodding his acknowledgement to Ella as he passed.

"Thank God for that," Linda announced from the top of the stairs. "Thought they'd never bloody go. Do us a favour will you? Put us some toast on while I have my morning constitutional. I won't be long, they're like an oil slick these days."

Now that sounded more like the Linda of old.

After failing to locate the toaster in any of the sparsely filled cupboards, Ella placed two slices of bread under the grill then wandered into the living room to retrieve her hangover remedy. Her hands slammed over her ears when her phone rang. *'Too loud'* her inner voice moaned. Seeing Rick's name flashing on the offending item, Ella took a calming breath before answering.

"Hi Ella, hope I didn't wake you."

"No such luck. I'm at Linda's.

"Oh in that case, I'll call back later," Rick answered nervously.

"It's okay, I'm on my own. Linda's upstairs and Joyce and Charlie are out. What can I do for you?"

"Actually, I was thinking I might be able to do something for you."

'Please, no teasing, my head hurts too much.'

"I want to offer my services," Rick continued. "Having read my letter I think Suzanne should receive hers and I'd like to deliver it."

"Can I ask why?"

"My son instructed me to look after her and their child. Reading his words gave me a sense of purpose and I'm hopeful Suzanne's letter will do the same for her. As you know, she's disappearing into her own little world, this could be our best chance of bringing her back."

"Possibly, but are you sure you want to deliver it?"

"What are your options? She doesn't know Jess. Dave and Louise will need to support her once she's read it and Joyce is receiving her own letter today. I think I'm your best option and more importantly I want to do it."

"I'm not doubting your suitability, it's just given the toll your letter took on you do you think you will be okay?"

Rick thought for a moment. "I'll be fine. Learning he'd written to me was the shock, reading it was quite therapeutic."

Ella could think of no reason to deny his request. Still, she felt she should check with Pete Waller before agreeing. She was still treading on eggshells over the will business so didn't want to alienate him any further by making this decision without his approval. "Rick, could you hold off until tomorrow. Jess has the letter but she's not planning on delivering it today. I promise you won't be gazumped, I'd just like to check with my bosses before agreeing to anything."

"I understand. I don't want to get you in anymore trouble than I already have."

The noise of the smoke alarm sent a shooting pain through Ella's skull and her stomach threatened to bring back her bacon sandwich. "Sorry, I'm going to have to go, I've burnt the toast," she explained running into the kitchen.

After throwing the flaming bread into the sink, Ella opened the kitchen window then went in search of the smoke alarm armed with a tea towel. Wafting the smoke away she was embarrassed to see Linda descending the stairs. "Not so bloody perfect after all, eh? Can't even make a bit of toast without burning the place down."

Ella chose not to answer until the noise ceased. "Sorry about that, I was on the phone. I'll put some more on. The tea's mashed. How do you take it?"

"White, three and mind I like my toast lightly done with plenty of butter."

'Yes your majesty'

Ten minutes later Ella passed Linda her toast and enquired how she was feeling today.

"Missing the bevy. The drugs help a bit but the doc says it'll take time. Could do without having to see a trick cyclist though."

"For the agoraphobia?"

"Yes, don't know why they're bothering. It's not like there's anywhere I want to go,"

"Six years is a long time without fresh air," Ella observed.

Linda resisted correcting Ella. It was actually sixteen years since she had left the house voluntarily.

17 July 1996

For over three years Linda and Rick courted by airmail. The arrangement suited Linda, since Bradley's birth her interest in the opposite sex had dwindled. The only boy she had eyes for was her son.

Determined to provide for him, and with the perk of having a mother for a boss, Linda quickly completed her hairdressing apprenticeship. The salon's clientele fussed and fawned over Bradley in-between their treatments so childcare was never an issue.

By the age of eighteen Linda was an accomplished stylist. Her appointment book was always full and she was highly regarded in a community usually so quick to judge. Yes, she was bringing up an illegitimate child but, as her mothering and professional skills were impressive, the ladies were prepared to overlook that. After all no one could create the 'Rachel Green' look like Linda.

Bradley softened Linda in every way. Now, instead of avoiding her, people actively sought her company. The fact she was devoted to the child's father was also commendable. Everyone concurred if it wasn't for the lad's snobby bastard of a father the couple would be together. Linda, not used to such praise from the older fraternity, basked in their words.

For the first time in her life she was content, she loved her son, her man and her job. Surprisingly she also found she could love herself. Not in the arrogant way she had as an adolescent teenager but as a mother.

Wanting to ensure they would have a respectable place to dwell when Rick returned, Linda had moved into her own two-bed semi around the corner from her mother and set about creating their perfect, albeit temporary, home.

Within a month of moving, Linda had redecorated and furnished the whole house. Other than Bradley's room, which was a shrine to Thomas the Tank Engine, everywhere was either pine, flowery or both. Charlie teased her that they lived in the city of steel not the fields of rye. Joking aside he was proud of his daughter's achievements. The house was homely and clean and his grandson thrived in his new environment.

Linda had been planning Bradley's fourth birthday celebration since moving on Kemmel Street. For the first three years of her son's life he had received his father's cards and money through the post, this year Rick's gifts would be delivered in person. For Linda, his attendance would be the icing on Bradley's oversized 'Thomas' cake.

She couldn't wait to show off her man. She knew some of her fellow single mothers scoffed at the tiny diamond ring she wore and her claim that Brad's dad would marry her once he qualified to be a doctor. She relished the opportunity to silence her doubters, especially her bitch of a neighbour, Cindy.

There was only one aspect of Rick's arrival that concerned Linda. In the five years since losing her virginity, she had only been sexually active for six months with one partner. Although returning to the bedroom made her apprehensive, the memory of long afternoons of nakedness meant Linda was in a constant state of arousal in the days leading up to Rick's return.

Determined to remind her absent beau what he was missing, she'd vowed to get her figure back with the help of Cher's 'New Attitude' video and cabbage soup. The exertion required to match the Diva's movements filled the living room with clues of Linda's current diet plan. Bradley's observation that mummy smelt like doggy cack prompted a dietary revision.

Opening the door to the gift-laden stranger, Linda held Bradley close to her hip. Rick's eyes searched for his son's, when he found them the huge grins exchanged between the two men in her life made Linda's heart leap. "Bradley, this is your daddy," she said handing over her son to a pair of eager hands. Rick closed his eyes as he held the boy tight. When he opened them he looked over his son's shoulder and took in the sight before him.

Once released the youngster toddled into the living room. Stepping into the house, Rick closed the door then grabbed his girlfriend. They had discussed in letters, and more recently in phone calls what they would do to each other the next time they met. Neither of them had envisaged how desperately they would want to. When Rick pulled her up into his arms, Linda wrapped her legs around him and ground herself against his penis.

Fifteen minutes later a horrified Linda stood in the shower. With only the essential items of clothing removed orgasms had been achieved on both sides in a matter of moments; whilst her young son was playing in the other room. How could she?

When she entered the living room the sight of her son happily sitting on Rick's knee whilst telling him how Emily, the lady train, had been naughty and pulled Annie and Clarabelle eased her guilt. Rick's nodding encouraged Bradley to explain about all of Thomas' friends at a hectic rate. Tears came to Linda's eyes. Mr Pashley could shove his money. This was all she wanted; Bradley with his dad.

During the party her neighbours kept the kids occupied whilst Linda tried to convince Joyce that Bradley was not in anyway disturbed by Rick's presence or his apparent need to constantly hug him. Joyce's anger at the boy who had abandoned her daughter subsided when she saw how comfortable her grandson was in his arms. Rick was also a hit with Linda's friends. Australia had been kind to him. The sun had bleached his hair and given him a healthy tan. His new hobby of surfing had certainly encouraged his body to fill out in all the right places. Add to this the hint of an Australian accent and the girls were positively drooling.

Linda happily waved goodbye the last of her flirty friends then joined Rick and her son in the child's bedroom. When they had first met, Linda's arrogance had convinced her she was doing Rick the favour. Now she accepted their roles were reversed. He could have his pick of the girls. Ironically, her best asset was no longer her formidable chest, it was the little boy he was now helping her tuck into bed. She had naively thought having Bradley would bring her financial security but now it was the emotional type she desired. When he had been conceived she thought Bradley a means to an end. Now he was her everything.

Bradley gave them both big hugs and wet kisses then yawned through the words 'Bestest birthday ever' before falling asleep. Rick stroked his son's hair. "God, I love him," he said more to himself than to Linda.

Linda led Rick to the bedroom. This time their lovemaking was slow and deliberate. Her beau insisted on kissing every part of her body. It was torture. By ten o'clock the pair had both climaxed three times. Linda was glowing from their evening of pleasure and just about to drift off when Rick announced he needed to let his mother know he wasn't coming back to his grandmother's house tonight.

Linda had stared at him in disbelief. After a few probing questions she ascertained the Pashleys had no idea of their son's whereabouts. Rick's insistence he intended to inform them of his decision to stay in Sheffield after his grandmother's funeral floored Linda. She had no idea the old bat was ill. When she enquired where that bastard thought he was, Rick responded his father wasn't concerned with that at the moment but his mother would be worried.

Linda finally relented when Rick told her of his plans to take her and Bradley to Blackpool the following day. Before she had become a parent she would have happily let Mrs P believe her precious son had been hit by a bus, now she was unable to cause another mother such pain, even Monica Pashley.

On hearing his father's voice, the colour drained from Rick's face. Fearing he would lose his nerve Linda wrapped her arms around her lover's waist, nuzzled her cheek into his bareback then lowered her hand to stroke his penis. Her show of support was effective. Pulling himself to his full height Rick informed his father in order to numb the pain of losing his grandmamma he'd consumed alcohol and was therefore unfit to drive. Claiming his friend's family were happy for him to stay the night, Rick slammed the phone down silencing his father's protests.

"You drove here?" Linda asked in awe.

Rick was shaking as he answered her question, "Yes, I passed my test last year. Dad put the hire car in my name. Probably thought I could drive him around whilst he drank with his old cronies. Well that's backfired on him," he said with false bravado.

Sensing his fear, Linda decided to take his mind off his father. Pulling away the white terry cloth standing between her and infinite pleasure she smiled suggestively. After a little coaxing her lover grabbed her hand and headed up the stairs. When the phone started to ring Linda shook her head and pushed Rick into the bedroom.

The sound of Bradley's sleepy voice deflated Rick's ardour. "Mummy phone," the young boy called from the doorway.

Due to her arousal, Linda had managed to ignore the constant ringing but now it had disturbed her son she was fuming. Not only because the caller had ruined 'the moment' but because they obviously were not going to ring off until they got an answer.

Storming downstairs she grabbed the receiver. "Can you not take a hint? When no one answers after five rings they're not fucking going to," Linda yelled.

"Still as charming as ever I see." Linda was too shocked to respond. "Well if you've finished your enlightening lesson on telephone etiquette do you think I could speak to my son?"

How the hell did that bastard get her number? When his request was not met, Richard Senior repeated it more forcefully. "Put my son on the phone this minute you little…"

Regaining her composure, Linda interrupted, "I'm sorry he's not available at the moment. He's putting your grandson back to bed. The phone disturbed him."

"Oh please, we both know your little bastard does not carry my genes. Still, I can hardly blame you for picking my boy out of a cast of probables to foot the bill."

"Bradley is your grandson," Linda screamed. "Rick is the only man I've ever slept with…" Rick's arrival at her side ensured he heard his father's response.

"As amusing as your protestations are I have no wish to hear any more of your lies. Just tell my deceitful, ungrateful, gullible son that I know exactly where he is and more importantly I know he has stolen the car. Unless both are back here tonight I will call the police and have him arrested. I know where you live so they will have no problem finding him. He needs to be back here tonight or so help me God…"

Linda slammed down the phone. "How did he get my number?" she screamed running up the stairs after Rick.

"He must have called 1471," he replied pulling his sweater over his head. "I'd better go."

"Go where? Not back to him?"

"I've got to. You don't know what he's like. It's not worth ..."

"Not worth what? Me and your son? Do you consider us as worthless as your father thinks we are?"

"You know that's not what I meant. I need to rethink this. He knows where you live. If I go back now he might..."

"What? Put you on the next plane out of here?" Linda followed Rick down the stairs. "Just stay. It's time we stood up to him."

"Not like this. Let me talk to him."

Linda slumped onto the bottom stair. "Like you did last time?" She angrily wiped at the tears threatening to fall. "He didn't listen then so what makes you think he will now."

"I'll make him." Rick's eyes were darting around the hallway. "Have you seen my car keys?"

Spotting the keys on the coat hook Linda grabbed them and held them behind her back. "He won't listen. You know that. Stay. Please," Linda pleaded. "Or I'll come with you," she added desperately. "We can talk to him together. Show him we're serious. We'll take Bradley."

Rick was panicking. "No," he yelled. "He'll lose it if he sees you. I'll go on my own, it'll be easier."

"For you maybe. What about us?" When Rick failed to answer, Linda flew at him. "You leave this house and you will never see us again. Do you hear me? I will not have you swanning in here, getting Brad's hopes up then pissing off again."

Rick grabbed Linda's shoulders in an attempt to calm her down. Wriggling free of his grip she pushed him into the wall. "Don't touch me unless you're staying."

"Please Linda, try and understand. I'll be back, I promise."

"When? In another four years?"

"I'm sorry I've got to go."

Defeated, Linda walked towards the stairs then knelt on the bottom one and placed her head in her hands.

"Mummy?"

Linda quickly wiped her eyes and looked up at her son. Seeing her distress his bottom lip started to quiver. Forcing a smile she responded, 'It's okay Pumpkin, Mummy's fine. You go to bed now. I'll tuck you in, in a minute."

"And Daddy?" Bradley asked hopefully.

Linda looked at Rick. The man who had slammed the phone down on his father only minutes ago was no longer present. Instead, there stood the boy who had crept out of her mother's house years earlier at his father's request. Once again, Mr Pashley was playing the tune while his son danced.

"No, not Daddy, Pumpkin," She held Rick's gaze. "Daddy has to go now and look for his bollocks." Linda said these words playfully in the hope the word bollocks would not resonate with her son.

"Linda, I…"

"Say goodbye to your son Rick. You owe him that much at least."

Rick ascended the stairs, lifted Bradley into his arms and headed towards the boy's bedroom. The sight caused Linda to double over. Her feeling of hopelessness was soon superseded by irrepressible rage. No more tears, she swore, as she opened her front door.

'95' car number plates were as rare as uncashed giros on her street so she soon located her target. Running to the hire car she ran Rick's keys over the paintwork. The gouge got deeper from boot to bonnet as her fury increased. Having circled the car once, she started to back heel each door. By the time Rick joined her she was on the fourth. Lifting her off her feet he carried her to the house. Linda wriggled to get free whilst scratching at his face with his car key. Accepting his punishment without comment, Rick placed Linda inside the doorway then fought to free the keys from her hand. Once successful he ran to the car with Linda at his heels. "I swear, if you drive away tonight you will never see your son again. I swear it Rick. I swear it."

Rick slammed the car door just as Linda reached it. When he refused to look at her, Linda moved to the front of the car and *sprawled herself across the bonnet. Still refusing to make eye contact, Rick averted his gaze. In exasperation, his girlfriend ripped off the right hand wiper then climbed off the car. When Rick sped away she hurled the wiper after him. When it failed to hit its target Linda fell to her knees and wept.*

Chapter 11

0932 hours, 30 September 2012

"Linda?" Increasing her volume, Ella repeated her question, "Are you going to refuse to see the psychiatrist?"

Linda considered the question. "I can't see the point. There's nowt out there for me. Mind, if I don't sort myself out them two will never bugger off or let Paul come back."

"You want him back?" Ella was astounded.

"'Course I do. They kicked him out, not me."

"Why didn't you stop them?"

"Oh I don't know," Linda snapped. "Maybe because I was drugged up to the eyeballs after a massive panic attack."

"You're capable of saying something now."

"How? Me and dad are getting on for the first time ever. Telling him will put us back to square one. Anyway, Paul's not been near. Maybe he's relieved to get away."

Ella grabbed her bag. After a minute of frantic searching, Linda demanded to know what the fuck Ella was looking for. The officer resisted the urge to swear. That morning she had grabbed Linda's letter from Bradley but not from Paul.' Ella looked up guiltily. If she told the truth, she'd get lynched. "Sorry, I was after painkillers. I've a bit of a headache." Seeing how unsympathetic Linda was to her plight, Ella decided to return to their original conversation. "Paul probably doesn't want another scene with your dad."

"Maybe. Could you get a message to him?" Linda asked. "On the QT like."

Great, now Linda wanted to use her as an errand girl too. "I don't think your mum and dad would be happy with me sneaking around behind their backs."

"I thought you were here to look after me, not them."

"I'm here to look after all of you." Ella reassured.

"Then tell Paul I love him and I want him back." When Ella hesitated, Linda continued, "Do you think I want to beg? I'm a prisoner in my own home. You're one of the few people they let through the bloody door. I'm sick of it. I can't go out and he can't come in." With that Linda burst into tears.

Although her first reaction was to comfort Linda, Ella stalled when she reached the couch. As the sobs grew louder, Ella couldn't hold back. Taking the seat next to Bradley's mother she tentatively placed her arm around the distressed woman's shoulder.

"What the fuck do you think you're doing?" Linda yelled. "Don't come all fucking concerned now. You don't give a shit about me. If you did you'd be out looking for my husband not trying to cuddle me, you fucking lesbian!"

Something inside Ella snapped. "Linda even though you make it very difficult, I am 'fucking' concerned about you. I want to help but I'm a CVO not a bloody marriage counsellor or a 'fucking' lesbian for your information."

Linda looked up, blinked away her tears then burst into laughter. "Haha, knew I'd break you eventually. Mind, I've got to admit you're a hard nut to crack. I'd have clocked me one ages ago."

Ella laughed. "I've been tempted, believe me."

Grabbing a tissue, Linda blew her nose loudly then picked up her toast. Inspecting the bread she nodded her approval. "Not bad, I'd have given it another minute but it's edible."

1023 hours, 30 September 2012

Fucking quacks. Why were they hell bent on him seeing a shrink? It was the stupid night nurse's fault. She gave no credence to Dinger's insistence his sleep had been disturbed due to the pain in his shoulder. According to her it was his mind not his pain causing him to scream out during the night. After all, he was being given enough pain relief and sleeping tablets to knock out a horse.

Yesterday morning after the nurse had bubbled him, he'd tried to assure the doctor there was no need for the psychiatrist to waste valuable time on him. Men with much more horrific injuries, both physical and mental, were in greater need. He'd been involved in other serious incidents and recovered with the minimum of counselling. He was aware of all the coping mechanisms and the signs he needed to look out for. He would unburden on his family when he got home. They were all the tonic he needed.

The doctor's insisted his refusal to receive counselling would delay his release date. Not trusting himself not to lash out, Dinger had sat on his free hand whilst the doctor harped on about the benefit of seeing the mind benders.

Last night, realising his only chance of escape was a trouble free night, Dinger had added a pill from his suicide stash to the two sleeping tablets the nurse had given him. It had had the desired affect but now he felt groggy and struggled to maintain his fake smile whilst telling the doctors he was feeling much better after a good nights sleep.

His pretence seemed to work. If he slept without 'pain' for the next few nights they would reconsider sending him home. Although this meant he would have to deplete his stash further, he consoled himself that once released he would not have to take another tablet until the fatal dose.

1157 hours, 30 September 2012

For a second Joyce thought she had walked into the wrong maisonette.

"And then, the cheeky little bugger passed her a tissue and told her to dry them. He was only three and already had no time for whining women," Linda shrieked.

"Sorry, I'm going to have to use your bathroom," Ella squealed jumping up from the couch. Charlie quickly moved his wife out of the officer's path. Tears of laughter running down her cheeks, Ella gratefully rushed past the elderly couple.

Returning to the living room, Ella was relieved when Linda didn't resurrect her barriers. Witnessing the playful banter between her and Charlie made Ella melancholy. Excusing herself momentarily she placed a call to her parents.

After making her dinner reservation, Ella joined Joyce in the kitchen. "How did your meeting with Father O'Sullivan go?" she asked.

The older woman's face lit up. "Oh it was a lovely letter. That grandson of mine was a bloody saint. I never doubted he loved us but..." Joyce's words caught in her throat. "Let's just say he made us feel very special," she finished then wiped her eyes with her hand.

"Do you want me to give Linda hers now?"

"No," Joyce replied decisively. "She's in a good mood, it would be a shame to spoil it. Why don't you leave it with me? I'll put it with Phil's and give it her when the time is right."

"Okay, if you're sure."

"I am. Now you get yourself back to that hubby of yours. You've done more than enough today. Never thought I'd see the day you two laughed together. Well done you."

1323 hours, 30 September 2012

Reaching the car park, Ella was disappointed not to see Larry waiting. Her disappointment turned to fury when Paul Douglas jumped out from behind a parked car.

"We'll have to stop meeting like this," she told Paul as she purposefully walked passed him and headed towards the car park's entrance.

Paul followed. "What did she say? Is she gonna write back?"

"I haven't given her the letter," Ella admitted turning to face her tormentor.

Paul stopped a little bit too close for comfort. "Why the fuck not? I know you were on your own. I saw the old bastards come back."

"I want to be sure she's in the right frame of mind when I deliver it." Ella said whilst looking over her shoulder. *'And to remember to bring the letter in the first place'*

"So you're a bloody shrink now?"

Standing up to Linda had broken a few barriers so maybe that was what was required with Paul. "No I'm not a shrink, or a bloody postman." Ella said forcefully.

"Well what the fuck are you then? Because I can't see why you're still hanging around here sticking your fucking nose in."

"I'm Linda's CVO. It's my job to look after her."

"No it's mine. I'm her fucking husband. I need to get back there. Sleeping on our Cindy's couch is doing my fucking head in."

"Now I'm confused, is it your couch or your wife you're missing?" Ella leered.

"Fucking hell that's a tough one, you'll have to let me think about it." Paul stroked his chin in mock contemplation. "My couch doesn't puke everywhere while moaning about being in pain. Oh and it doesn't have interfering fucking tarts like you turning up to see it. So, I suppose the couch has it."

"I can't imagine why Linda wouldn't feel the same. It's a darn sight more supportive than you."

"You cheeky bitch, I've supported her for fucking years," Paul raged. "They weren't interested when she was shaking like a shitting dog after that twat left. I had to pick up the pieces then. What thanks did I get? Diddly squat."

"If, by picking up the pieces, you mean filling her with booze, it's hardly surprising they weren't grateful."

"She chose to be an alky, I didn't make her one. She poured it down her own neck. I was just the skivvy she ordered to fetch it," Paul said defensively.

"You could have refused."

"Don't you think I tried? Listen, whatever you think, I love that woman!" Paul yelled.

"Of course you do," Ella replied sarcastically.

"Are you saying she's not good enough to be loved? She's a diamond, that girl. My soulmate."

"Well I suppose you've a lot in common. You both seem to get pleasure from throwing abuse at people."

"And why do you think that is?" Paul asked lowering his tone. "Come on, you're a clever woman, figure it out." Ella's blank look encouraged Paul to continue, "She's not daft, she knows what people think of her so she gets the knife in first. The ruder she is the quicker they piss off. You were different though. Didn't matter what we threw at you, you came back." Paul snorted. "Don't worry, we knew it weren't through choice."

Aware the curtains on the estate were once again twitching, Ella decided to alleviate the tension. "Listen, to be honest I would have given Linda the letter today but the opportunity didn't present itself. I'll try again soon. Just promise me it doesn't contain anything that might upset her."

"It doesn't, I swear. She's nowhere near as hard as she makes out. I just want her to know someone gives a shit. She just lost one of the few that did so she needs me whether you believe it or not."

The emotions in Paul's voice silenced Ella.

2121 hours, 30 September 2012

Cuddled up on the couch with Larry, Ella reflected on her day. Other than Paul's appearance it had been an enjoyable one. Having a civilised conversation with Linda had definitely been the highlight followed closely by her mother's sumptuous roast dinner.

Ella had expected Larry to strop because she'd failed to consult him before changing their dinner plans. Fortunately, he was too wound up to complain. After she'd revealed the identity of the man she'd been deep in conversation with when he had finally arrived to collect her, Ella had had to resort to threats of violence in order to convince him not to exact some on Paul Douglas.

His mood quickly improved when they arrived at the Johnstone's. Ella knew his sullenness was just pretence when he complained that her yorkshire pudding was twice the size of his and she had more roast potatoes. Mrs Johnstone's defence of her favouritism amused Ella. Saying it was nice to be able to feed her daughter again was priceless, it had only been three weeks since she had last visit to her mother's table.

"And what about your favourite son-in-law?" Larry moaned.

Ella's father informed Mrs Malone, who was now to be a regular for Sunday lunch, that Larry was their only son-in-law so the bar wasn't high.

Joking aside, Mr Johnstone was relieved to see his daughter and her husband laughing together. He'd feared the reappearance of the girl he had once regarded as a surrogate daughter, could easily have caused the collapse of his real daughter's marriage. He'd also been fearful of Ella's reaction if she learned the part he had played in covering up Larry's deceit. His son-in-law's assurances that his daughter would never speak to Nicky again only eased his burden slightly. He suspected Ann and Hazel were both holding their pins in the air, waiting to burst Ella's bubble.

2151 hours, 30 September 2012

As she passed her study, Paul's letter taunted her. She would have to deliver it but not tomorrow. Bradley's letter would be enough for Linda to contend with.

What about Suzanne's letter? Would the hierarchy have any objection to Rick handing it over? A worrying thought crossed Ella's mind. What if they thought she had somehow convinced Bradley's father to make the request?

The bollocking she had received three days ago had shaken her. She was paranoid any wrong move on her part would land her back in front of her boss. Given her impelling sense of self-destruction she questioned why she was so determined to continue with her other little mission.

2342 hours, 30 September 2012

Self-destruction was never far from Dinger's mind. As he willed the meds to take effect he prayed for an uneventful night. Earlier he had dozed off and awoke screaming. Fortunately, the young nurse on duty had accepted his claim that he badly twisted his shoulder. The real catalyst of his nightmare had been his vision of Jabbaar snatching Suzanne's red knickers from Bradley's dead body.

The identity of Bradley's assassin had inspired Dinger's belief the bullet that killed his friend was meant for him. Since Jabbaar's arrival on the base it had been Dinger that had scorned, ridiculed and humiliated the Afghan Army recruit. It wasn't personal, all the trainees received the same treatment from Corporal Bell. For him, his presence in Afghan was about protecting his friends not making new ones. He made no effort to hide his contempt for men who would readily raise arms with their enemy against their countrymen. If a foreign army invaded Britain he would die before volunteering to fight against his own.

Bradley was the complete opposite. It was vital to him their mission had a purpose. He believed all the drivel about enhancing the Afghans' quality of life and making it a safer place for their children to grow up. He constantly babbled on about 'hearts and minds' - win their hearts to change their minds. Dinger didn't see why they needed to. It was their country, their faith, and their funeral. Why should he constantly repeat himself to people who claimed not to understand him one minute, then managed to repeat verbatim every unkind expletive he directed their way? He'd already been in front of the Platoon Commander on three occasions to discuss his temperament around the devious little bastards. Of course, one of the formal complaints had come from Jabbaar.

Poor, timid, Jabbaar who struggled to comprehend the Corporal's orders. For someone so afraid of friction, Dinger had noticed he was always in the thick of any discord and constantly poking his nose into things that were none of his concern. Dinger had reported the slimy bastard's over interest in their weapon systems, patrol patterns and personal lives but his superiors had failed to heed his warning. Stupidly, Dinger had made no secret of his suspicions to Jabbaar. In fact he took every opportunity to tell the parasite to get out of his space and mind his own business.

The day before the shooting, Dinger had physically removed the pest from lurking around the ISO containers. Bradley had warned him this time his rough treatment of the trainee might warrant a punishment. Ironically, when considering what his penance might be, a bullet through the brain never entered his mind.

In Bradley's brain but meant for mine, Dinger thought. He had pushed Jabbaar too far and by doing so had lost his best friend. He needed to redress the balance but in order to do that he had to get home. There were too many eyes on him in the hospital and more chance of being resuscitated or having the tablets pumped from his stomach.

Chapter 12

0844 hours, 01 October 2012

Thankfully, Pete Waller was back to his jovial, supportive self and readily signed up to Rick's request. "I think it's a great idea. It will be good for Mr Pashley to have something productive to do. He must be feeling like a spare wheel at the moment. He's probably right about the letter motivating Suzanne. The family usually take great comfort in hearing from their loved ones one last time."

"Okay, I'll call Rick now to let him know." Ella replied.

0852 hours, 01 October 2012

Checking the caller's ID, Rick was tempted to take it. The delightful Captain Harris would be a pleasant distraction but not one he needed right now.

Switching his phone to silent Rick concentrated on the task he was about to undertake. It was imperative he performed well. His grandchild was depending on him and he would not fail him the way he had Bradley. Nothing and no one was going to stop him from playing his part in the child's upbringing.

It was not lost on him that he had been equally determined sixteen years earlier.

2105 hours, 17 July 1996

Rick had seen no advantage in confessing to Linda that his father believed he was in England to make his peace with his grandmamma and not because he intended to move in with his girlfriend and son.

Learning of Georgina Pashley's impending demise, Rick had pleaded the opportunity to apologise for the shame he had brought upon the Pashley name and the way he had spoken to her during their last encounter. He now understood why his grandmamma had banished him and desperately wanted her forgiveness before she left for the fires of hell. Of course he failed to mention his preferred destination for the old dragon.

Since the strict matriarch of the Pashley dynasty had orchestrated his exile to Australia, Rick had shown nothing but contempt for his grandmother so Richard Senior was unconvinced by his son's newfound remorse. He only relented to the boy's request when Monica announced she would also like to say her farewells.

The Pashley's arrived in Sheffield the day before Bradley's birthday, four days before Georgina Pashley's funeral and three hours after her death. Rick was the only one who found solace in missing his chance to say farewell; he would have struggled to portray any sincerity in the apology he would have been forced to make.

Shortly after their arrival, Richard Senior had locked himself in his late father's study armed with a letter from his mother and a bottle of Bunnahabhain 25.

As her husband's emotional spectrum matched his mother's in lack of sorrow, guilt and empathy, Monica was shocked by the singing, sobbing and snoring that emanated from the study. She could however see the benefit of her husband's incapacitation. For once, she and her son could come and go without his consent.

The following morning, when Richard Senior showed no signs of leaving the sanctuary of the study, Monica seized an opportunity she'd not dared to hope for. Her son soon followed suit, informing his uncle he was off to visit an old swimming buddy and might stay overnight. Uncle Edward readily agreed to the boy's absence. He wanted to talk some sense into his brother and pry him away from their late father's expensive whiskey collection.

Getting into the car Rick couldn't believe his fortune. His original plan to sneak out of the house that morning and face the consequences later had concerned him for two reasons. Firstly, he suspected his father would be watching his every move. Secondly, he was worried he would lose his nerve when the time came to break free. Now he was leaving with his uncle's blessing and his suitcase: Result! His mother's discomfort at him witnessing his father's erratic behaviour was obvious, so with a bit of luck she would later agree to him staying with friends until the day of the funeral. He figured he would be able to hide his intention to remain in Sheffield right up until 'she who must be obeyed' was lowered into the ground. By the time his father realised he had no intentions of paying his respects he'd be in Blackpool.

Thanks to the generosity of his mother's family, Rick's bank account would afford his young family a pleasant holiday until it was safe to return to Linda's home. Richard Senior was due to perform a pioneering new surgery on his return to Australia. As his professional ego was insatiable, returning to Australia to ensure his place in medical history would easily triumph over his need to remain in the UK to find his errant son.

Now, as Rick erratically fled Linda's home, he chastised himself for believing things were finally going his way. Had he stuck to his original plan to leave as soon as Bradley's party ended, he would be in a Blackpool B&B and his father would be clueless.

His father; what had happened there? How had he sobered up quickly enough to track him down? How did he know where Linda lived? What sort of a reception would Rick receive when he arrived at his grandmother's?

The thought of facing Richard Senior led Rick to stop the car. Maybe he should turn around, grab Linda and Bradley and head for Blackpool? If he did, would they make it there before the police picked them up? No doubt his father would call them. After what had just transpired would Linda agree to leave with him? After the damage she had just caused, did he want her to?

Why was he such a coward? Now, as well as being afraid of his father, he was petrified of his girlfriend. He inspected the welts on his face where the car key had slashed. He'd always known she had a temper but never expected it to escalate to violence. What if she hurt Bradley? The thought made his blood run cold. After one brief encounter he could not envisage his life without his son. He wanted to provide for him, tuck him in at night and laugh when the boy jumped on him in the early hours of the morning. He wanted to teach him how to ride a bike, read a book and tie his shoelaces. He wanted to be his father.

Turning the car, he headed back to Linda's. He wasn't sure she was the woman he wished to spend the rest of his life with but spending it without his son was not an option.

0853 hours, 01 October 2012

At the beep Ella left a quick message asking Rick to contact Jess regarding Suzanne's letter. As her colleague was not at her desk, Ella left a detailed note for Jess then scuttled back to her own office. Firing up her computer she quickly logged on to the Human Resources site and called up the records of the two names Beetle had provided; Privates David Patterson and Samesa Waqanisau.

Scanning the first record, Ella struggled to suppress her excitement. When the information in Private Waqanisau's file reflected his comrades, Ella clapped like a demented seal.

Her excitement soon diminished when she recalled the CO's warning. How could she pursue her investigation without his knowledge? Why was she so determined to do so? For the sake of her career she should walk away but what of her sanity?

0952 hours, 01 October 2012

Although grateful for the distraction, Ella felt less so when Joyce revealed the purpose of her call. She had a doctor's appointment and, as Charlie was at work, wondered if Ella would mind sitting with Linda for an hour. "Seeing as you two seem to be getting on so well I thought it might be nice. Linda's on board. Think she'd be glad to get me from under her feet." Joyce lowered her voice then walked into the hall. "We're going to give her Bradley's letter tonight so we're trying to keep her upbeat."

"Why? Do you think she will take it badly?" This time last week Ella would have expected Linda to show as much concern for her son's letter as she did for the moustache she cultivated. Now, having witnessed the woman's mini breakdown and her tears regarding her errant husband, Ella believed Bradley's mother did possess a heart capable of being broken.

"I don't have a clue how she'll take it. If he's half as sweet in hers as he was in ours I'm sure she'll be okay." Joyce caught her breath then continued. "Given what he's asked us to do for her I think he's gone easy on her. He never was comfortable with hurting anyone feelings, least of all his mother's."

"What did he ask you to do?"

"I'll tell you all about that later. I need to get a shift on if I'm not going to miss my appointment. That's if you can come round of course."

"I'll be twenty minutes."

1023 hours, 01 October 2012

After motioning for Ella to come inside, Joyce rushed through the open door yelling her bus was due at half past and the tea was in the pot.

As Linda was engrossed in an episode of Homes under the Hammer she was oblivious to both her mother's departure and Ella's arrival.

"Hi Linda," Ella said brightly. "Fancy a cuppa?"

Linda looked up and smiled. "Oh, so you're on guard duty now." Her smile faded. "Bloody daft if you ask me, it's not like I could go anywhere if I wanted to."

"It's nothing like that, I just thought you might fancy a chat with someone other than your parents." They both knew she was lying but thankfully Linda chose not to challenge her.

"Have you seen this?" Linda asked, pointing at the television. "They buy shitholes, do them up and then sell them for a killing." She looked around her dated living room. "Made me think it's about time I did summat with this place. It's been like this since we moved in. Council gave us a decorating grant but we spent it on booze." Linda smirked, "Obviously."

"Sounds like a lovely idea. Any designs in mind?"

"Not really. Last time I went in a furniture store everything was pine and chintz. We left all our stuff at the old house. Part of the house-swapping agreement we made with the sly old git that lived here before us. Obviously he got the better deal. At least my stuff was from the nineties not the seventies. 'Course, Paul promised we'd get new but that never happened."

Not keen to discuss Linda's husband, Ella ignored the woman's wistful look when mentioning him. "Well I'm sure it wouldn't take much to bring this place into the twenty first century."

"Problem is, I'm hardly up for a trip to MFI."

"They've closed down."

"Really? I suppose I could ask me mum to bring a catalogue round. Is Littlewoods still on the go?"

"Yes, but they don't really do catalogues anymore. They've got a website. In fact there are loads of shops on the Internet. You can get some bargains on Ebay and they deliver."

"I've never bothered with the Internet. Bradley tried to show me once on his phone. Said I'd be able to Skype him, whatever that is. I couldn't be arsed. We don't have a landline anyway so there was no point. Wish I'd listened to him now," Linda said flatly.

"We'll if you'd like to try again, I might be able to help. I've got a dongle."

"Sounds painful," Linda laughed.

After drinking their tea, Linda asked if Ella had considered her request regarding Paul.

Ella nodded, "Listen, why don't I tell him you miss him and want him home but right now you need your mum around to help with your meds. Maybe he could come back in a couple of weeks."

"I don't want to leave it too long. There's bound to be some bitch sniffing after him."

Ella managed to stifle a snort. "Oh, I think the women of Sheffield will be able to resist his charms a while longer," she grinned.

"I don't appreciate you taking the piss," Linda warned. "You might not think much of him but he was the only one that gave a shit about me when that bastard left us."

"Rick?"

"Yes, I have Rick the Prick to thank for Paul coming into my life. Paul took care of me and Brad when he decided he couldn't be bothered to."

17 July 1996

It never crossed Linda's mind to be embarrassed as Paul lifted her to her feet and guided her down the path. Barefoot and naked, under her mud stained dressing gown, the possibility she might have flashed her naked body to the twitching curtain brigade did not faze her. Her only regret was that she'd released her fury on Rick's car and not his body. Tomorrow she would feel the damage she'd done to her feet, and her pride, but for now she felt nothing but hatred.

Paul passed Linda a glass of wine. It was unusual for alcohol to be in the house but some of her friends had used Bradley's party as an excuse for an afternoon aperitif. As they had failed to factor in needy toddlers around their ankles, four bottles of white had remained unopened.

After Linda greedily glupped down two glasses, Paul disappeared into the kitchen then returned with a bowl of soapy water. "You okay, love?" he asked placing her dirty feet in the bowl.

Linda looked at the man who had come to her aid with vague recognition. "Thanks," she mumbled as she refilled her glass.

"You wanna go steady with that. Won't look good if you're pissed when the coppers arrive," Paul warned.

"Coppers?"

"One of those nosy sods will have called them. If not, Flash Harry will when his no claims bonus goes down the swanny." Paul wrapped a towel around Linda's feet. "Do you want to go upstairs and clean up? I'll wait here in case the filth turn up."

Once showered, Linda donned a clean pair of pyjamas, placed her feet in her slippers then whimpered. The sharp pain in her heels worsened as she descended the stairs.

Paul handed her a coffee mug. "I've put a drop of whiskey in there for you love. Help calm your nerves."

Linda had never drunk whiskey. She didn't really drink coffee either but as her mind, as well as her taste buds were not functioning properly she quaffed the drink without complaint.

"The old bill turned up whilst you were in the shower. Think they were going to lift me, but I explained I was looking after you because of what your bell end of a boyfriend had done. They're over at our Cindy's now checking I am who I say I am."

Linda was relieved she could now identify her saviour. A month ago, after their mother's death, Paul had moved in with his sister across the road.

When the police returned, Linda was adamant she didn't want to pursue the matter so they left after issuing a warning and said they would return if Rick made a complaint. Joyce arrived as they pulled away. Whilst Paul relayed the few facts he knew, Linda drank. After conveying her gratitude, Joyce dismissed her future son-in-law.

"I've got work in the morning so I'll be off now," Paul informed Linda. "I'm just across the road if you need me."

Linda filled her glass.

1155 hours, 01 October 2012

Ella had received an edited version of that evening's events. Linda had omitted the presence of whiskey, wine and the state of her feet and over emphasised how Paul had looked after her, dealt with the police and offered his services in her hour of need.

"The following morning my 'so called' friends got me out of bed. They couldn't wait to tell me the gossip they'd heard. In some stories, I was naked, spread-eagled across Rick's car bonnet begging him for one last shag before he left. Thankfully, Paul popped in on his way to work and kicked the bitches out."

"How did Bradley handle his father's disappearance?" Ella asked.

Linda looked pained. "I haven't got a clue," she admitted. "Mum turned up and took him to the salon. She said I wasn't in a fit state to look after him. Later on, I decided to go and get him but I couldn't leave the house. The thought of everyone in the street laughing and pointing..." Linda studied Ella's reaction. Could she trust this woman? The doctor had said talking about it would help but she was yet to tell him that her first panic attack had happened two days after Rick Pashley abandoned her, not years later as they all suspected. "I tried again, actually got through the front door but as soon as the fresh air hit me I froze. That's where Paul found me. He helped me to the couch then swore I'd never have to face the bitches again. He packed his job in to look after me."

Chapter 13

1218 hours, 01 October 2012

To Joyce's dismay, Ella insisted on leaving as soon as she returned. Had the older woman known why the officer was reluctant to engage her she would have been more upset.

Diving in her car, Ella cursed herself for promising to speak to Paul on Linda's behalf. By doing so she risked losing the trust of someone she adored, in order to appease someone she despised. When she tried to block the image of a disappointed Joyce, Paul's smug face replaced it. At least he hadn't been lying in wait for her today.

Gathering her thoughts, Ella closed her eyes then pushed her head against the headrest whilst contemplating her next move. The rap on her passenger window caused her to scream. Seeing the worried face on the other side of the glass, Ella opened the door.

Rick jumped into her passenger seat. "Sorry if I startled you," he said holding up an envelope. "Thought you'd want to know I'm on my way to deliver this."

Ella could see the apprehension in Rick's eyes. "Are you sure you want to do this?"

"Definitely. Dave said Susie hasn't got dressed since the funeral. Other than crying, all she does is eat and sleep. If it wasn't for the baby, he doubts she would do either. This letter has to give her a boost." Rick said hopefully. "I'm just a bit worried about how to broach the subject. What if she falls apart?"

"I'm not sure I'm the right person to ask. I thought the direct approach was best but now I wish I'd been gentler."

"I think my reaction would have been the same."

"I take it Dave will be there?"

"And Louise. He's also got the doctor on standby. Just in case she reacts badly."

"Will you let me know how you get on?"

"Of course. In fact I was wondering if I could treat you to dinner tomorrow night to say thank you for all your support."

Ella felt the heat in her cheeks." There's no need to thank me. I'm only doing my job."

"To be honest, you'd be doing me a favour. It's my last night in Sheffield and I don't want to spend it wallowing in my room. I doubt Susie will be up for company once she's read this and I don't know many people under eighty in Sheffield."

Although Ella pitied Rick, something told her no good would come of her spending time alone with him. Still she did want a first hand account of Suzanne's receptivity to Bradley's letter. "I'm sorry I already have dinner plans but I could meet you for coffee later."

Although disappointed, Rick nodded. "Okay, I'll call you when I leave Susie's."

Driving away, Ella was frustrated. Waiting for Rick's call and visiting Paul meant there was no chance of catching up on her ever-increasing backload of work.

1226 hours, 01 October 2012

Vacantly staring out of the kitchen window, Joyce nearly had a panic attack of her own when Rick Pashley came into view. Why was he on the estate? Did he know where Joyce had really been that morning? When Rick turned toward Suzanne's maisonette Joyce allowed herself to breathe normally. She really would need a doctor if things carried on like this.

That boy had enough to answer for without sending her to an early grave. Linda had hardly touched alcohol before he'd abandoned her, yet hours after he'd done so Joyce had had to carry her drunken daughter to bed.

18 July 1996

Linda's sobs had been replaced by gentle snoring around two am. Worried her daughter might choke on her own vomit, Joyce slept fitfully by her side.

The following morning, after placing two slices of toast, paracetamols and a mug of tea on Linda's bedside cabinet Joyce informed her she would cancel her morning appointments. "See you after lunch," She yelled before heading home to prepare Charlie's breakfast.

When her daughter failed to materialise or pick up her phone, Joyce told Penny to cancel her daughter's afternoon appointments then grabbed her coat.

Discovering Linda and Bradley cuddling on the couch in their pyjamas, Joyce demanded to know what her daughter was playing at. On the verge of tears Bradley answered, "Mummy's very poorly" he said stroking Linda's hair, "Nasty Daddy gave her something to make her sick."

Linda was sobbing so vocally her mother struggled to hear her grandson's words. When the infernal racket briefly ceased, Joyce replied. "I don't think it was daddy that made mummy sick sweetheart, I think it was the nasty juice."

"For God's sake mum keep it down will you. My head's splitting, I threw up my breakfast and my stomach's giving me gyp."

"That's what you get for slinging two bottles of wine down your neck," Joyce snapped. "You need to go back to bed. I'll take Bradley in with me."

When Bradley protested he wanted to look after mummy, Joyce squeezed in between her daughter and grandson then put her arms around them both. "I think you're right Bradley, mummy's very poorly. She needs to take her medicine and get some sleep. That's how we get better remember?" Bradley nodded knowingly. "It'll only be for one night," she told Linda.

"You won't have the energy to keep up with him mum. You must be knackered yourself, you were up all night with me." Linda replied guiltily.

"How about I ask Penny if you can have a sleepover at hers?" Joyce asked Bradley.

Her grandson's eyes lit up. "Will Benny be there?"

"Where else would he be?" Benny didn't necessarily reciprocate the boy's adoration but he was a placid dog and never objected to Bradley's excessive petting.

Bradley jumped from the settee. "I'll need to pack," he yelled, running into the hall.

"Wait for me, Pumpkin." Once vertical, Linda stumbled, put her hand to her head and fell back on the couch. "Got up too quickly," she explained.

After a more successful attempt, Linda joined her son whilst Joyce wandered into the kitchen. It didn't take a CSI team to figure out what had happened there. Given the amount of Frosties on the worktop, the spilt milk and open fridge, Joyce deduced Bradley had prepared his own breakfast. Not ideal, but only a slight misdemeanour compared to his mother's crime. It was evident Linda had consumed a 'hair of the dog' whilst Bradley was in her care. The half full bottle of wine had not been on the worktop when Joyce had left that morning. After pouring the remainder down the sink, Joyce eradicated the evidence of both crimes then joined her daughter in the hallway. Taking Bradley's hand, she instructed Linda to drink plenty of water and to eat.

"I made Frosties," Bradley told his grandmother proudly.

"I know you did sweetheart, but you really shouldn't be in the kitchen on your own." Joyce threw Linda a disproving look. "You'll be in tomorrow?"

Linda burst into tears. "Where else would I be? Not bloody Blackpool, that's for sure," she cried. "He conned me mum. All these years, he conned me, and I fell for it. He's never coming back. His Daddy won't let him. I hate him, I fucking hate him."

"What have I told you about using that language in front of Brad? I know you're upset but you need to pull yourself together. For his sake, if not your own."

Linda looked repentant. "Sorry mum, I'm tired." She bent down and kissed Bradley's cheek. "You behave yourself for Penny, okay? I'll see you tomorrow, Pumpkin. Love you."

Chapter 14

1256 hours, 01 October 2012

Finding a possible source of gossip on her doorstep, Cindy Douglas quickly ushered Ella inside then called her brother's mobile. On learning the identity of his visitor, Paul told his sister to keep Ella there until he arrived.

Aware of her time restraint, Cindy started her interrogation. "How's Linda?"

Ella didn't feel it fitting to talking about her charge, so ignored the question. "Is Mr Douglas going to be long?"

"He said ten minutes," Cindy answered sharply leading Ella into the living room and signalling for her to take a seat. "I'm not surprised she's got agora-whatsit. She always was a bit strange." Ella took the proffered chair but remained silent. "I remember when our Phil was due. She insisted on a bloody homebirth. I was worried sick. The amount of ale she'd chucked down her neck. No wonder he's a little runt."

'Like his father,' Ella's inner voice observed. Her outer voice refused to be drawn.

"If our Paul hadn't stopped her drinking and smoking, that kid would've never made it. Mind, what did he receive for his trouble? Dog's abuse. As soon as Phil popped out she was back on the ale and expecting him to change shitty nappies."

Realising she was providing more answers than her guest, Cindy tried a different tack. "I heard God's gift's back on the scene. Surely Linda doesn't think she's got a chance of hooking him again. He was well outta her league before she turned into an alcoholic, chain smoking loony." Ella's lack of response was seriously pissing Cindy off. "You don't say much do you? Well? Is Rampant Rick back on the scene or not?"

Aware Cindy had the same temperament as her sibling, Ella thought it best to respond. "Mr Pashley did fly in for his son's funeral but he will be returning to Australia soon."

Cindy stared at Ella aghast. Was that it? No juicy details? "So, if that's that case why have I ended up with my useless brother again? Linda's not going to find anyone else. The days of the lads chasing her are long gone. That was her problem, too far up her own arse. Bitch used to look down her nose at me. Do you know the last time she allowed me in her presence?"

As obvious as the answer was, Ella realised she was expected to supply it. "No," she obliged.

"Two days after our Phil was born. I took my mate with me. Snotty cow was fine when we were cooing over the baby but the minute Sally suggested she get our Paul down the aisle the bitch lost it." Cindy shook her head. "I told her Sal was only saying what everyone else thought. I know our Paul's no catch but when you've two kids to two different dads you can't afford to be choosy, can you?"

Once again Cindy stared awaiting a response. "I suppose not," her guest concurred.

"Exactly," Cindy shouted as if she and Ella were speaking the same language at last. "Then Paul comes over here gobbing off because I'd upset her ladyship. Said she'd had some sort of attack. If you ask me it was just an excuse for her to get back on the booze. 'Course Paul blamed me for that as well."

Being happy to see Paul Douglas was an emotion Ella hadn't thought possible until that moment. "Sorry if I kept you," he apologised. "What did she say? Did you give her the letter?"

Ella looked towards Cindy. She didn't want to discuss Linda in front of her sister-in-law. Especially as the woman's dislike of Bradley's mother was so evident.

"What?" Cindy yelled then turned to her brother. When he looked uncomfortable she blew. "You can fuck right off. I'm going nowhere. It's my fucking house. If you don't want me to hear, you fucking leave."

"We could talk in my car?" Ella offered.

"Seriously?" Cindy snapped. "You'd rather sit in a freezing cold car?"

Motioning for Ella to follow him Paul headed for the door. As the officer attempted to close it behind her, Cindy snatched it from her hand. "You better hope to God that bitch wants you back because you're not getting your sorry arse in here again!" she screamed.

Paul and Ella jumped into her car. "Well did you give her the letter?" Paul asked.

"Not yet, but we've spoken. She does want you back, just not yet."

"Why the hell not?"

"She's still recovering from her panic attacks and battling the booze so she wants her parents to help for a little longer."

"So I'm out on the street? I've a good mind to break into Joyce's house and kip there."

"Surely that won't be necessary? Cindy won't really throw you out, will she?"

On cue, a carrier bag was flung into the street. "Ungrateful little shit!" Cindy screeched.

Paul sighed, "This is the excuse she's been looking for. She hates me being there as much as I do. First few days are fine 'cos it gives her something to gossip about. After that I'm about as welcome as syphilis." Paul jumped out of the car to retrieve his bag. Once back inside he shrugged. "So once Linda's back to her old self I can go home?"

"She's hoping not to return to her old self. If you go back, she'll need your support."

"WHEN I go back, I'll give it her. I always have."

"This is different. Fags and booze won't cure it. It'll just make thing worse."

"Oh, so it's all my fucking fault?" Paul raged. "I can't bear to see her sober because it means I might have to be? Pisses me off, everyone thinking I throw it down her neck even though it's the other way round. She makes me drink with her. Thinks you're only an alky if you drink alone."

"And you really hate the stuff, right?" Ella asked sarcastically.

"I used to enjoy getting pissed but she's ruined that. For one thing, we can't afford for us both to be permanently shitfaced and for another someone's gotta get her to bed at night."

"Oh come on, every time I come around you've got a beer in your hand?"

"Have you ever seen me start a second? I sit nursing the same can all night. She's too pissed to notice."

Ella was getting flustered. Could Paul be believed? She might be gullible but not to that extent. Digging deep she found her counter-argument. "You were drunk the night of the funeral."

"That was a one off. I was pissed off because Charlie wouldn't let me see Linda so I went to the Flying Horse to find Phil. Thought he might be able to talk his grandad round." Paul threw his hands up in exasperation. "To add fucking insult to injury I was also banned from seeing my lad. Rick the Prick was flashing the cash in the function room so the landlord wouldn't let me go in. Made me wait in the main bar. Some silly tart came over saying she wanted to buy Bradley's step dad a drink. Kept my glass full until my gob opened. Then she asked me how I felt about the neighbours saying Linda couldn't even be arsed to turn up to her son's funeral. Cheeky bitch, I wasn't having that so I put her right. I told her..." Paul screwed up his face as he remembered exactly what he'd told her.

Ella snorted, "You told her I wasn't looking after Linda and Bradley wasn't the father of Suzanne's child?"

Paul looked down at the carrier bag on his lap. "Something like that, yes." Recovering, Paul turned to Ella. "See, if I was used to the ale I wouldn't have gobbed off," was his poor defence for nearly ruining her career.

She had to admit that Paul might have been a lot of things during their previous encounters, but drunk wasn't one of them. "I don't understand. Why pretend?"

"To make her feel better. She'd be gutted if she knew I sat there sober watching the state she gets into."

"I take it Charlie and Joyce don't know this?"

Paul shook his head. "I think Brad did." Paul seemed uncomfortable mentioning his stepson. "Not that he'd stick up for me. Blamed me for his dad leaving. Funny really, seeing as I turned up after the bastard had run off."

"It must've been hard for Bradley," Ella pointed out.

"Hard for him? What about me? Within a year of moving in I was juggling a newborn with a pissed up wife. I didn't have time to worry about an ungrateful little shit who kept saying I'd broken his mummy."

'Of course you didn't', Ella thought. "But why keep bringing her the booze?"

"Because if I hadn't I would have missed out on the joy of carrying her to bed every night and the early morning showers when she pissed herself," Paul replied sarcastically.

This was all too much to take, Paul the victim? Even Ella struggled to swallow that.

Pulling his hands through his hair Paul sighed. "As soon as she tried to stop drinking she went all fucking paranoid. Listening at walls, then screaming the bitches were slagging her off. After that she'd kick the shit out of me until I agreed to fetch her booze."

"So you were a battered husband?" Ella was surprised at the malice in her voice.

"That's right, take the piss. She's fucking vicious when she wants a drink. That wasn't what got me to the shops though. No, it was when she took a fucking knife to her own throat that I gave in."

Ella admitted defeat. The more answers Paul provided the more she questioned herself.

Paul glared at Ella. "You don't believe me?"

"It's a little hard to take in. If all this is true, why stay?"

Paul looked incredulous, "Er, because I love her? Always have."

The vibration on her thigh made Ella jump. Careful not to alert Paul to the identity of the caller, Ella arranged to meet Rick in Dan's cafe then hung up.

"I'm sorry, I need to go," she explained.

"Sure," Paul said but made no attempt to leave the car.

"Can I drop you somewhere?" Ella offered.

"Nowhere I can think of. Cindy's my only family in Sheffield. Drop me off at the tram, I'll go to Meadowhall. Keep warm there until chucking out time. There are a few benches outside."

That was the last straw. If there was any truth in the story she had just heard, Ella couldn't bear Paul sleeping rough. She wracked her brain for an alternative.

Take him home? – Larry would leave.

Take him to Linda's? – Joyce would have a fit.

Plead with Cindy? – Not enough time to crack that nut.

Ask Hazel and Ann? – They'd already had their fair share of waifs and strays that week.

Who else? She needed more time to think. Handing Paul her business card, she instructed him to call her in a couple of hours then dropped him at the tram stop.

1459 hours, 01 October 2012

Joyce had had Suzanne's place under surveillance since Rick had entered two hours ago. She wished Charlie was home. If there was any possibility of a member of the Pashley family knocking on her door she wanted her husband by her side. Thank God he'd turned up the last time Richard Senior had arrived at her door.

1517 hours, 18 July 1996

Having spent the previous night on Linda watch, Joyce was dead on her feet. With the encouragement of her staff she cancelled her last two appointments, told her grandson to behave for Penny then rushed home in the hope of getting her head down for an hour before Charlie got home. Arriving at her doorstep she wished she hadn't.

Mr Pashley followed her into the house, then exploded. Did she know what her vindictive little bitch of a daughter had done this time? Had Joyce known they were still in touch? Why hadn't she put a stop to it? The more Joyce tried to appease the older man the angrier he became, then the threats started. If Linda ever contacted Rick again she would be cut off. Not that she'd be receiving any money in the foreseeable future; her wages would be used to cover the repairs to the hire car. If Linda objected, he'd call the police and have her arrested for criminal damage. If that resulted in her ending up in prison the child could be taken away.

The thought of Bradley in care reduced his grandmother to tears.

Charlie burst through the door. He had seen the damaged car outside and heard the shouting from the path. Once he had the gist of the situation he issued his own ultimatums. Charlie had been rattled with guilt at his inability to protect his girls when Mr Pashley had last visited them. This time, he informed Richard Senior, he would have to deal with the man of the house and not his wife and pregnant daughter. Charlie was seventeen years younger and four inches taller than his adversary. His manual job gave him a stocky build and Mr P was right to feel intimidated by his physique, especially as Charlie was sorely tempted to knock the arrogant bastard into the middle of next week.

Charlie relished the opportunity to get four years of pain off his chest. "So, let me get this right. Your son swans back here after God knows how many years; takes advantage of my daughter, again, and then runs off with his tail between his legs as soon as daddy shouts and you're the one that's pissed off?"

"They were not supposed to see each other again. We had a deal. It's in the contract, I'm well within my rights to terminate your wife and daughter's employment..."

"I think you'll find it was your snivelling little prat of a son that broke your precious agreement. He was the one who turned up at our Linda's door."

"She shouldn't have let him in. I send her money every month."

"And so you should. Your son knocked her up then fucked off to Oz. She deserves some support and it's not like you haven't got the means." Charlie's anger subsided long enough to apologise to Joyce for his bad language.

Joyce shrugged. Under the circumstances she was prepared to overlook his swearing. The only other time he got away with such profanities was when Sheffield Wednesday let in a late minute equaliser. In those instances she'd pretend to be as devastated as her husband and act as if she had failed to hear his outburst.

Mr Pashley, on the other hand, seized the opportunity to point out Charlie's uncouth behaviour. "Do you think we could keep this conversation out of the gutter?"

Charlie scoffed. "No, I don't think we can. After all you've made it quite clear you think that's where you think we belong. Happy for your grandson to be brought up there too. Anything to keep him away from your precious son."

"Let's not be naive. We both know your daughter trapped Richard. It's her own fault she's relying on the tax payer to bail her out."

"For your information, she isn't relying on anybody. She pays her own way, and Bradley's. She's a fantastic mother. She was doing fine before your excuse of a son turned up." Charlie stepped closer to his antagonist. "Don't worry he won't be welcomed back. I want my daughter to have a fella she can rely on, not some lily livered arsehole who runs back to daddy when things don't go his way."

Mr Pashley edged towards the door. "So we're in agreement then. They will stay away from each other?"

"You'll have to ask your son. Not that he's got the bollocks to tell you." Charlie's laughter was forced. "He's not big on the truth, is he?" Moving closer, Charlie leaned forward so that he was on eye level with Richard Senior. "You see, we knew about them being together because our lass doesn't lie to us whereas your son's big on false promises and bullshit."

Mr Pashley had no intention of being spoken to in such a manner by an ex convict. Violence wasn't the only weapon that won wars he thought. Glaring back at Charlie he sneered, "I meant what I said, if this carries on I will go to the police. I'll have the child taken away." The eyes that bored into him made Pashley's knees shake. Charlie Craig was not a man to be intimidated. Fortunately, for Rick's father, Joyce stopped her husband raising the fist he was about to launch.

Charlie sneered, "Tell me, how it will look to your hoity toity mates when it gets out your wonderful son got the local scrubber pregnant then you sent him to the other side of the world? Oh, and then, when the lass manages to provide her child with a decent home, you get the kid taken into care." The brief sagging of Pashley's shoulders told Charlie he had the upper hand. "I've a feeling not many in your circle know about your lads little walk on the wild side. I might have to have a chat with the papers, sure they'd pay good money for a story like that."

Mr Pashley was flustered. "I'll sue. You and the papers."

"For what? Printing the truth? I'm sure a man in your line of work knows all about DNA testing. Then there's the hundred and fifty quid that lands in Linda's account every month. How do you explain that?" Sensing victory, Charlie continued, "Now I'll tell you what's going to happen. You will keep paying my daughter for your grandson's upkeep and it'll increase regularly. That little lad's going to make something of his life without your input but not without your money. As for that deadbeat son of yours, tell him he's lucky it was the only car that got damaged. Mood our Linda's in, I don't fancy his chances if shows up here again."

Charlie matched every step Mr P took backwards. When the men finally reached the door, Charlie opened it and pushed the older man outside. "Now get out of my house and never come back."

Mr P stumbled and landed on his backside. Standing up, he wiped imaginary dirt from his trousers, glared at Charlie then headed for his car. "I should've know you would resort to violence," he shouted indignantly as he opened his car door.

"Yeah, and you should also know that I intend to kick ten barrels of shit out of you if you ever set foot near my wife or daughter again!" Charlie yelled as he ran up the path waving his fists.

The car screeched away just as Charlie got to the gate. Laughing heartily he turned to his wife. "Our Linda did some job on that car. Good for her. Now she can get on with being a mother again. She's good at that." Charlie beamed.

The pride they felt for their offspring was short lived. Joyce soon found it hard to recall the last time she wasn't ashamed of her only child.

Chapter 15

1513 hours, 01 October 2012

Ella ordered an Americano then took the seat opposite Rick. "So, how was Suzanne?" she asked.

"We did the right thing," he announced with obvious pride.

"I don't remember doing anything," Ella quipped.

"I mean giving her the letter was the right thing. She's a different girl," Rick beamed.

He then went on to explain how, after her initial disbelief, Suzanne had taken Bradley's letter to her bedroom to read in private. Apparently, it was the first time she had voluntarily left the couch since the funeral. After half an hour, Dave had gone to check on her and found her fast asleep clutching the note. When his looming shadow awoke her, Suzanne had jumped up, kissed his cheek then headed for the shower. Twenty minutes later she had joined the men in the living room, having ditched the dressing gown and started issuing instructions to everyone.

"That's good to hear." Ella smiled. "So the letter helped?"

Rick looked awkward. "That and my agreeing to her demands."

Ella sensed Rick's reluctance to elaborate but pushed anyway, "Demands?"

Rick tapped the bridge of his nose whilst deciding how to proceed. "You're not going to like this," he warned. "She asked me not to pursue the baby's claim on Bradley's estate."

It made sense. A DNA test was inevitable if Rick pursued the matter and something Suzanne was eager to avoid. Ella shrugged. "Well if that's what she wants."

"I thought you'd be angry," Rick confessed.

"Why? If anything you're doing me a favour. One of the reasons I got suspended was because my bosses suspected I orchestrated the baby's claim."

"I hadn't thought of that. Still, I know you were keen for Susie to get the money."

"Can I remind you I never actually said that?"

Rick grinned, "Of course you didn't. If it helps, I promise you, Susie and the baby will want for nothing. I've no one else to spend my money on and without wanting to sound vulgar I have plenty. That reminds me, I really should see about changing my will. Do you think I should wait until after the baby's born?"

"I suppose if you want to name him or her, you'd have to."

"I don't want to leave it too long. My current one leaves everything to Bradley. Unless I draft a new one my father is bound to state his claim. He was furious that my mother left so little of her estate to him. If he gets his hands on my inheritance he will consider it divine retribution."

"Surely he has enough money of his own?"

"He has, he just couldn't bear the thought of Linda's offspring getting his hands on it. Even to this day he's adamant Bradley wasn't mine. Wish I'd insisted on a DNA test. Too late now."

"I would have thought a photograph would have been all the proof required. Bradley was the spit of you."

"Father would never look at one."

"Well he must have seen one recently, Bradley's face has been in all the newspapers and on television."

"Even if he has, he'll still deny it. Probably say sleeping with someone who looked like me was part of Linda's master plan. Anything but admit he was wrong." Rick's face lit up. "If I get a DNA test on Brad's baby he'd have to accept he's a great grandfather then."

"No, you can't," Ella blurted out forcefully.

"Why ever not?"

Ella stared at her coffee. "I... Well... It's just... I don't think you can initiate a test without parental permission."

"I'm sure if I explain to Susie she'll agree."

'I'm sure she won't.' "Maybe, but she's in a delicate place at the moment. What if she thinks you don't believe Bradley is the father?"

Rick cringed. "Because of what Paul said? She knows I would never take any notice of him."

"Does she? She's asked you to drop the child's claim to Bradley's estate. Maybe she's annoyed at being forced to prove the child's paternity."

"Linda was the same. That's why she was okay with my name not being on the birth certificate. Said she knew the truth so sod everyone else."

"There you go then, Suzanne might get upset if you mention the test."

"You're right. It's early days, I'll wait until she's feeling better, then speak to her. She'd probably relish an opportunity to prove my father wrong. Obviously they've never met but I think Bradley's hatred of him rubbed off."

"If I was you I wouldn't mention it until the baby's born. You can't do anything until then so why risk upsetting her?"

When Rick agreed, Ella felt sick. She might have bought Suzanne some time but he was sure to be suspicious if the girl refused his request at a later date. Ella decided a change of subject was in order. "So how was Suzanne when you left?"

Rick smiled, "Making lists. She wants to reply to her letters of condolence, sort out Brad's headstone and create a scrapbook with the newspaper clippings regarding Brad's VC nomination and his funeral. She's a bit all over the place but at least she's being productive."

"That's good."

"She's also really keen to visit Dinger. Do you know when he'll be released from hospital?"

"No idea. I'd need to ask Jess." Ella was relieved her colleague hadn't been in her office earlier. Asking questions about Dinger on Rick's behalf would be safer than admitting her conversation with Louise. "On that note, I really should get back to the office. I've been out all day and I've a lot to catch up on."

107

Rick looked disappointed. "I'm sorry for taking up so much of your time. I keep forgetting you have a day job."

Climbing into her car, Ella was confused when Rick jumped in her passenger seat. "Did you want me to drop you off somewhere?" she enquired.

"No, I've got my hire car. I wanted to speak to you in private. You know I'm going back to Australia on Wednesday?" Ella nodded. "Well there's something I need to say before I go. You are aware of how much I appreciate all you've done for Susie and I over the last couple of weeks." Again Ella nodded. Rick looked uncomfortable. "What you're probably not aware of is how I feel about you." Seeing Ella's shock, Rick grabbed her hand, "I'm sorry to blurt it out like that. It's just with your husband leaving…"

"What? Who told you…?" Ella shrieked snatching her hand away.

"Jess. Don't be angry with her. She didn't exactly tell me. I guessed. It was too much of a coincidence. One minute your husband marches you out of the wake and the next day you're no longer CVO. In her defence she insisted his leaving was nothing to do with your removal."

Ella couldn't comprehend her sudden need to cry. "It wasn't."

Rick stroked Ella's hair from her eyes when he saw her tears forming." I'm sorry, I didn't mean to upset you. I just wanted you to know I think your husband is crazy for letting you go." Placing his hands either side of Ella's face he stared intensely. "When you turned up at the hotel looking so sexy on Saturday night," Rick shook his head. "If it hadn't been for Brad's letter I don't think I would've been able to stop myself."

Ella tried to blink away the tears. "Rick, I…"

"Ella, please, let me finish. I haven't allowed myself to feel this way about anyone in such a long time…"

It was Ella's turn to butt in. Grabbing Rick's hands she pulled them away from her face. "Rick, please stop. Larry hasn't left me. It was just a misunderstanding." Seeing his doubt she continued. "We had a small blip because of Nicky but I swear we are still together. He picked me up from the hotel for God's sake."

"No he didn't, you had a meal with your friend. I saw you," Rick challenged.

"So you were spying on me?"

"No. Well not exactly. After I read Bradley's letter I needed someone to talk to. I nearly asked if I could join you but you were laughing so much I didn't want to spoil your night. Jesus, I thought she was your pick-me-up friend. The one you call when your marriage falls apart. Anyway the point is I didn't see any husband," Rick snapped.

"Well if you'd have hung around, you would have." Ella needed to put a stop to this conversation. "Rick, whether you believe me or not is of no consequence. I am with Larry and that's that."

Rick turned to look out of the window. "You could have stopped me earlier."

"I'm sorry. Hearing I'd split up with my husband threw me."

"So I misread the signals?"

Rick's sulky tone infuriated Ella. "What signals? I wasn't sending any bloody signals."

"If you say so," Rick replied petulantly. When Ella failed to respond he turned to face her. "Listen, you've done nothing wrong. I'm in a shitty place so I was probably clutching at straws." He touched her hand. "Sorry if I offended you."

"Actually, I'm flattered," Ella admitted as she removed his hand. "But still unavailable."

"Well let's put it down to wishful thinking. No harm done?" He put his hand on her chin and tilted her face towards him. "You are gorgeous, you know."

'Right back at you sexy, now please stop with all the touching.'

Ella smiled shyly but refused to meet his gaze. "Thank you."

Removing his hand, Rick plastered on a huge grin. "Well, I'd better get off before I make an even bigger fool of myself." Attempting to lighten the mood he added, "Just promise me if Captain Ella Harris ever has a space on her dance card she'll give me first refusal."

"It's a long way to come for a Waltz," Ella quipped.

"You never know, I might be nearer than you think," he said leaning over to kiss Ella's cheek. When he lingered too long she playfully pushed him away. "Safe journey, Mr Pashley." She laughed nervously as he left her car.

1608 hours, 01 October 2012

'Oh my God, Oh my God, Oh my God.' Ella's inner voice was demented and her cheeks beetroot. What the hell was that about? Rick Pashley wanted her? Rick Pashley wanted her and she had said no! Of course she had, she was happily married. Was she? If so, why did she feel so guilty? Was it the brief moment when she had imagined his tongue in her mouth? More guilt. She shouldn't be aroused by the thought of an illicit tryst with Rick; she should be revolted.

'Yeah right, like there's anything revolting about Mr Pashley. Stop beating yourself up you're only human, unlike him, he's a God.'

Parking up in the barracks, Ella took a deep breath before opening her car door. It did nothing to relieve the tension building up in her nether regions so she remained in her car, closed the door and willed her pulse to settle.

She had turned down Rick's proposition. Larry was the love of her life, her soulmate. Her previous affair was due to the IVF. That's what the shrink had said and that's what she needed to believe. She had sworn never to betray Larry like that again and she never would. Still, she thought God was extremely cruel sending a piece of ass like Rick to test her resolve. *'Let's not go there.'*

Once able to focus on things other than Rick's torso, Ella headed for her office. Finding Paul Douglas a bed for the night would be her first priority then she would need to tackle her increasing backlog of work. There was no way she was going to make it home before seven. In some respects she was relieved.

110

After her encounter with Rick she was in no hurry to speak with her husband. Still, she couldn't put it off. Larry would need to know she was going be late home. She considered sending a text until she discovered the seven missed calls, two voicemails and three texts she had failed to acknowledge.

Had she not been feeling so contrite about her liaison with Rick, Ella might not have accepted Larry's scolding so willingly. She understood why he was annoyed by her lack of communication but he needed to accept she couldn't drop everything for him. Since her failed IVF, subsequent collapse and affair, Larry constantly checked up on her. She in turn, constantly reassured him she was well, had eaten her lunch and happily revealed whose company she was keeping.

The CVO duty had seemed to curb his compulsion to talk to his wife hourly. Ella had been impressed by his restraint and then heartbroken when he'd ceased all contact just before the funeral.

Right now, Larry was labouring on how he had spent the last five hours worrying Paul had attacked her. When she eventually pointed out she'd been busy dealing with Bradley's family Larry complained about her still spending time on 'that'. "I thought things were suppose to ease off now. Don't tell me you've been with those people all day," Larry barked.

"Most of it, yes. Joyce had a doctor's appointment, Paul's sister kicked him out and Rick delivered Suzanne's farewell letter." The mention of Rick made her cheeks flush. That was a habit she needed to break.

"What does any of that have to do with you?" Larry demanded. "I'm sure Joyce managed to get to the doctors before you came along. As for Paul, he's nothing to do with Linda anymore so why should you be concerned if he's homeless? More to the point, you shouldn't be anywhere near Suzanne or her letter. You were warned to stay away, remember?"

"I do and I have. What you have conveniently forgotten is that I am still Rick's CVO." *Damn still blushing.* "He needed someone to talk to after delivering Suzanne's letter. As for Joyce, getting to her appointment wasn't the issue; she needed someone to look after her daughter whilst she attended it. You know, Linda, the woman who has lost her son, is battling alcohol abuse and has just admitted she hasn't left her house in years." Ella's temper was in full flow.

Larry sensed he was on a hiding to nothing but wasn't prepared to submit just yet. "And Paul? What did you feel you needed to do for him so desperately?"

"Not for him, for her. For some strange reason, Linda thinks her life is better with him in it. Personally, I think she should make the most of him not controlling her every move. I for one know how bloody irritating that can be."

That was it. Ella was battle ready, Larry needed to retreat. "I'm sorry Babe, you've obviously had a shit day. It's just, I was worried sick. You normally answer my texts straight away."

That was the problem, she did. She needed to assure him she wasn't going anywhere as much as he needed to hear it. Her previous infidelity had wounded him badly, she had no wish to cause him further pain. "I know, I know. I should've texted you back. It's just been one thing after another. I never seem to get a minute. That's why I'm calling now. I'm sorry, but I'm going to be late. I've a pile of work to get through."

"What time?" Larry fought to hide his annoyance.

"I don't know. Seven, maybe eight."

"Okay. What about dinner? If you call me as you're leaving I could rustle up fajitas."

"Sounds great, but only two please. I'll struggle to sleep on a full stomach and I've a feeling I'll need an early night."

"I like the sound of that."

"Down tiger, Mrs H's libido doesn't fire on all cylinders when fatigued. You know that."

'Was firing just fine half an hour ago' Ella's inner voice teased.

With normal service resumed in the Harris household, Ella went in search of the unit's Quartermaster. It was a long shot but she'd thought of a possible solution to the Paul problem.

At first, Major Tattler was unimpressed with Ella's suggestion. He had no objection to her visitor staying on camp but questioned if the transit room was the right abode? Surely, as her guest, the Officer's Mess would be more suitable than the junior ranks overspill room.

Ella explained that the rich tapestry of Mess life might be a bit daunting and her visitor would probably feel more at home with the junior ranks. Although begrudged to reveal Paul's identity, Ella broke under the QM's interrogation. Whilst he was still reeling from the shock that she wanted him to accommodate Linda's husband, Ella explained Mrs Douglas had taken the loss of her eldest son badly and the doctors felt her parents were best placed to look after her, leaving no room for Paul.

Major T prided himself on being a 'typical' hard hearted Quartermaster, so was not about to be won over with sob stories. What did make him relent was his belief in Ella. He trusted she must have a good reason for such a bizarre request.

Permission given, there were strict rules Paul would have to adhere to. He would be escorted on and off camp and only allowed to frequent the transit block, the NAAFI shop and Ella's office. Deviation in any way would result in his extraction from camp. This offer expired on Friday. As the majority of the camps occupants disappeared at the weekend, Major T was not prepared to allow any resident of the Haddington free reign over his barracks.

Half an hour later, accompanied by the Duty NCO, Ella escorted Paul to his room. As the bed spaces were only used on a temporary basis the furniture was sparse; four areas each contained a single bed, bedside table and locker.

Two sheets, pillows and pillowcases were laid out on each bed along with a mattress protector, quilt and duvet cover. The ablutions were across the corridor from the room. After a quick demonstration on how not to burn your arse in the shower the NCO departed.

Whilst helping Paul assemble his chosen bed, Ella used the opportunity to quiz him. "Did you ever consider speaking to a doctor about Linda's condition?"

Paul sighed, "Whenever I suggested it she'd lose the plot. The thought of being dragged off to the 'funny farm' with that bunch of bitches gawping was too much."

"Fair enough, but if you did want her to stop drinking, why did you hide lager in the house when she tried?" Ella probed.

Paul looked annoyed but answered, "I couldn't risk another meltdown. Did you know she tried to stop the day after Joyce's little blackmail attempt?" Ella nodded. "Within a couple of hours she was screaming the place down. When I refused to fetch her booze she took a knife to her wrist. Fortunately, I had a couple of cans hid under the sink. I gave her them then shot off to Asda. You were there when I got back."

Ella remembered. She had opted to go to the café with Joyce instead of visiting the warring pair. "Okay, I'll give you that one. But explain to me, if you were so concerned why, when she managed to stop, did you frequent the pub every night?"

Ella's constant interrogation was vexing Paul but he was determined to convince her he had Linda's best interests at heart. "I didn't go to the pub. I just had to get out of the house. Her meds wore off at night so she'd get leery and start demanding booze. We both knew I'd give in but not Joyce, she's a tough old bird. I stayed out of the way until Linda had taken her bedtime drugs. It was her idea. Same with the funeral. She knew the stress of it would push her over the edge so didn't want me around in case I gave in and fetched her ale."

"But she said her stopping had nothing to do with Joyce offering her the money to go to the funeral."

"It didn't." Paul sighed. "It was the letters."

"What letters?"

"I think they're called condolence. There were loads of them. The ones that really touched her were from other mothers. She also got some from the army top brass and Prime Minister. Even the Queen sent one," Paul said in mock disbelief. "I think she thought that if Her Majesty said she should be proud, the likes of Cath the Mouth and our Cindy could swivel."

Ella was aware that senior members of the military and state sent letters within twenty-four hours of a soldier's death, but she had not contemplated strangers doing so. "I never saw any letters."

"She hid them in our bedroom along with the flower, cards and other gifts. Whenever she weakened she'd run upstairs re-read her favourites and then look at pictures of Brad." Paul grimaced. "Of course they weren't all sweetness and light. Some sick bastards wrote he deserved to die. Then there were the religious nuts ranting that he shouldn't have been there in the first place. I weeded those ones out so she didn't see them."

"How did they get your address?"

"Some just said Bradley Craig's mum, the Haddington, Sheffield. Guess the post office were on the ball."

Chapter 16

1732 hours, 01 October 2012

Although Linda had waxed lyrically to Ella about her husband, now reminiscing the events of Paul's arrival in her life she struggled to recall when she had decided he was 'The One'. Certainly not after their first intimate encounter.

0602 hours, 19 July 1996

The sickness in the pit of Linda's stomach was not due to alcohol alone. Recalling the events of the previous evening brought bile to her throat. What had she been thinking? Paul Douglas of all people!

The previous day, after her mother had taken Bradley away, it had dawned on her she'd met Cindy's brother before. At school she had often caught 'Pervy Paul' hanging around the girls' cloakroom. The recollection led her to vow never to invite him into her home again.

Within hours of making that vow Paul had lifted her from her doorway and carried her into the living room. For a brief moment she had considered asking him to leave. The three bottles of wine he'd also carried, and her lack of companionship since he'd chased all her friends away, weakened her resolve. Realising she detested her own company more than she hated his she gratefully took the glass of wine he offered then started to vent. As she enlightened her guest about what a self-absorbed little prick her ex boyfriend was her opinion of Paul changed. He was so understanding, so attentive and so complimentary. Hearing how beautiful she was had made her… No, she couldn't bear to think about what it had made her do.

She'd freaked when she'd awoken to find Paul staring at her bare chest. Disappointed by her obvious distress, he'd rearranged her shirt then helped her to her seat and another glass of white. Staring at her intensely, he'd assured her she was the sexiest woman he had ever had the pleasure of. When she'd burst into tears he'd given her a cigarette and told her to draw deep. The instant hit steadied her momentarily

When the effects of the nicotine had worn off the panic had begun. Who would he tell? His sister? The neighbours? What if her dad heard; her mum; Oh my God what if Rick found out?

Topping up her glass, Paul promised it would be their little secret.

To her relief there had been no lights on in the street when he had left. Before heading for her bed she'd poured the remnants of her glass down the sink. If alcohol made her sleep with the likes of Pervy Paul she would never drink again.

The following morning, although her head was splitting, Linda decided she would have to return to work. Wallowing in self-pity was not an option when you were a mother. Her boy must come first, she needed to bring him home. Sod his useless father.

Tears sprung to her eyes when she thought of Rick. Had she been too hard on him? Was it wrong to expect his love for her and her son to outweigh his fear of his father? Why had he not called since driving away? Had she lost him for good?

One thing she didn't question was her love for him. All the booze and cigarettes in the world could never make her forget how right it had felt being back in his arms. As much as she hated herself for being so weak, she knew she would take him back in an instant. That was what made her liaison with Paul Douglas even harder to understand. How could she have let him touch her when she was still in love with Rick?

2008 hours, 01 October 2012

In an attempt to make amends for his early strop, Larry ushered Ella into the living room then pressed play on the Sky remote. Minutes later he returned with a tray containing two tightly packed fajitas and a glass of diet coke. Having missed lunch, Ella eagerly tucked in.

For a short time she enjoyed watching someone else's drama unfold. Annoyingly the storyline soon brought her back to reality. When did Emmerdale become so racy? Carl was blackmailing Chas because of her affair with Cameron and for some strange reason she thought marrying Dan would remedy the situation.

Blackmail, infidelity, love triangles! Ella's mind was in turmoil. Watching Chas marrying a man who was so obviously wrong for her just to stop herself throwing herself at the man who actually got her juices flowing, made Ella uncomfortable. Still if Chas chose Cameron, it would destroy the lives of everyone she loved. Dan didn't deserve that; his only crime was loving her too much.

As for creepy Carl, when did that happen? He used to be one of her favourite characters, how could someone's personality change so radically? Paul Douglas sprung to mind. Had she misjudged him? Living with Linda's illness couldn't have been easy yet he had remained devoted to her throughout.

2201 hours, 01 October 2012

Sneaking his third tablet from his tin, Dinger reflected on a productive day. That morning when the doctor had told him the psychiatrist was still concerned by his unwillingness to mix with the other injured soldiers or allow visitors, Dinger had decided to rectify the situation.

Instead of giving himself indigestion in his haste to return to his room he'd made a concerted effort to interact with his fellow patients during breakfast. The amputees' arrival had caused him to squirm but not for the reasons they suspected. It was not pity but envy that provoked his discomfort. Maybe if his injuries had been as serious he wouldn't feel so guilty. Then again was losing limbs payment enough for denying a mother a son, a fiancée a husband or a child a father?

At lunch, whilst struggling to swallow his pizza, Dinger had chatted to the lads with false enthusiam. When one arrived with a 'One Foot in the Grave' T-shirt and a holdup stocking on his only leg, Dinger was annoyed by his own reaction. As the joker had explained the sexy silk covering on his remaining extremity stopped people from focusing on his missing one, Dinger had left the table.

Fake hilarity was vital if his plan was to succeed but he had no right to feel genuine pleasure. In the past he'd been a strong advocate of the use of black humour. It was the squaddie way of dealing with hardship and he'd had a particular penchant for it. Today, however, he resented his uniped comrade's pun. The nurse witnessing his hearty laughter was his only consolation. With luck she would report his interaction to the doctors.

2216 Hours, 2 October 2012

In his hotel room, Rick was berating himself. He was such an idiot. Whatever was he thinking making a pass at Ella? His perception of the female species was no better in his thirties than it had been in his teens.

With Linda, he'd seen a sexy, vivacious, loyal girl who loved him and his child in equal measures. Wrong. She was a manipulative tart whose only interest in him had been financial.

With Ella he'd seen an attractive, available, intelligent woman who appeared as drawn to him as he was to her. Wrong. She was a happily married woman; her interest in him was purely professional.

Discovering he was wrong about Ella had only harmed his pride. Sixteen years earlier discovering the truth about Linda had broken his heart, spirit and stolen his ability to trust.

18/19 July 1996

Driving back to Linda, Rick hoped she'd calmed down enough to agree to go to Blackpool with him. His heart missed a beat as he turned into her street. Slamming on his brakes he cursed his father. The arrogant bastard hadn't even given him time to get home before involving the police. He had no option but to drive away.

Now driving aimlessly around the back streets of Crooks Rick, he assessed his options. With the police on their case, driving to Blackpool was too risky. Given the state of the hire car, after Linda's little tantrum, it would be easy to spot on the M61. Plus, if it rained,he only had one windscreen wiper.

His best option was to call Linda, ask her to pack her bags then order a taxi. He'd ditch the hire car and she could pick him up en route. It was too late to get the train to Blackpool so they'd have to try and get a hotel for the night or sleep in the train station. Decision made, he drove to the nearest pay phone.

Believing he was speaking to a police officer, Rick claimed to be a concerned relative. It soon became obvious the man who replied was not wearing blue.

"She's upstairs washing your spunk from her fanny," Paul told Rick.

Too shocked to address his vulgarity, Rick enquired to whom he was speaking.

"The man who's going to shag her next," Paul replied then slammed down the phone.

Rick was not deterred, when he considered enough time had passed for Linda to wash whatever she was washing, he called again.

Whilst an oblivious Linda retrieved a bottle of wine from the fridge, Paul told the father of her child she never wanted to speak to him again. After replacing the receiver he then took the phone off the hook.

After twenty minutes of listening to the engaged tone, Rick admitted defeat. As tempting as it was to return to Linda's he couldn't risk being lifted by the police. All was not lost, he might be unable to escape tonight but Linda's little outburst might have been a blessing in disguise.

Inspecting the vehicle, Richard Senior savoured the moment. He was not in the least fazed by the damage Linda had done to the Audi. He was however disappointed not to have witnessed the altercation that had caused her to flip. Seeing his son informing the harlot he was only concerned about his child's wellbeing and had no interest in resuming their relationship would have been priceless.

Rick labelling Linda a conniving little tart and suggesting they should have her arrested for criminal damage added to his father's delight. If his son was prepared to see the girl behind bars the torch he had carried for her had definitely been extinguished. Rick's further declaration that as much as he would love to see her rot in prison he did not want to bring further shame on the Pashley name was music to his father's ears. At last Richard Junior understood how important it was to be respected in the community. Maybe there was hope for the boy after all.

The following morning the Mayor called to offer his condolences and invited the Pashley's to a fund raising event that evening. In honour of Richard's late mother, the Mayor was keen to donate a sizable contribution to one of her favourite causes. He would be honoured if Richard Senior agreed to receive it on her behalf. After accepting the invitation, Rick's father instructed his wife to hire tuxedos for himself and his son then sort out her own outfit. He had some errands to run but he would be back in time for them to leave at six thirty sharp.

While Monica carried out her husband's orders then trawled the salons of Sheffiled trying to find someone capable of setting her hair, Rick sat in his bedroom purposefully picking the scabs on his cheeks. He intended to use Linda's attack with his car keys to his advantage.

His parents' reaction when he joined them in the drawing room, eased the pain of angry sores on his face. As his mother gently wiped the blood away from his cheeks, his father accepted it would be difficult to explain his son's injuries to Sheffield's elite. Rick feigned disappointment when he was told to take off his tux as he would no longer be joining them at the Mayor's table.

Thankfully, Monica's pleas to stay with her son were swiftly rejected. Her husband assured her he had no intention of leaving Richard Junior unsupervised. The boy's Uncle Edward would keep an eye on him. Although Richard Senior's brother might not be the most reliable member of the Pashley dynasty, Edward knew better than to disobey his older sibling's orders.

Later, after watching his nephew climb out of his bedroom window and drive away in the battered Audi, Uncle Edward cheered. Only Richard Senior would be arrogant enough to think he could slip into his mother's shoes without resistance. Now the old witch was six feet under, Edward had no intention of following 'strict instructions' from anyone, especially his pompous prick of an older brother. Unlike Richard Senior and their bitch of a dead mother, Edward found the battle to uphold the family name extremely restrictive. With a bit of luck Rick would succeed in bringing total shame upon it.

Not wishing to make his grovelling apology in front of an audience, Rick decided to sneak around to the back of the house to check she was alone. He was out of luck; Linda had company. Unfortunately for him, he did not realise until he had peered through the living room window. The sight of the abhorrent little weasel wiping his penis on his soon to be ex girlfriend's chest brought Rick to his knees.

Once in the safety of his car, he released the words he had desperately wanted to scream outside Linda's window. "Slut. Whore. Bitch!" he yelled. Looking at the windscreen he pointed at his reflection, "You're an idiot. A complete mug. As if a whorebag like her was ever going to wait for you."

Banging his head against the steering wheel, Rick cursed his father. He had warned him Linda was a money grabbing tart. Why did he always have to be right?

She might be dead to him now but what about his son? Even though the child's mother had been pricked more times than a second hand dartboard, he was confident of Bradley's lineage.

The resemblance was too strong, as were his feelings when holding the boy. Bradley was his son and he expected to leave him behind to be brought up by a whore?

2237 hours, 01 October 2012

Laying on the thin mattress, 'wank mag' in his left hand, Paul Douglas congratulated himself. Captain Smarty-Pants had fallen for his bullshit, hook, line and sinker. Even though his scheme to get home had faltered, the fake eviction from his sisters had gained him his own room for a few nights and an unlikely ally to fight his corner.

Paul hoped the news he was sleeping rough would encourage Linda take him back. To facilitate this, he had promised Cindy a cut of the profits if she threw him out in front of Ella. It had been his intention to return to his sister's couch but the officer's intervention had been an unexpected bonus. Thanks to her, he didn't need worry about his nieces catching him with his cock in his hand.

Captain Harris certainly had her uses. It was just a pity she responded better to bleating than threats. He found the role of bully much more entertaining than victim. Still, as the interfering bitch was his best hope of getting his hands on Bradley's fortune, he would polish his 'woe is me' routine.

Suzanne's refusal to take a DNA test and, by virtue, the lads money had made Paul more determined to regain his pole position at number thirty-three. He'd done his homework. After a few discreet enquires to PAX and the Pensions Department he'd discovered that if Brad had maxed out his insurance there could be best part of two hundred grand up for grabs.

Once he got home, getting Linda back on the ale would be Paul's top priority. In the past, as long as he provided booze and fags, she'd always handed him the money she received from the social and Bradley's grandfather. As long as she still had her vices, he believed she would be just as trusting with her inheritance.

It had been a huge mistake to succumb to Joyce's bribery. Twelve thousand pounds was loose change in comparision to the amount they would receive from Bradley's estate. He'd been so caught up with the possibility of revisiting the whorehouse he had failed to contemplate the possible repercussions of Linda's sobriety.

Thinking of the fortune within his grasp, Paul though it ironic that he'd first lifted Bradley's mother from the tarmac in the hope of relieving her of a few trinkets.

The week before Bradley's birthday party, Paul had become concerned that Cindy's tolerance of him was dwindling at the same rate as her grief over the loss of their mother. She was now demanding he pay his way. As his job was fictious and the paltry amount his mother had left him depleted his finances, he would need a quick boost if he were not to be rendered homeless.

Linda turning fruit loop in the middle of the street had given him the opportunity to see if she owned anything of value. Seeing she was naked under her mud stained dressing gown led him to reconsider his options. Some girls tended to be more accommodating after they'd been dumped. A mixture of proving they were still attractive and wanting to stick two fingers up at the guy who'd rejected them could lead the chastest lady into an unlikely tryst. If he played his cards right he might be able to get his end away with a decent bird instead of the whores he'd spent the majority of his mother's money on. Like all the lads at school he'd thought of Linda Craig whilst pleasuring himself, how cool would it be to use her hand instead of his own?

Although the wine and foot massage didn't have the desired affect, Paul noted as long as her glass was full, Linda seemed happy enough for him to hang around. Had it not been for Joyce, Paul was pretty sure he would have stayed the night.

Not to be deterred, he called on her the following morning. Once he'd chased the cackling bitches from her living room he'd suggested a hair of the dog then left to get new supplies. Unfortunately, her mother was entering the house when he returned.

Hours later, when he'd noticed Linda standing in her doorway he had grabbed his resupplies then dashed across the road. When he took her hand, Linda seemed oblivious to his presence. The girl was practically catatonic. As he had the previous night, he guided her inside and onto the couch. Once seated,

Linda's faculties began to return. When she started to twitch he suggested a cigarette might help to calm her nerves.

After an initial coughing bout Linda puffed and slurred her way through two bottles of Pinot and half a packet of B and H whilst bleating on about her evil ex. Paul's interest peaked when Linda mentioned Rick's parents were loaded.

Eventually, Paul found a way of silencing his target. Massaging Linda's ego reaped far more rewards than massaging her feet. She was happy to puff away whilst hearing she was the most beautiful girl he had ever seen. How all the boys at school had voted her the sexiest girl in town. There had been no other candidates he assured her. She was sex on legs and only a moron would walk away from a piece of skirt like her. He told her Rick was a fool to let her go. If he was ever fortunate enough to court a girl like her, he would think himself the luckiest man on the planet.

As Linda absorbed every syllable, Paul chanced his arm. His gamble paid off. Fifteen minutes after leaning in for a quick kiss, the pair were rolling around the living room floor. Even though Linda was a little tipsy, she was an awesome shag. Her tits were amazing and she didn't even complain when he came all over them.

Chapter 17

0910 hours, 02 October 2012

'*Best of nine?*' Ella's inner voice suggested. What the hell was wrong with her? The decision she needed to make deserved more consideration than the toss of a coin.

Professionally, heads was the best result but if she was ever going to sleep again, tails was her favoured option. It was currently four – two in favour of heads.

Last night, she had been unable to shake off the thought of Rick's father dragging Suzanne through the courts then celebrating when he proved her child was not a Pashley. Could they force Suzanne to take the test? Maybe if she had a good lawyer she could fight them but she would need money for that.

Now Ella was asking a coin to decide whether she should resume her quest for Bradley's will. She had to face it, as hard as she tried she could not remain impartial, nor could she justify her inaction because the child might not be Bradley's. Even though her opinion of Paul Douglas might have softened she still fervently believed Bradley would turn in his grave if his stepfather pocketed the money.

To hell with the consequences, if the will existed she had to find it. Annoyingly, in order to do so she would need assistance. Therein lay the problem. Who could she trust not to run to Pete Waller or her CO? Placing the coin on the table she dialled Sergeant Major Cooper.

The CSM readily agreed to Ella's request. "I'd rather it were my feet in the CO's intray than yours," he assured her. "For the record, I think it stinks you can't see Susie anymore. I wouldn't be surprised if Hoity-Shite had a hand in that, spiteful little turd."

Although Ella knew Lieutenant Horton-Smythe's father had played a part in her removal she blamed herself, not the young officer, for her predicament. "No, Sergeant Major, my removal was down to me but fortunately I'm still able to be there for Bradley's parents."

Given Rick's recent declaration and the ongoing Linda and Paul debacle, Ella inwardly questioned if that was something to be grateful for.

Being informed by the guardroom that Paul was waiting at her car was extremely frustrating. When was she going to get a minute's peace? Joyce had already been on the phone asking her to pop around with her dingly thing so Linda could look at furniture.

Boxing gloves or handkerchief? Ella wondered as she entered the car park. "Good morning Paul," she said with false cheer. "I was just off to Linda's can I drop you somewhere?"

"Her place would be nice," he replied with a half smile.

"Sorry, but I think you know the answer to that."

"In that case could you drop me off at the housing office, I'm going to declare myself homeless."

"Isn't that a bit premature? Linda said she wants you back."

"And you said she needs to get better first. That isn't going to happen overnight." Paul held out a mobile top-up card. "Can you give her this with my letter? She's never got any credit on her phone."

"Do you intend to call her?"

"She doesn't need credit for me to do that," Paul said flatly. "I'm hoping she'll call me."

The sadness in his voice weakened Ella's resolve. "Before I give her anything I need your assurance you'll support her in her sobriety."

"If that means I'll keep her off the ale, you have my word. I probably want that more than she does. It can't be good for her liver."

Ella looked down at the top-up card. "It might be difficult for her to call."

Paul grimaced. "She'll find a way. If she doesn't want me back I need to hear it from her. It'll hurt like hell but I'll do it if it means she'll get better."

Paul's admittance he was capable of human emotion caught Ella off guard. "I do want to help but it doesn't feel right sneaking around behind Joyce's back."

"In that case you're not going to like my next request."

"Which is?"

"I need money." Seeing the horror on Ella's face, Paul laughed. "Don't worry I'm not trying to tap you. I've a stash in the house. I was saving up to get Linda some treatment. Thought I could get a professional to come to the house."

"Seriously? And you thought she would agree to that?"

"Thought it was worth a try. The money's in a suitcase under Phil's bed. I was wondering if you'd grab it for me."

"No way. I'm not taking money from Linda's. Anyway, how do I know it's yours?"

"Because she's got no idea it's there."

"I can't go snooping around Phil's room."

"Just ask Linda to put me some clothes in the suitcase. The money's in a secret compartment in the bottom, she won't spot it. It's not like I don't need clean clobber. I've been walking around in the same stuff for six days. I'm stinking. My undercrackers have already been inside out and back to front."

"Seriously too much information," Ella said pulling a disgusted face, then inspecting the card in her hand, "If I do give her this and your letter, I will have to tell Joyce what I'm doing. As for the money I won't take it from the house without Linda's consent."

"Are you mad? She'll go ballistic if she finds out I've got that sort of money stashed away."

"If not, it is theft. Thanks to you, I'm in enough trouble without adding that to my list of misdemeanours." Ella pointed out.

"Oh, so it's revenge you're after?" Paul snarled. "Me being homeless not enough for you? Now you want to see me starve as well?"

Maybe Ella should have thought twice before getting in the car with Paul. He might have mellowed recently but he would still rate highly on the list of people she would least like to get stuck in a lift with. "Paul, I promise you this isn't revenge. Without overplaying my worth, I'm your only link to Linda, if I jeopardise that, you're sunk too."

Paul forced himself to calm down. As hard as it was playing nice with this bitch, she was right. Placing his head in his hands, he pretended to wipe his eyes. His composure regained, he looked pitifully at Ella. "I'm sorry I shouldn't take it out on you, it's just I miss her so much."

Ella recalled how she had felt when Larry had abandoned her. "Let me see what I can do. I can't see anyone objecting to the clothes. If Linda knows about the money..."

"She doesn't."

"Then neither do I. If you tell anyone otherwise, I'll deny it and you'll get no more assistance from me. Understand?" When Paul nodded, Ella continued, "What I was about to say was, if Linda did know about the money she would probably stop me from taking the case therefore if she doesn't mention it, I won't."

Paul looked up. "Thanks," he said meekly.

1122 hours, 02 October 2012

Deciding it would be prudent to keep Pete Waller in the loop, Ella dialled his number.

"Give Mrs Douglas the top up card and the letter," Pete instructed. "If she wants to write back or call her husband it's not our place to stop her."

"But it's okay to warn her mother about it?"

"If you feel you must but either way Mrs Douglas receives the letter today."

1143 hours, 02 October 2012

When two raps of the letterbox failed to bring anyone to the door of number thirty-three, Ella began to panic. Paul's earlier revelation that Linda turned violent when refused alcohol was at the forefront of her mind. Imagining Charlie and Joyce lying in pools of blood, Ella tentatively tried the door. Finding it unlocked she opened it a few millimetres. No way was she setting foot inside until she was sure Linda wasn't wielding an axe. "Hi, is anybody home?" she yelled.

"Yes, come through," 'Joyce called out.

'Don't go in', her inner voice pleaded *'Linda's got her mother pinned against the wall with a knife to her throat.'*

"Watch your step," Joyce advised whilst climbing down the stepladder and wafting dust away from her eyes. "Sorry I couldn't move quick enough to answer the door, half the bloody wall fell off with the paper," she explained holding up a pallet knife.

"We're redecorating," Linda announced cheerily holding up a plastic scraper. "Do you have that dingle thing with you? Thought I might check out some wallpaper on line."

"It's in my briefcase."

"Coffee break," Linda declared. "Be a love will you mum?"

Joyce smiled and headed towards the kitchen.

"Best we sit at the table," Ella suggested then fired up her computer. Once online, Ella pulled up the B&Q website. "There are other sites but this will give you some ideas."

Linda soon got to grips with browsing the Internet. Sensing her presence was more of a hindrance than a help, Ella joined Joyce in the kitchen.

"Grab the other end of this will you love?" Joyce asked, holding out a well-worn duvet cover. "We'll have to ring it out over the sink. Spin cycle's none existent on her machine. Summat else to add to the list."

"List?"

"Yes we're going to do up the whole house. New everything. Linda's in her element." Joyce grinned. "It's Bradley's idea." Her smile faded at the mention of her grandson.

"His letter?"

Joyce put her finger to her lips, quickly checked on Linda and then closed the kitchen door. "Yes. That's why he left the twelve grand to me," she whispered. "Wants his mum to do up this place and turn his bedroom into a hairdressing salon. Didn't want to leave the money to her as he suspected wallpaper wouldn't be at the top of her shopping list."

129

"Why are you whispering?"

"Linda doesn't know. Thinks the makeover was my idea. He never said he wanted me to tell her so thought it best not to."

"And he didn't mention it in Linda's letter?"

"I don't know." Joyce pulled another sheet from the washing machine in order to avoid eye contact with Ella. "I haven't given her it yet," she admitted.

"Why ever not? You were supposed to get them at the same time. Please tell me you've given Phil his."

Joyce looked contrite, "Not yet. He's bound to let something slip to his mother and I'm not sure she's strong enough to hear it yet. She's getting there. She's even being pleasant to you," Joyce added in the hope to appease Ella. "The letter could contain something she doesn't want to hear and …"

"It contains something Bradley wanted her to hear, isn't that more important?" Ella asked forcefully.

"Please, just a few more days," Joyce pleaded. "Let's get the house done up and then give it to her. At least that way, if she does react badly, we'll have managed to carry out some of Bradley's wishes."

As Ella wasn't about to ruin the older woman's day she decided to concede. "So, other than a new washing machine what else is on the shopping list?"

Relieved Ella had submitted to her request Joyce answered enthusiastically, "Whatever you can get for twelve grand. I've told Linda whilst there's money in the pot she can have whatever she wants and believe me she wants a lot."

Spotting the hole in the sheet she was about to hand to Ella, Joyce rolled it up and threw it in the bin then retrieved the duvet cover from the laundry basket and deposited that too. "Sod it, I'll pop to the shops and get her some new bedding. Pour the tea will you love?"

Ella did as requested then turned to Joyce, "Before I take this to Linda, I need to speak to you about Paul," Ella warned.

Joyce slouched back on the kitchen stool. "Why have I got a feeling I'm not going to like this?"

"He wants to come back."

Joyce shook her head. "Well tell him he can't."

"It's not that easy. He's written a letter to Linda and I've been told to deliver it."

"By who?" Joyce asked fervently.

"My bosses."

"So they know what's best for my lass now?"

"No, but like me, they feel we have no right to withhold correspondence."

Joyce pursed her lips. The accusation wasn't lost on her. "So you're not asking me, you're telling me."

"I just wanted to warn you."

"Can't you just ask him to stay at Cindy's a few more weeks? He could come back once we've done the place up? He won't want to be around here whilst we're decorating." Secretly Joyce was hoping in a few more weeks Linda would see the benefits of not having Paul around.

"Cindy's kicked him out."

"Can't say I blame her. Where's he staying?"

It was Ella's turn to avoid eye contact. "I got him a room on my camp but only until Friday."

Joyce was flummoxed. "Why in God's name would you help him?"

Ella shrugged. "I did it for Linda. I don't think she wants him out on the streets."

"Told you that has she?" Joyce asked suspiciously. When a denial wasn't forthcoming, Joyce patted Ella's hand. "It's okay, I understand. It not like she'd get a fair hearing from me or her dad." Grabbing a cloth from the sink, Joyce started to wipe away imaginary crumbs from the worktop. "You think she wants him back?"

"Yes."

"Maybe I could stay on for a bit? Move into Phil's room. Just until Paul's up to date with her medication."

"He's promised he won't let her touch a drop," she assured Joyce.

"And you believe him?" Joyce asked skeptically. "He'll not stand up to her when she demands booze."

"Will he need to? Like you said she's doing well."

"She's still got a long way to go. We've had some right ding dongs." Joyce opened the cutlery draw. "Not a knife in sight, see. She keeps threatening to top herself or, when she at her worse, the both of us."

"I didn't realise it was that bad." And she had thought herself being overdramatic when nobody had answered the door!

"You can't kick a habit like hers overnight. Worse still, after her little tantrum she ends up having a bloody panic attack because she feels bad about threatening us. How's he going to cope with that?" Tears gently trickled down Joyce's cheeks as she spoke.

"I'll speak with him, you never know he might surprise you. According to Linda it wasn't Paul that drove her to drink he just facilitated her need."

"That's a load of tripe. Paul didn't facilitate it he created it. Feeding her wine for breakfast. And fags! My lass never touched either of those before he came along. Within days of meeting that little shit she was skiving off work so she could smoke and drink with that layabout."

Chapter 18

1212 hours, 02 October 2012

"Hey come and have a look at this paper you two," Linda yelled from the living room. "Bit expensive but we can afford it, can't we, mum?"

Joyce quickly wiped her eyes. "Just coming, love. Do you want a bit of Bakewell?" She mouthed 'Dave' to Ella then raised her eyebrows.

"Go on then, you've twisted my arm," Linda replied.

Although unimpressed with Linda's chosen colour scheme Joyce decided to take advantage of Ella's presence and left in search of red bedding. "Give her the letter whilst I'm out," Joyce told Ella in the hall. "I can't trust myself not to rip it up if I'm here."

"Are you sure?"

"You've got your orders. Anyway, if she wants him back there's nothing we can do to stop her. Us trying will just cause more aggro. I'm going to insist on staying for a bit though."

Linda was unimpressed when Ella closed the laptop. "I wanted to look for a new settee," she moaned.

"And I want to give you these," Ella informed her taking the letter and phone card from her bag. "They're from Paul."

Snatching the items, Linda ripped open the envelope. "Go and make a brew will you? I don't need you breathing down me neck whilst I'm trying to read."

'You're welcome.' Ella's inner voice snarled back.

Whilst waiting to be summoned Ella checked her phone. Not knowing how long Linda would be she decided to return the missed call from the Sergeant Major.

Coops was keen to impart his news. "I got Beetle to call APC this morning. You were right, they haven't received his will either."

"What about the other two names I gave you?" Ella asked excitedly.

"As you suggested, I asked the clerks to ring APC on the other lad's behalf. They did but then went running to the Chief Clerk. Sorry, ma'am but I think she's on to you," the CSM cautioned. "When I said I was only making enquiries because Beetle had said his will was missing the Chief asked what, or more precisely who, had made me ask about the other two guys. According to her, only someone au fait with clerical procedures think to do that and she's pretty confident that someone was you. I denied it but she wasn't convinced."

"Don't worry Sergeant Major, Jules and I are old friends, I'll talk to her later. Right now, I'm more concerned about the other wills. What did the clerks say?"

"Same as Brad and Beetle. They are listed as being sent to APC but not as being received."

"So they could have been sent to the wrong department at Glasgow. Not to worry, wills are sent by Recorded Delivery so they should be able to track them down." The prospect excited Ella.

"I'm afraid not. There's no record of them being sent. That's why Jules got involved. The clerk had to tell her the documents hadn't been correctly dispatched. I pity whoever's at fault, the mood she's in someone's going to get their nuts fried."

"That might make her feel better but it doesn't help Suzanne." Ella was livid. The last thing she wanted was this fiasco to be a clerical error. The Post Office messing up she could've handled but her own cap badge being responsible was unforgivable.

The Sergeant Major tried to reassure Ella. "They're not giving up. Jules is investigating. She's promised to get back to me. I'll let you know what she says."

"Thanks, but now the cats out of the bag I may as well speak to her myself."

1323 hours, 02 October 2012

Linda's enquiry into how long it took to make a bloody brew resulted in Ella saying a hasty goodbye to the Sergeant Major.

Receiving her tea, Linda announced Paul wanted to come home. Surprisingly the prospect didn't appear to be filling her with glee.

"I thought you'd be happier. Have you changed your mind about wanting him back?" Ella asked hopefully.

Linda shook her head, "The thing is, when he sees me like this, will he still feel the same?"

"Sees you like what? Sober? You were sober when he left."

"Was kicked out," Linda corrected. "Yes, I was sober. That was bad enough but now with the agoraphobia I'm even worse. I can be a right cow when I'm coming down off my meds."

'As opposed to being a right cow all the time?' Quipped Ella's inner bitch.

"Come on, I'm sure Paul's skin's thick enough to handle that."

"Really? Why? Because he's used to me being a bitch?" Ella wondered if Linda could read minds. "Well I might be a bitch to everyone else but not to him."

"I suppose you two are quite tight," Ella conceded.

"We've had to be. He's the only one that gave a shit about me when Rick buggered off. Them pair were no use. Mum kidnapped Bradley and dad sold me down the swanny to Rick's tosser of a father."

"What?"

"He cut a deal with the evil bastard. I got to keep my job at the hairdressers plus a bit of money for Brad and Rick got to pretend we didn't exist."

"They were probably thinking about you. Long distance relationships rarely work."

Linda sneered, lit a cigarette then shook her head. "They might have been thinking about Brad but not me. Other than hurling abuse through the front door, dad never spoke to me. He never failed to yell what a disappointment I was when he came to pick up the boys." Linda took a long drag on her cigarette then continued, "He wasn't telling me owt I didn't know but it still hurt."

Ella squirmed. She had a genuine affection for Charlie and felt she should defend him, but how? Although she found Linda's claims hard to accept she could hardly accuse her of lying.

"You don't believe me do you?"

'Derren Brown eat your heart out,' Ella thought. "I… Well it's not that I don't… It's just..." Thankfully a sentence passed through Ella's mind that she could complete without stuttering. "He stayed with you on the day of the funeral. He's looked after you ever since. He wouldn't have done that if he didn't care."

"I'm still trying to get my head around that. He's been lovely. Not that I deserve it, I've been a total mental case. Did mum tell you I threatened to kill them both in their bed?"

The lack of shock on Ella's face enraged Linda. "'Course she did. Tells you everything, doesn't she? Thinks the sun shines out of your arse. No secret who'd she'd rather have for a daughter." Linda drew hard on her cigarette reducing its size by half. "I'm such a fucking disappointment. She's no better than dad. Saint fucking Joyce, on her knees every Sunday. Doubt any of her prayers were for me. She didn't even try to understand how upset I was when Rick pissed off. She just snatched Bradley. If it hadn't have been for Paul I'd have probably never got my lad back. As far as she was concerned I was an unfit mother and Bradley needed to stay away from me. Well her precious God has answered that prayer. I'll never see my boy again."

When Linda started slapping her forehead and shouting "Fuck" over and over again Ella removed the cigarette from her hand, placed it in the ashtray and grabbed the woman's wrists. "Linda, calm down please. Whatever happened is in the past. You're getting on better with your parents and Paul's coming home. That's a good thing, isn't it?"

Linda blinked then stared hard at Ella through teary eyes. "Who am I to slag her off? I was a useless mother. Too busy necking my own bottle to give Phil his." Linda's shoulders sagged. "I breast fed Bradley. I loved being a mum then. It was great when it was just the two of us. He was so perfect."

Bursting into tears, Linda stood and headed for the stairs. Ella felt like a bacon butty at a bar mitzvah, unwelcome but unable to leave. Should she follow Linda? Probably not, the woman obviously wanted to be alone and given her volatile nature Ella wasn't brave enough to go against Linda's wishes.

Once upstairs Linda desperately scrabbled under her bed. She needed a fix. As alcohol wasn't an option, reading a supportive letter from a total stranger would have to suffice. Her favourite, a letter from another mother who had also lost her son, was at the top of the pile. The woman was able to eloquently put into words the guilt, pain and utter uselessness Linda felt.

The woman also talked of an unbreakable connection between mother and son. Linda had convinced herself it had been such a bond that had heightened her fear when that toffee nosed git had turned up at their door. That morning the tenseness she'd felt far outweighed her usual distress on hearing the doorbell. She couldn't put her finger on it but her whole being was telling her not to go downstairs, even the thought of Paul opening the door made her shake.

When she'd finally allowed Paul to leave their bed, she'd sneaked to the top of the stairs and listened intensely as Lieutenant Horton-Smythe blurted out her Bradley was gone. Placing her fist in her mouth to stifle her screams, she'd slid down the wall then lay on the floor absorbing every painful detail. Her mind was racing. Not her Brad. Not the child whose birth had evoked emotions she had felt herself incapable of. Not her beautiful Pumpkin.

The few happy memories she had of her life all included her first born, yet she had been totally blasé when waving him off to that hellhole. Just like his father, he had bolted at the first opportunity and her bitterness would not let her convey the pain she'd felt. She had not even told him to stay safe or how much she loved him. Was this her punishment for the years she had neglected him because he resembled the man she loathed so much?

Listening intensely, Linda convinced herself Paul's couldn't give a shit attitude was for the benefit of the officer. They always showed that level of disdain to any visitors. He was probably as heartbroken as she was but there was no way he would show weakness to the likes of that snobby bastard.

The revelation that another unwanted arrival was about to descend on them sent Linda crawling to her bed. Some snotty bitch was going to look after her? As if! She didn't need looking after by the likes of them. Paul would take care of her, he always did. The sooner they got rid the better.

When Paul climbed back into bed, Linda blamed the previous evening's curry for her distress then crept off to the bathroom, once inside she wretched violently. It was not the previous evening's chicken balti she was trying to rid herself of but the feeling of self-loathing. Her boy was gone and she couldn't remember the last time she had uttered a kind word in his presence.

Rubbing Linda's back whilst telling her to, 'Get it all up before the money woman arrived' had been the extent of Paul's concern.

Reading the condolence letters was Linda's only hope of deterring another panic attack so she wiped away her tears and focused on the words. Since her first episode in 1996 Linda had always feared she would fail to wake when her demons visited, these days she found she couldn't care less if she didn't. Maybe if her first panic attack had finished her off Bradley would still be alive.

0813 hours, 19 July 1996

Linda couldn't breathe. Her body seemed to reject the air offered. Dropping the phone she attempted shorter breaths. This was it; she was going to die. Whilst wondering who would find her maggot ridden body Linda lost consciousness.

Once again Paul Douglas came to her rescue. He'd decided to pop in on his way to work to assure her nobody was aware of their previous night's liaison. It was just as well he had taken a key he told her.

None of Paul's words registered as he guided her towards the couch. Rick's on the other hand were replaying over and over again in her mind.

Because she had been so excited to receive his phone call it had taken her a moment to register the venom in his voice. The insults then came thick and fast. Amongst other things she was a whore, a money-grabbing slapper and a terrible mother.

It was the questions, not the abuse that had caused her to drop the phone. When asked where Bradley had been whilst she was entertaining her client the previous evening, Linda had failed to understand the reference to 'client' and replied their son had stayed at a friend's. Rick's next query 'had she washed the spunk from her chest yet' caused her throat to constrict.

Chapter 19

1348 hours, 02 October 2012

The sight of Ella scraping away at a stubborn piece of wallpaper amused Joyce. "What are you doing, lass?" the older woman asked.

"Sorry. Linda went for a lie down so I thought I'd make myself useful."

"Cheese and onion or steak bake?" Joyce enquired heading for the kitchen. "I popped in Greggs on my way to the bus stop," she explained.

Although pasties were not a normal lunchtime snack for Ella she knew better than to refuse. "Cheese and onion please," she replied following the tempting smell.

"Has she been down long?" Joyce asked.

"About half an hour."

"Sorry about that. I know she normally has a nap in the afternoon but I didn't think she'd be so rude. Not with you here. Don't know why really, when is she anything else?"

Although before her conversation with Linda, Ella wouldn't have given the comment a second thought, now she now noted how easily Joyce belittled her daughter.

"I think Paul's letter upset her," Ella offered as a defence.

"Does that mean he's not coming home?" Joyce asked hopefully.

Ella shrugged.

The microwave's ping coincided with the kettle's whistle. "Let's have coffee for a change," Joyce suggested. "You must be fed up of tea."

Carrying her lunch into the living room, Ella joined Joyce around the dining table then bit into her pasty. Melted cheese exploded in her mouth and spilled down her chin. Ella quickly spat the hot liquid into her hand prompting Joyce to run into the kitchen.

"Bloody hell, that's hot." Ella shouted then tossed the contents of her burning hand on to the plate. "Oh my God, Joyce. I'm so sorry. It was just too hot to swallow."

Joyce returned with a glass of water. "Quick, drink this. It's me that needs to apologise I should've warned you it would be hot."

Apologies dispensed, Ella gratefully drank the water. "I think I'll give that a minute." She told Joyce disappointedly. Having tasted the artery-clogging treat her stomach was crying out for more.

"So, what were you two chatting about?" Joyce asked.

As the only response Ella could think of was, 'What a rubbish mother you were.' She inspected the blister forming on her hand until she could come up with a suitable lie. "We were talking about doing up this place."

"Did she mention changing Bradley's room into a salon?"

"Not really. She was looking at furniture for the living room."

"I hope she does. She was a great stylist back in the day. It's in her blood. As soon as she could walk she was sweeping up hair. Once she got a pair of scissor in her hands there was no stopping her. My boss promised to take her on as an apprentice as soon as she finished school."

"Rick's mother?" Ella knew the answer but wanted to glean more information from a surprised looking Joyce.

"That's right. Did Linda tell you about her?"

"No, Rick mentioned her."

"I see. Told you how our Linda targeted the boss's son, eh?"

"Not at all. He just said he thought his mum missed you for more than your hairdressing when they moved away."

Joyce sighed at the mention of Mrs Pashley's departure. "She was a lovely lady. Very particular about her hair but other than that she was as soft as snow. Let our Linda run rings round her. I should've nipped it in the bud. If I had maybe she wouldn't have set her sights on Rick.

The subject of Rick caused Joyce to declare their discussion over. "If Linda catches me talking about you know who she'll have a fit," she told Ella. "Think I best go and wake her she's been on her own long enough."

"Before you do that, can we talk about Linda and Phil's letter? I'm sorry, but I'm not happy about delaying delivery."

"Trust me it's not the right time," Joyce answered heading into the hallway.

"Those letters were entrusted to me to deliver!" Ella yelled after her.

Rushing back through the living room door Joyce closed it. "And you did, you gave them to me," she whispered. "If anyone complains, I'll take the flack."

"I'm not worried about complaints," Ella snapped. "Bradley obviously had a message for his mother and brother and they have a right to hear it."

"I've got my reasons," Joyce replied.

"Well I'm sorry, but I think I'm entitled to hear them."

The older woman sighed. "Fair enough, but not here. Can you pick me up later?"

"What time?"

"Sixish?" Once Ella agreed, Joyce yelled upstairs and ordered her daughter to join them.

When Linda joined them in the living room, Joyce jumped up from the table, "Are you hungry, love?" she asked. "I've got some pasties from Greggs or I can make you a sandwich."

"Stop feeding me, mum. I can hardly fit in my jeans. Thought lager was supposed to be fattening. Since I've stopped drinking, I've clapped on weight."

"Double edged sword love, you've been compensating with crisps, chocolate and cake." Joyce told her daughter.

"Think I'm going to need some new clobber soon," Linda said loosening her belt. "You two don't fancy another trip to

Meadowhall do you? Think it's time I brought my wardrobe, as well as my wallpaper, into the twenty-first century."

"You could look online," Ella suggested opening her laptop.

"I've gotta get myself one of these things, mum." Linda said whilst scanning the Next Directory, "If I order today its gets delivered tomorrow. Means I don't need to go out."

"Not yet love, but one day it'll be nice to walk around the shops together."

Linda looked thoughtful. "Maybe, but for now I think I need one of these," she said holding up Ella's laptop.

When Joyce headed for the kitchen, Linda turned her attention to Ella. "I called Paul. He said he needs clean clothes so I've popped some in a case. You can take it when you go," Linda lowered her voice. "He's coming home on Friday." When Ella frowned Linda sighed. "Where else is he supposed to go? Your lot are kicking him out and thanks to you he can't go back to Cindy's."

"Don't you want your mum to stay a bit longer? She knows all your meds and she's helping with the makeover," Ella pointed at the bare walls.

"Paul can do that."

"When I said help, I meant financing. I doubt your mum will give Paul her credit card."

"Fair point. I suppose it would be nice to have her around a bit longer but I'll need some time alone with Paul," Linda winked. "He's a bit of a moaner, don't think mum would like to hear him."

Ella managed to hide her disgust. "You could send her into town for wallpaper. It's at least half an hour each way. That should give you plenty of time to get reacquainted."

"Yes, and if he's up for seconds I can always tell her she forgot something," Linda laughed.

Desperate to end their conversation, Ella snapped shut her laptop. "I'll get off now. Please consider letting your mum stay. I know she'd like to, she worries about you."

"When she's not lecturing me about leaving plates on the floor. Does my head in." Linda softened. "I suppose I will miss her a bit, and the old man. Don't you dare tell them though."

"I've a feeling they'll both be around more."

"What about you?"

"I'll be on the end of the phone if you need me."

"Might need a hand doing up this place. Don't suppose you're any good with a paintbrush?"

"Not particularly. Spent plenty of time in hairdressers' chairs though so if you need a hand planning the salon, I'm your woman."

"Might have to put that one on the back burner. I can't see anyone letting me near their barnet with a pair of scissors?" Linda held out her hand, "Half the time I'm shaking like a leaf."

"You're not shaking now and it's going to get better. Tell you what, once you've made Bradley's room into a salon, I'll be your first customer. If you do a good job I'll recommend you to my friends."

"What? A sort of show and tell?" Linda sneered. "Let them see the mad cow you've been saddled with?"

"Behave. You know how important a woman's hair is to her. Do you honestly think I'd let you near mine, or risk losing my friends, just to gain a bit of gossip material? Your mum told me you're a natural stylist so I'm willing to risk it." Ella picked up Paul's case. "Still, if you don't want to."

"No. I mean, yes. I do. I'm just not very good with strangers. Maybe just you for now."

"Okay. Get that room done and I'll start looking at hair magazines," Ella replied.

1617 hours, 02 October 2012

Ella was alarmed when the gate guard stated her presence was required in the CO's office. If her boss couldn't wait for her to arrive in the building before demanding her company it was obviously important. Unfortunately, Paul Douglas would have to wait to change his underwear.

The look on Jess's face told Ella this was to be a 'beret on' encounter. Entering the CO's office Ella saluted. "You wanted to see me sir?"

"I did. Close the door." Placing the letter he had been reading to one side he stared at the officer before him. "Would you like to explain to me why Mr Douglas is currently residing on my camp without my knowledge?"

Ella's bowels lurched as she fought with her bum cheeks to stop her fear making a more vocal appearance. "I'm sorry, sir... I meant to tell you... I thought the QM would." Shaking her head she resigned herself to the truth. "I didn't think."

"Got there in the end. You didn't think."

"No I didn't. Well, I did, but only about the consequences of not having him here."

"Which are?"

"Mr Douglas sleeping on the streets, days after his stepson's funeral, might stir Press interest. Then there's his wife. She didn't want him kicked out in the first place."

"Then why was he?"

Ella went on to explain the whole story.

"So he's definitely going home on Friday?" The CO asked.

"Yes, sir."

"In that case, you did the right thing but you should have spoken to me first. How do you think it would have looked to the Press if they had found out I had no idea he was on my camp? They might think by giving him a bed, you were trying to bribe him regarding his allegations."

"Sir, that's not why I did it."

"I know that, but the Press do not. You need to be more careful."

"I realise that now." Ella sighed. "This whole thing is a minefield. I feel like I can't do right for doing wrong," she admitted.

145

"You've allowed yourself to get too involved. I think we need to pull you back a little. You're there to support the family with regard to their son's death not their marital disputes and medical conditions. Personally, I would like to see a bit more of you around here. Staff Coleman's doing a cracking job but he cannot cover two desks indefinitely. Jess doesn't seem to be half as busy with the fiancée and I thought she was the one who had taken it the worst."

Prior to their conversation, Ella had considered asking if the decision to remove her as Suzanne's CVO could be overturned. Now she was grateful of it. If she still needed to run between Garvey Grove and Garvey Close she wouldn't have a minute's peace.

Jess pounced as Ella left the CO's office. "Everything okay?"

"I think so, I forgot to tell the boss Paul was on camp."

"Yes I heard." Jess grinned. "If I was you I'd avoid the QM. He got it in the ear earlier."

"I'd rather not think about that right now. How's Suzanne? Rick said she's doing a lot better."

"Yes, about that. You dealt with Sergeant Major Cooper during the repatriation?"

"Yes. He was also Suzanne's notifying officer."

"Good guy?"

"I think so."

"Well, he's not being very good to me right now. He's Corporal Bell's Unit Visiting Officer and he point blank refuses to let Suzanne see him. He claims the lad's not fit enough for visitors."

At last something was going her way. Ella had intended to broach the subject of Dinger on her return to the office now she could do so without appearing to interfere. "I didn't realise his injuries were that serious."

"They're not. The bullet only chipped his shoulder blade. They're confident they have removed all fragments and the wound is healing nicely. There doesn't appear to be any nerve damage so on the whole he's been pretty lucky. He'll start physio soon."

"Then why no visitors?"

"That's what I'd like to know. Louise is convinced seeing Corporal Bell will get Suzanne back on track so she's constantly on my case."

"I thought Bradley's letter had helped Suzanne."

"Her hygiene and diet have certainly improved but she still can't sleep. She's on edge all the time. Louise reckons she's riddled with guilt. She wants Dinger to convince Suzanne that Bradley had forgiven her. I have no idea what for and no one feels the need to enlighten me." Jess complained. "Would you have a word with the CSM? See if he'll give you more info."

"Leave it with me, I'll see what I can find out," Ella offered.

1629 hours, 02 October 2012

Seeing Paul Douglas loitering outside her office, Ella inwardly groaned. "I take it you're here for your case?"

"Linda said you were going to bring it to my room," he replied sulkily.

"Sorry, something important came up." She raised her hand to stop the abuse she expected. "I do have other things to attend to, I can't put you first all the time."

Noting the exasperation in Ella's voice, Paul feigned sympathy, "Fair enough, I know you're a busy lady. Could I get it now?"

"It's in the car. Follow me," Ella instructed. "Linda said she didn't pack much because you're going home soon."

"Do Joyce and Charlie know?"

"Joyce does."

"Bet that went down like a lead balloon."

"She's only worried about Linda's recovery. She's scared you'll buy her booze."

147

"I won't, I swear. I just wish they would trust me." Paul decided he needed to launch his charm offensive. "Listen, now I've got some money do you fancy grabbing a coffee at the NAAFI, my treat."

"Sorry, I wasn't exaggerating earlier, I've got a pile of work to get through and a meeting at six o'clock." Ella passed Paul his case. "Do me a favour, we need the QM sweet so keep your head down for the next couple of days."

Paul nodded. "Okay. Seeing as you've blown me out, I'll pop round and see my grand daughter. You have a nice evening and don't work too hard."

Ella stared in disbelief as Paul headed towards the transit block. She'd expected him to blow a gasket when she hadn't delivered his case but instead he'd offered to buy her coffee! What the hell was going on?

1635 hours, 02 October 2012

Pacing the kitchen floor, Joyce wondered how Charlie would react to the news of Paul's return. No doubt he would want to leave before his son-in-law reappeared. How would he feel about returning home alone? When Linda had agreed to Joyce staying in Phil's room, she had been overjoyed. Now the realisation she would have to run between her daughter and husband in order to keep the peace made her anxious. It would be just like the days of Charlie's incarceration, only worse; now she would have Paul to contend with. He might have Ella convinced he'd played no part in Linda's addiction but Joyce knew better.

Her first encounter with 'Linda the Lout' was only days after Paul Douglas's arrival in their lives. Joyce still reeled at how far her daughter had fallen in such a short space of time.

0912 hours, 19 July 1996

Slamming down the phone, Joyce instructed Penny to cancel her next two appointments and all of Linda's. "Tell them there's been a family emergency. Better still a death. There just might be if she hasn't sorted herself out."

Coughing exaggeratedly, Joyce walked in to find Linda puffing away. "And when did you start smoking young lady?" she demanded. Seeing the glass in her daughter's hand Joyce shook her head, "So you're too ill to come to work but not to swill alcohol. For God's sake girl it's not even ten o'clock."

"Mum, Rick phoned and he was so nasty." Linda whined. "I collapsed in the hall. Paul gave me the wine and cigarettes to calm me down."

"How kind of him. Where is he now? I'd love to thank him," Joyce sneered.

"He's gone to the off licence to get some…"

"What? To get some what?"

Linda squirmed. "More wine," she answered begrudgingly.

Joyce couldn't believe her ears. "More wine? More bloody wine? That's the last thing you need. As for the fags, if you think I'm bringing Bradley back here to breathe in these fumes, think again."

"Actually, I was going to ask if you could keep him for a few days. Just until I'm feeling better."

"Better or sober?"

Linda cringed. "Both. I don't think I'm up to looking after him right now."

"Well at least that's something we can agree on. I'll keep him, but not for your sake, for his. Lad doesn't need to see you in this state." Joyce looked at her daughter in disgust. "Are you planning on getting dressed today?"

Linda looked down at her filthy dressing gown and shrugged.

"I've got to get back to work," Joyce snapped. "I don't want to let MY clients down. You need to be careful young lady, if you carry on like this, you'll lose yours."

Along with everything else, thought Linda as her mother stormed from the house. She'd already lost Rick, her self-respect and her sobriety so why not her clients? Worse still, she'd lost Bradley. How could she face the child she had let down so badly. The boy whose resemblance to his father caused her physical pain; her gorgeous, funny, well-mannered, little Pumpkin.

She had so many dreams for him. He was going to be the first Craig to go to university, to own his own house, to be looked up to instead of down on. She'd ruined that for him before he'd even started school.

149

School? She'd often wondered how he would react to swapping the salon for the classroom. Would he be excited, apprehensive, frightened? A new fear constricted her throat. She would have to face the other mothers when dropping him off. How could she after what she had done last night? The thought of people knowing she had let Paul Douglas... And they would know, if Rick had found out, they certainly would.

Paul had sworn he had not breathed a word to anyone about their liaison. If he was to be believed, his theory that Rick's father must have hired a private investigator was the only logical explanation. He must have taken photographs for Richard Senior to show his son. Knowing that bastard, he'd probably circulate his evidence around the neighbourhood to cause her further humiliation. If the other mothers saw them...

Maybe she could ask her mother to take Bradley to school. In fact, maybe she should ask Joyce to take care of him permanently. It might be time for Linda to return to the gutter but that didn't mean she had to drag her son there with her, he deserved better.

What he really deserved was his father. Sadly she no longer did. Whatever anyone else thought, she had loved Rick Pashley. The money had faded into insignificance soon after she had snared her prey. The love, laughter and security she'd experienced during their short time together had shown her, it was not money that brought happiness, but people. Rick Pashley was an affectionate, funny, loyal guy who had made her feel worthy of the adoration he bestowed upon her. The disappearance of his devotion had returned her to the worthless piece of scum she'd always known herself to be. Who was she to turn her nose up at the likes of Paul Douglas? It was time for her to accept the hand she'd been dealt. For a short period she might have basked in sunshine but now it was time to return to the shade.

Draining her glass, Linda panicked, where was Paul with the wine? Rushing to the fridge she was relieved to find a can of lager next to one of her son's favourite yoghurts. 'Pumpkin', she whispered then took a long slurp of lager. Fighting tears, she drew hard on her cigarette. Crying served no purpose, Bradley was better off with his grandparents and that was that.

Chapter 20
1631 hours, 02 October 2012

Although the Mr Nice Guy routine was killing him, Paul accepted he would need to keep GI Jane sweet for a few more days if he didn't want to spend his nights on Cindy's lumpy couch. Not that he intended to spend much time in the bed Ella had supplied. Thanks to her, he could afford to visit the whores with roofs over their heads instead of the ones that ply their trade in dark alleys. Maybe he'd splash out on two girls tonight, he deserved a treat after sucking up to that silly tart.

Thank God Linda had handed over the case. He'd been stressing about the loot in the bottom of it for days. It had been stupid leaving the money there but waltzing around the Haddington with the best part of two grand in your pocket wasn't sensible either.

1633 hours, 02 October 2012

After placing her order for a light evening meal with a disgruntled Larry, Ella called Sergeant Major Cooper.

"Hi ma'am, freaky or what, I was just about to call you. Jules has just left my office. It gets worse. The wills you asked about aren't the only ones missing. Jules carried out a full trawl and it seems there are five more unaccounted for. What's weird is, three were sent off before Bradley's and two were sent after so that's three envelopes unaccounted for."

"I take it all three envelopes weren't sent by Recorded Delivery?"

"Correct. Jules can't get her head around it because everyone else's was."

"Maybe they were never dispatched or one of your clerks might not know the correct procedures. He or she could have sent them to the wrong department. They could be somewhere else in Glasgow awaiting action."

"I hope so and not just because of Bradley's will, Jules is worried sick."

"I can imagine. She'll get it in the neck if it turns out to be a clerical error. I'll give her a call later and see if there's anything I can do to help. In the meantime, I wanted to talk to you about

Corporal Bell. I believe you've been assigned as his Unit Visiting Officer?"

"Yes, ma'am."

"How is he?"

"Hoping to be released soon. It'll be a bonus for me if he is. Took me three and half hours to get to Birmingham yesterday and four to get home."

"I don't understand, if he's well enough to go home why isn't he well enough for visitors?"

"Ah, you've been talking to Captain Lowry. I knew she didn't believe me." The CSM sighed, "It's a tricky one ma'am. He's refusing visitors. He didn't want to see me. Fortunately, as I'm his UVO he has no choice. Not that he said much. Lad's undergone a total personality transplant, usually you can't shut him up. Think his head's screwed up more than his body."

"I take it he's seeing the psychiatrist."

"He's refusing treatment."

"Can he do that?"

"Apparently. Including Bradley, the unit has had four fatalities this tour. Dinger witnessed two, plus he was there when I was injured. He reckons he's all counselled out. Sees no point in going through it all again. Says it just makes him worse."

"Do you believe him?"

"That it makes him worse? Possibly, but not that he doesn't need it. I understand he's been in the chair a few times but this is different. His best mate died in his arms and he was injured himself. When I took my bullet it messed me up big style. I'd prepared myself for my lads dying but not me."

"So do you think that's the problem, he's contemplating his own mortality?"

"Maybe. Right now he won't admit he's got a problem. The doctors are reluctant to release him without a full psychiatric evaluation but at the same time they can't keep him there indefinitely. Plus, being around seriously injured soldiers might not be helping. They've suggested I ask the Occupational Health

Officer to see him once he's home. Maybe he'll be able to talk Dinger into having treatment in Preston."

"I suppose there's no point in me pleading Suzanne's case?"

"I've already tried. She's the last person he wants to see. He says he's not strong enough to deal with her. I can't say I blame him. She's bound to ask about Brad's last words. They're not going to be easy to recall."

"I guess not."

"He doesn't want Suzanne to know he's refusing to see her. That's why I told Captain Lowry he was unfit for visitors."

"Do you mind if I tell Jess the truth? She won't tell Susie I promise."

"Okay ma'am. On the upside I suppose it will stop her calling me."

After saying goodbye Ella called Jules.

"WO2 Robinson speaking."

"Jules, it's Ella."

"I thought I might hear from you, ma'am. I take it the CSM has informed you your interference has paid off."

Ella knew denying her involvement would only add insult to injury. "Come on Jules, I get you're annoyed with me but you can drop the ma'am crap. We're still friends aren't we? I'm sorry I didn't call you direct. If I'd have thought for one minute the problem originated from your office I would have."

"That would've been my preferred option. Still as your nosiness was warranted, I might just forgive you."

"Pretty please, Jules. I promise not to interfere again."

Jules laughed, "Don't make promises you can't keep. Seriously though, I hope you don't mind me taking credit for figuring this out. It might go some way to repairing my staff's reputation and I'm guessing you won't want Major Waller to find out you're still chasing wills."

"You've spoken to Pete?"

"He called me shortly after you, er, resigned from CVO duties. Made it clear if you contacted me regarding the will I should let him know."

"Bloody hell, I didn't think he'd take it that far. You're not going to tell him, are you?"

"Of course not. And not just to save your bacon. As I said I want the hierarchy to think my staff uncovered the truth. The problem is I can't get my head around it. The three missing envelopes were dispatched by two different Lance Corporals. Both have previously sent the documents by Recorded Delivery so why would they change procedures?"

"What have they got to say for themselves?"

"They're both in Afghan. The Ops Room are going to get them to call me. I was hoping it was them when you rang."

"So you need me to get off the line?"

"Afraid so. Seven of the lads whose wills are missing are still out there. They'll need to write new ones. How bad is that? Writing them before they leave is hard enough but now they're in the thick of it the thought of their letters being read will be more poignant."

"Don't you want to wait until you're sure they're missing before asking them to draft new ones?"

"I've considered it but I couldn't live with myself if anything happened to one of them. We're going to have to come clean to the unit. We'll probably lose the trust of all the guys but what choice do we have? I feel such an idiot. I checked and re-checked everyone had made a will and that they had been dispatched. It just never entered my head to confirm they'd made it to APC."

"Don't beat yourself up, I wouldn't have thought to do that."

"No, but you did think to question why Lance Corporal Craig's didn't get there. I just accepted he never completed one. You might have just saved another family going through this."

Even though her tenacity had paid off for the other eight soldiers, Ella had mixed feelings about having her faith in Bradley justified. Confirmation he had written a will made the thought of his money not ending up where he intended harder to take.

'And his letters haven't either' she thought. She was due to pick Joyce up in an hour. Bradley's grandmother better have a good explanation for her delaying delivery.

1812 hours, 02 October 2012

Placing a plate of custard creams in front of Ella, Joyce took a seat then cleared her throat. "I suppose I'd better start with a confession. I didn't go to the doctors the other day, I went to see a solicitor."

"About Bradley's estate?"

"Partly."

"You wasted your time. Rick's no longer going to stake a claim for Suzanne's baby."

"It wasn't about that. The solicitor I went to see was Monica Pashley's."

"I thought she was dead."

"She is. This guy was the executor of her will. I just wanted to check with him if Bradley's death changed anything."

"Because?"

"Maybe I should tell you about the last time Monica sat in this kitchen."

1537 hours, 20 July 1996

Sheepishly entering Joyce's home, Rick's mother was astute enough to realise she would not receive the same level of hospitality as she had three days earlier. Ironically, on that day, she had visited Joyce in the hope of meeting her grandson on his fourth birthday.

Since discovering the hidden photographs in the monthly paperwork Joyce sent her for the salon, Monica had fixated on holding the little boy who bore such a strong resemblance to her son. As with Rick, her eagerness to join her husband on his visit to Sheffield had been fuelled by the possibility of meeting her grandson and not to say farewell to her overbearing mother-in-law.

155

Joyce had been over the moon when Monica had turned up on her doorstep asking to meet Bradley on the same day he had reconnected with his father. She assured his other grandmother that now the Pashley's were prepared to accept Bradley into their hearts, the Craigs would let bygones be bygones. All that mattered was their offspring's happiness.

As Joyce twittered on about how quickly Bradley and Rick had bonded she failed to notice the change in her guest's demeanour. Her statement that she was sure the young family would thrive with the support of both sets of parents caused Monica to bolt but not before she had wheedled Linda's address from her unsuspecting mother.

Later that evening, Joyce realised the part she had played in her daughter's downfall. Prior to her visit, Monica obviously had no idea of her son's whereabouts, if Joyce hadn't revealed he was visiting Linda, Bradley would now be enjoying himself at the Pleasure Beach instead of sitting in her living room worrying about his mummy.

Today, Joyce would not be so accommodating. "Charlie will be home soon, so you better be quick," she told Monica. "If he finds you here, he'll have no qualms about kicking you out."

"Do you mind if we sit at the table?" Monica asked taking an envelope from her bag. She and her husband had agreed on the terms she was about to propose but had different motives for doing so. Monica hoped her offer would afford her grandson a better life. Richard Senior hoped to ensure his own son's name would never be linked to Linda's child.

Joyce was confused by the contract in front of her. It stated that Mrs Joyce Craig was to have total control over the running of the salon. She could decide who was hired, fired or awarded bonuses and wage increases. She would also receive seventy-five percent of any profits made. Joyce quickly pointed out they had entered the wrong name on the contract. It was Linda who craved control of the salon not her. Monica assured her the contract had been drawn up as a reward for her exemplary service. However, if Joyce wanted to award Linda a pay rise or gift her a monthly share of the profits she would be free to do so.

Linda's name only appeared once on the document. Along with her mother and father she was to sign up to terms and conditions. According to Linda, Rick would never speak to her again so Joyce thought there was a chance she would agree to the no contact clause. Not that Joyce believed she would stick to it if Rick changed his mind. That said, Linda was adamant Bradley's father wanted nothing to do with them so if Joyce promised to give her the profits from the salon she might take the Pashley's up on their offer. Without Rick around it was the best hope of her securing a better future for Bradley.

Nearing the end of the document, all Joyce's hopes of her daughter signing it vanished. Linda would never agree to denying that Rick was the father of her child to the press or anyone else.

Though Joyce insisted it was pointless, Monica demanded she read on. Reaching the last clause Joyce stared at her old boss in disbelief. Given their obvious intention to distance themselves from the child, why would they gift Bradley the salon on his eighteenth birthday?

Monica smiled, "In appreciation for your long and dedicated service we wanted to give your grandchild the best possible start in life." The patronising tone of Monica's voice grated on Joyce. Both women knew the real reason for the Pashley's generosity. Charlie's threats to talk to the newspapers about Bradley's parentage and the monthly payments the Pashley's made into Linda's account had obviously struck a nerve with Richard Senior. This new contract would allow him the deniability he coveted whilst making his family look like benevolent benefactors to a faithful employee.

Monica failed to divulge that it was Rick who had insisted the salon be left to his son. She and her husband had intended to give Linda what she had always craved in the hope she would disappear for good. Rick, however, was determined his ex would not profit from the pain she had caused him. He was also concerned that his son might become surplus to requirements once she became the owner of 'Hair Perfection.'

Monica's reassurances that Joyce would have control of the money and the salon until Bradley turned eighteen did nothing to appease Rick. Whilst satisfied Joyce would look after Bradley during his formative years, he wanted to provide for his son beyond that. Gifting Bradley the salon would allow him to.

Once again, Joyce voiced her doubts over her daughter's co-operation. It had mortified Linda having to write 'father unknown' on Bradley's birth certificate. Fortunately, only her

157

parents and the Pashley's were aware of this. To her friends, and more importantly her enemies, she had been extremely vocal about the father's identity and of Rick's intention to marry her once he became a doctor. She might agree to not speak to the newspapers but she would never give the other kids in the neighbourhood ammunition to tease Bradley for not knowing who his father was, especially as the boy had now met him.

Joyce pushed the document towards Monica. "She won't sign it, and not because Bradley's getting the salon instead of her. She won't do it because she wants Rick to be a part of Bradley's life."

"That is never going to happen. Rick has no intentions of seeing Bradley or your daughter again. This offer is the best she can hope for. You need to convince her of that."

"And if I can't?"

"I will sell the salon, then sue Linda for breaching our original contract. Finding the money to pay for a lawyer capable of taking on ours when you are both unemployed could prove difficult. If, as your husband threatened, you try and raise money by running to the newspapers we will also sue him for libel. Our son wasn't named on the birth certificate so it would be your word against ours. If the worst comes to the worst and Richard Junior is forced to carry out a DNA test we will make our own statement to the press. We will tell them how your daughter targeted our son in the hope of getting her hands on our money and attempted to blackmail us into handing over the salon. Everyone will see our son as a victim and your daughter as the harlot she is." Although Monica had rehearsed her response if her proposal was rejected, it had still been difficult to deliver. She hated to see her old confidant suffering.

Joyce felt trapped. "You've certainly thought this through," she said dejectedly.

"I'm sorry, but I can see no other solution. Linda and Richard were never a match made in heaven. Fortunately, Richard now accepts this. A clean break is better for all concerned, including Bradley. A total stranger turning up every couple of years would only confuse the boy."

Joyce saw sense in her words but would Linda? If Rick was lost to her, would a share of the profits and the prospect of the

158

salon one day being owned by a Craig, albeit Bradley, soften the blow?

"I'll talk to Linda," Joyce offered.

"There is one more thing we need to discuss. I had my lawyer draw up another contract," Monica said placing a sheet of paper in front of Joyce. "I would prefer the contents to remain between you and I. Neither Rick nor my husband must know of our agreement."

Joyce read through the document then tore it up. "You don't need my signature to agree to that?" Joyce said.

"So you'll do it?"

"Of course." Joyce said squeezing Monica's hand reassuringly. "Now enough of all this blessed paperwork. How would you like to meet your grandson?"

The prospect of finally holding the boy she had fantasised about since his birth was too much for Monica. Joyce waited patiently until the woman's tears subsided then led her into the living room. "Probably best to sit quietly until his programme's finished," Joyce advised. "You won't get any sense out of him while Thomas the Tank Engine is on."

Monica didn't mind waiting. When the boy noticed her presence he grinned. Taking the seat beside her, Bradley gave her a brief insight into the plot thus far then giggled when she asked which one was Thomas. At that moment Monica thought her heart would burst.

1854 hours, 02 October 2012

"So Rick doesn't know his mum met Bradley?" Ella asked when Joyce had finished regaling her story.

"Nor that I sent Monica monthly updates and photographs. That is what she asked for in the contract I tore up."

"Did Linda sign the other contract?"

"Yes. She signed."

"So Bradley owns the salon?"

"Yes."

"Why didn't you mention this before?"

"Bradley made me swear not to. When he took over ownership he insisted he didn't need handouts from a family that had disowned him. I got the impression he'd signed the salon over to his father but something in his letter made me think again. That's why I called Mr Prentice."

"The solicitor?"

"Yes."

"What did he say?"

"He was a little confused at first. He thought I'd asked to see him to discuss Bradley's will."

"So he has it?" Ella squealed.

Noting the excitement in the officer's voice Joyce shook her head, "I'm afraid not, love but he did say he'd put Bradley in contact with a colleague who he thought had drafted one for him."

"So this other guy could be holding Bradley's will?"

"Mr Prenctice doesn't think so. He's sure if he had it he would have presented it by now."

Her hopes floundered, Ella sighed, "So if there's no will, Linda will get her salon after all?"

"If Bradley still owned it. As I said, he might have returned it to Rick. I asked Mr Prentice but he said he'd need to clear it with his bosses before discussing Bradley's estate further. He promised to give me a call when he had more info. That's why I don't want to give Linda Bradley's letter. If he's mentioned the salon, she's going to fire questions I can't answer."

"What about the will the other lawyer drafted? Is there any chance of getting a copy?"

"If Bradley hasn't signed it, what use would it be?"

"At least it would give us an idea of what his wishes were."

Chapter 21

2056 hours, 02 October 2012

Larry placed a cup of tea and two chocolate hobnobs on the bedside cabinet. Looking up from her book, Ella complained, "I'll get crumbs in bed."

"And I'll bounce them out again," Larry said whilst attempting to nuzzle Ella's neck.

"Not tonight you won't sex pest, I'm shattered."

As Larry dived on top of his wife she hit him with her book.

"Hey, why all the aggression? I was only climbing over you to get a biscuit." Larry held up a hobnob. "After all, it's all I'll be getting tonight."

Ella passed him the plate, "Fill your boots," she said then closed her book. It was pointless reading on. She had so many questions running through her head but sadly none were related to the plot of the novel.

Turning off her bedside light, Ella contemplated the fallout of what she had learned today. Did Bradley still own the salon? Was that the reason he wanted Linda to return to hairdressing? If he had left the salon to his mother maybe she had been his intended beneficiary all along. If so, Ella had unnecessarily tortured herself about his wishes not being fulfilled. What Ella couldn't get her head around was Linda's failure to mention the salon. Having signed the contract surely she was wondering what would happen to it now?

Ella stared at the ceiling. How was she expected to sleep?

2217 hours, 02 October 2012

The news that the CSM would be visiting the following day had crushed Dinger. If anyone was capable of breaking down his wall it was Coops. He hadn't trusted himself to speak during their last encounter but if he didn't this time that would hinder his release date.

When the CSM had been shot, Dinger had ordered his lads to retreat so he could assess the risk before sending them on a possible suicide mission. Technically, by running through intermittent gunfire, Bradley had disobeyed his order but there was no chance of disciplinary action after he carried Coops to safety.

161

The Sergeant Major's insistence that he was proud of Dinger for following protocol in the most extreme circumstances did nothing to expel his guilt. Coops might have felt able to absolve his sins but Dinger had spent many a night contemplating the outcome had Bradley not rushed in.

He understood why the CSM had drummed into him the importance of putting the lives of many above that of one, but not when that one was Coops. Most of the lads regarded the Sergeant Major as a second father, for the likes of Dinger and Beetle he was the nearest they had ever come to having a first.

Like a father, Coops demanded respect; unlike some, he deserved it. The CSM loved reminding the lads that the only difference between what he was asking them to do and what he had done at their age was that the weapons were lighter, the attire more comfortable and the menu more palatable. His boys got to enjoy bacon and beans whereas he'd had to survive on brown biscuits and paste.

Coops knew exactly how to get the best from the men under his command. A single compliment from him could make a soldier's stance a foot taller, not that commendations easily tripped from his tongue. He only praised the worthy. The unworthy would have their deficiencies pointed out in a voice loud enough to deafen passing seagulls.

Coops rejected the concept of treating all men as equals. He would never punish or reward before considering the soldier's possible reaction. They were individuals. Leaving the lad to brood, affording him the opportunity to redeem himself or administering a pep talk was always decided before he voiced his displeasure.

Dinger had witnessed parents telling their children they only shouted because they cared. He never doubted the Sergeant Major had similar reasons for his justifiable outbursts. The lads had to learn the errors of their ways quickly. Failure to do so might result in the loss of their own or their comrade's lives.

In order to get the best from his troops, Coops had to know who responded best to sugar or salt. To achieve this, he took a keen interest in his lads. He knew their family background, hobbies and friendships and studied carefully their reaction to conflict, embarrassment or affection. To be an effective fighting force the guys needed to care for and respect each other so he grouped together those he believed would bond and separated those who might clash.

Placing Dinger, Bradley and Beetle in the same section had been an easy decision. Coops considered Dinger the most effective soldier in his company. His head ruled his heart and therefore he could make the difficult decisions. Bradley was an exceptional soldier but on occasions struggled to discipline those beneath him so placing him with Corporal Bell, who never let a misdemeanour go unnoticed, was inspired. Bradley also had the ability to talk his friend down, therefore ensuring the punishment didn't outweigh the crime and Dinger's over exuberance didn't result in bullying complaints. The good cop, bad cop routine ensured the lads in their section flourished, especially Beetle.

Bradley's compassion and the fear of reprisal from Dinger had turned Beetle into the unit's top sniper. His ability with a rifle had resulted in his original nickname of 'Dung Beetle' being shortened. Once in possession of an SA80 rifle, the timid, awkward, unassuming boy would turn into a cool, calm, killing machine. Due to this he was revered and respected by his colleagues. His rifle truly was his best friend but followed closely by his two NCOs.

Dinger shook as he remembered the sight of Bradley carrying the CSM's broken body. As much as his friend's actions had made him feel inferior, he was ever grateful for Bradley's disobedience. How could he have lived with himself if he had caused Coops death? How was he supposed to live now knowing he had brought about Bradley's? "I will make this right." He promised his friend.

2258 hours, 02 October 2012

Dinger wasn't the only one speaking to Bradley. Rick was currently thanking his boy for showing him more compassion than he deserved.

In his letter, Bradley insisted he had never blamed Rick for going to Australia. He knew his father had been tricked into leaving and at fifteen years old had no hope of returning without his parents' assistance. Bradley told him to stop punishing himself for Richard Senior's sins.

On the subject of custody, Bradley claimed to be grateful Rick had never pursued it. Had he failed, Joyce would not have allowed them to spend time together at her home. At least the way Rick had approached their reunion had guaranteed them some memorable times together.

Bradley had ended his letter by thanking his father for his love and support and made one last request; Rick must play an active role in his grandchild's life.

Staring at the ceiling of his hotel room, Rick told his boy how proud he was of the man he had become, how much he loved him and how much he wished he had taken him back to Australia on his tenth birthday.

May 2002

The contents of his mother's safe deposit box had floored Rick nearly as much as her death. Learning of her deceit and not having the opportunity to challenge her caused him both rage and regret. He'd devoured every word of Joyce's letters and committed every photograph to memory. The journey his son had made from toddler to adolescent was captured in over sixty pictures that his mother had failed to share. How could she? Wasn't she the one who'd claimed it would be easier if they forgot about Bradley? Not that he ever had.

Seeing the boy playing football, flying a kite and building sand castles crippled Rick. The happiness exuding from the letters did little to ease his suffering. Charlie had taught Bradley to ride his bike, cast a fishing line and how to avoid the off side rule. Bradley loved the beach, football and Spiderman. He hated sprouts, cricket and girls. At times, his temper could match his grandfather's but he had inherited Joyce's capacity for compassion. There was no evidence of the part his mother played in his upbringing. Joyce was either omitting Linda to appease Monica or because her daughter had no interest in Bradley. Rick hoped it was the latter.

At least there was no mention of a father figure. Was that because he had a number of uncles? As he often did, Rick fought to block out the memory of Linda's chest glistening whilst Paul grinned inanely.

He should have fought harder when his parents refused to apply for custody. What if he wasn't named on the birth certificate? A strand of hair or swab of saliva would have proved his paternity.

He'd agreed that dragging the child away from everyone close to him would be distressing but surely being in the bosom of a loving family who could provide him with a privileged upbringing would have eased the blow? That was the problem. He didn't have a loving family to bring his son to. Richard Senior had made it clear there would be no room adorned with Bradley's name in his home. Even, with his parents' support it would have been difficult to gain custody. Without it, it was impossible. Linda had Joyce and Charlie; he had no one.

The death of his mother made that statement more poignant. On a good day he and his father tolerated each other, on a bad one the atmosphere in the house was toxic. Due to this he had been an infrequent visitor during his university years and internship at Canberra hospital.

Now, thanks to his mother, he would never have to visit the tyrant again. He could afford to purchase his own home and Bradley could have his own room. Re-reading Joyce's letters, Rick made a monumental decision. His boy belonged with him and he was going to fetch him.

Chapter 22
0936 hours, 03 October 2012

Not in the office two hours and Ella was considering breaking one of the two vows she had made the previous evening.

An hour ago, when she'd asked what Bradley had said in his letter to prompt Joyce's visit to the solicitor, the older woman had curtly told her the contents of her grandson's letter were private and not up for discussion. Ella's next question - why hadn't Linda queried ownership of the salon received an even frostier response. She was informed that was also none of her business and advised to drop the subject. Joyce ended their conversation by stating they planned to decorate all day so would appreciate her not getting under their feet. This meant her first vow, to complete a full day at her desk, was a distinct possibility.

Her second vow, not to hassle Jules, was proving more difficult to uphold. Ella checked her watch. Why hadn't Jules called her? Surely she would have spoken to the clerks in Afghanistan by now. Patience was never a virtue Ella held in high esteem and hers had reached its limit. Three times her inner voice had ridiculed her notion of driving to Catterick to search the units post room, desks and mail sacks.

The last thing Ella needed was to be accused of interfering. Jules would be well within her rights to tell Captain Harris to butt out or worse still, inform Pete Waller she was still pursuing the will. Pushing for answers was too risky: She would have to wait.

Turning to her 'To Do' list, Ella searched for something to deter her from calling Jules. She'd already completed tasks two to five. The first entry 'Call Rick before he leaves for Australia' was proving difficult. Why? It would be a quick courtesy call to wish him a safe journey and assure him, if he needed her, in a professional capacity, she would always be there for him.

Picking up her mobile, she scrolled through her contacts list then returned the phone to her desk. What if he misread her signals again? What if he suspected she was just using his departure as an excuse to speak with him? What if he brought up their last meeting? Asked her to reconsider his offer?

With too many 'what ifs' Ella moved on to number six on her list; 'Stationery demand.'

The ordering of pens and paperclips did nothing to distract her thoughts. Phoning Jules might be a non-starter but there were other ways to skin a cat.

Ella listened carefully as Coops relayed the little information he had gleaned since they had last spoken. Jules had been given a stay of execution. She had forty-eight hours to investigate before the soldiers affected would be requested to draft new wills.

"They think it's worth the risk," Coops explained. "Asking them to rewrite their wills could seriously damage morale."

"Does Jules think she can resolve this in forty-eight hours?" Ella asked.

"Reckons if she can't, she never will."

"Have you any idea what the clerks in Afghan said."

"Sorry, no."

That subject exhausted, Ella asked about Dinger's progress.

"I'm on my way down to see him now. Technically, I only need to visit once a week but I can't stop thinking about the lad. I remember how lost I felt when I woke up in hospital. I only had my injuries to deal with, he's got the death of his best mate to contend with as well."

"Can't be easy."

"I spoke with his doctors. They're looking at releasing him soon. His shoulder is healing well so any further treatment can be provided from home. There's an excellent facility in Preston but I'm not sure his mother's is the right place for him. Her house is full to bursting."

"Surely it's better than laying in a hospital bed."

"At least when you're in hospital people aren't constantly bombarding you with questions. Why you so quiet? Why won't you eat? When did you start drinking whiskey? Plus the other patients don't pester to hear what happened or how you feel about

167

it. They understand if you don't want to tell your story. If you do, you can without having to worry they'll get upset hearing it."

"So I take it you found it hard when you got home?"

"It was harder for the missus than me. Although she hated it, she was used to waving me off. She was also used to me returning in one piece. My getting shot terrified her. I tried to act as if nothing had changed. I pulled it off during the day but the nights beat me. Drove her mad, me smiling in the sunshine and screaming in the dark."

"You're better now though?"

"Getting there. After a lot of nagging, I agreed to counselling. Talking about it helps but it's not easy. As you know we soldiers prefer to laugh it off than cry about it."

"And Dinger's still refusing to talk to anyone?"

"Yes, I'm going to try to change his mind. Just hope he'll listen. The doctor thinks he's turned a corner but I want to see for myself. Last time I was there I struggled to get a word out of him."

1103 hours, 03 October 2012

Without pondering the possible outcome, Ella picked up her phone. Rick's flight was leaving in a couple of hours. Personal feelings aside it was her duty to touch base with him. A quick call, to wish him a safe journey and assure him she was available to answer any future queries he might have regarding his son's death was all that was required. Maybe she could also ask about the salon. If Rick confirmed Bradley had returned it to the Pashley estate, Joyce might be willing to give Linda her letter. The problem was she'd promised Joyce she wouldn't discuss her visit to the solicitor with anyone.

"Hello. Captain Harris, how are we today?" Rick said with false bravado.

His question threw Ella as she had mentally prepared herself for their conversation but discussing her wellbeing hadn't been in the script. "Hi, yes, it's me. Ella I mean, I…" Ella stopped rambling and allowed her brain to catch up with her mouth. "Hi, I just wanted to touch base with you before you left. Make sure there were no outstanding matters you wanted to discuss and wish you a safe journey."

"Okay, right, I see." Rick responded, her obvious discomfort rubbing off on him.

"So was there?"

"What?"

"Anything you wanted to discuss?" *Shit what if he thought she meant his proposal?*

"No, I don't think so. You?" Rick asked hopefully.

"No, no. Well yes, maybe." Telling herself Joyce need never learn of her betrayal, Ella blurted out, "I was wondering if you owned the salon Joyce and Linda used to work in."

"No. Why do you ask?"

'Shit, wrong answer, now what?' Ella thought it too late to backtrack. "Is there a possibility Bradley might?"

"Oh my God, I never thought about that. He was supposed to inherit the salon when he was eighteen. I thought it had been sold and included with my mother's assets when she died. Bradley never said anything on his eighteenth so I guessed he hadn't inherited it."

"I see," Ella responded regretfully. Once again her interfering had garnered no results.

"So does he own it?" Rick enquired.

"I don't know."

"What made you ask?"

"Erm, nothing really. It was just a thought."

"Quite a random one. Who have you been talking to? "

Ella gulped. "Nobody. It's just…" *'what?'* What could she possibly say to convince him?

"Sorry Ella, but I find it hard to believe Bradley owning the salon just popped into your mind without coercion."

"I'm sorry, I made a promise," Ella confessed. "I shouldn't have mentioned it."

"Okay, I won't ask you to break a confidence but I will need to know if it is included in Bradley's estate. For Susie's sake I will accept Paul Douglas getting his hands on Bradley's compensation money but not my mother's."

After promising to keep Rick up to date with her findings, Ella wished him a safe journey before saying goodbye. When Rick responded, "I think you mean Au Revoir, Captain Harris," her cheeks flushed. Why did his intention to be back in the country before his grandchild's birth affect her equilibrium so?

1153 hours, 03 October 2012

'Showtime,' Dinger thought when he heard the clicking of the CSM's stick. He intended to keep their conversation light and jovial. If the subject of Bradley arose he would happily reminisce about his former friend whilst steering the conversation away from their final moments together. It wasn't going to be easy; the happy memories were always clouded by the last.

"You up for a walk?" The CSM asked. "I could do with stretching my legs after three hours on the train." When Dinger didn't move, Coops held up a jacket. "Come on, I've spoken to the nurse, she reckons some fresh air might do you good. Put this on. It's Baltic out there."

Stepping outside, Coops felt his injured knee object to the cold. He hoped getting Dinger outside would be worth the pain. "So, how are you today?"

"Great," Dinger over enthused. "My wounds are healing nicely so there's not a lot more they can do for me here. Just need phsyio and I can get that in Preston."

"And counselling?"

"Not necessary."

"If that's your answer I think it certainly is necessary," the CSM joked.

Dinger had expected Coops to try and persuade him to see the shrink so had rehearsed his response. "Can't see the point. I've had plenty of counselling in the past. Never got much out of it," he said casually.

"In the past you didn't get shot."

"Me getting shot isn't the problem."

"What is then?"

Dinger wasn't going to fall into the CSM's trap. "Nothing. I just meant it's only a chipped bone and a bit of a scar. It's not like I lost a limb or anything."

"True, but do you never wonder 'what if'? What if the bullet had caused more damage or hit you in the head instead of Bradley."

Dinger had hoped for a little more small talk before discussing his friend but he was ready, "If it had hit me I wouldn't be here thinking about it at all, would I?" He replied trying to sound nonchalant.

"So you do think about it?"

"What?"

"If the bullet had hit you instead of Bradley?"

"No, I do not," Dinger replied with more venom than he had intended.

"Really? So you don't have flashbacks?"

"What is this? Twenty fucking questions?"

"Watch your language Corporal Bell. I'm here as your UVO. It's my job to see how you're coping. As you're not your usual chatty self I need to ask 'fucking' questions to figure that out. So far, I'm guessing you're not as 'fine' as you're making out."

Dinger needed to contain his rage. "I am until people start badgering me," he replied in an even tone. "I got shot and my best mate died. I'm dealing with it in my own way. Why can't they just leave me in peace?"

Spotting the bench ahead Coops suggested they sit. "Because you're not at peace. As much as you think otherwise, you're not the first person to go through this. You are, however, the first person that's been 'fine' afterwards. No one walks away unscathed. Some handle it better than others but we all need help," the CSM said rubbing his knee.

"Including you?"

"Yes, including me. I wasn't keen either but the wife likes her sleep."

"Sorry?"

"My dreams are so real. I hear the gunfire, smell the fear and I always see Bradley. Sometimes he doesn't come back for me. Other times he does but takes a bullet on the way. I wake up screaming the house down. Strange thing is, my dreams never reflect what actually happened. According to the shrink I'm subconsciously blocking that out."

"So you've had counselling?" Dinger asked suspiciously.

"I'm having counselling," Coops corrected. "These things don't right themselves over night. The reason I asked you about 'what ifs' is because they plague me all the time. What if, by coming back for me, Bradley would've been killed? What if he'd left me? Lad risked his life to save me."

"But at least he knew he was doing that. When he took a bullet for me…" *Shit, shit, shit.*

Coops turned sharply and stared at Dinger. "I'm not following you lad. What do you mean he took a bullet for you?"

Dinger looked away without answer. Coops considered the boy's statement. Since Bradley's death the CSM had spent many an hour berating himself for not heeding Dinger's warning about Jabbaar. After being evacuated from Afghan he'd heard Dinger was still voicing his suspicions about the trainee. "So you think Jabbaar wanted to kill you?"

Dinger's eye's glistened as he nodded. His eyes pleaded with Coops not to push him further.

"Well, at least you're right about that," Coops replied flippantly.

Dinger exhaled the breath he had been holding so tightly. Maybe voicing his thoughts wasn't so bad. At last someone agreed with him. "I knew it, there was no way he'd want to kill Bradley."

"Oh yes he did. His mission was to kill as many British soldiers as possible. You and Bradley weren't his only targets. Five others took a bullet. Jaabbar managed to let off over forty rounds before Beetle slotted him. He fired at random, it was anything but personal."

"But he hated me most."

172

"You're probably right but he didn't need to sacrifice himself to kill you. If you were his only target he could've slit your throat and left camp before anyone realised."

"But the first bullet was aimed at me," Dinger argued.

"You don't know that. He sprayed bullets all over camp. Maybe you were the first soldiers in his line of sight. Once he started firing everyone ran for cover. Moving targets aren't so easy to hit. It makes sense he only injured the rest."

"I wasn't moving," Dinger admitted.

"And yet he didn't come back for a second go," Coops answered triumphantly.

Dinger looked away. He should never have let his guard down. It was unsafe to let the CSM inside his head. This visit needed to end. "You're right, I don't know why I said that." Dinger stood. "I think I want to go back now. My meds make me drowsy."

"Let's sit here a bit longer. My leg's sore, I need a minute."

Dinger stood rigid, Coops had confused him with his lies so he had no wish to hear anymore.

"Sit," Coops barked forcefully.

Slamming down beside the CSM, Dinger glared. When Coops returned his stare the young soldier looked to the ground. The Sergeant Major had got all he was going to get. Dinger would block him out. He needed to focus on the truth. In his mind he repeated, 'It should have been me.' He was unaware that he was rocking in time with the sentence.

When Dinger failed to respond to further questioning, the CSM took his arm and guided him back to the ward. Once there, the injured soldier climbed on the bed and feel asleep.

Watching the boy twitch, the CSM recalled Jabbaar had been one of three who had made a formal complaint about Corporal Bell's attitude. Coops had tried to reel the lad in. He understood why Dinger had his suspicions but believed them unwarranted. Had they been then? It was the chicken and egg scenario. Had Jabbaar infiltrated the camp in order to kill as many soldiers as he could or had Dinger's behaviour toward him turned him against the force he had sworn to serve. The investigation into Jabbaar's background was in its infancy. They had traced links back to known Afghan rebels but that wasn't unusual. Whatever Jabbaar's reasons Coops could not let the lad blame himself.

Dinger started to mumble and jerk, then his eyes shot open. The horror was evident. Whatever had stirred him was more painful than his physical injuries. As the reality of his location sunk in, the soldier sat upright. "You're still here," Dinger's tone conveyed his disappointment.

"Nowhere else to go. How do you feel? Better for having a sleep?"

"A bit, yes," Dinger lied.

"Good, because I wanted to talk to you about Jabbaar."

Dinger shook his head. Suspecting the lad was about to zone him out again, Coops rushed on. "Please, just listen to what I have to say. If you do, I'll never bring the subject up again, I promise."

Dinger nodded. "Okay. But after that you need to leave. I'm all talked out."

"Deal," Coops answered. "Before I continue, you must swear not to repeat anything I say. I could get in serious trouble. What I am about to tell you isn't in the public domain and probably never will be."

"Okay, I'll keep it to myself." It was an easy vow to make, Dinger had no interest in discussing anything with anyone.

"Bradley was Jabbaar's intended target."

Dinger looked at Coops in disbelief. "No way, they loved Brad. He was great with them."

"Exactly. That's why Jabbaar was told to execute him. He was winning the battle for hearts and minds. Brad recruiting guys into the Afghan National Army wasn't good for their cause."

"So they took him out?"

"Yes. You, on the other hand, had the opposite effect so he wouldn't wish to remove such an effective deterrent permanently. He probably hit you where he thought he would cause the most pain then moved on to other targets." Coops felt no guilt as the lies tripped off his tongue. It could be the truth. "Think about it. Bradley was the only one to die and the first person he shot. After he hit his intended target he stuck one in your shoulder then fired intermittently at anyone else within range. You never moved so he could have come back for you at any time."

As much as Dinger wanted to protest, the CSM's claims were hard to refute. Bradley did have a way with the locals and had gained their trust. Take personal feelings out of the equation and he would have been the more logical target. If that was true, why did this information make him feel more compelled to join his friend?

Chapter 23

1652 hours, 03 October 2012

Ella had spent her day ploughing through unanswered correspondence, rescheduling cancelled meetings and returning unanswered calls. Staff Coleman had done a sterling job. All the end of month checks had been carried out and all the accounts balanced. She had a few personnel reports to write and a case study to initiate but they could wait.

As tempting as it was to pack up her desk, she knew she couldn't leave until she heard from Jules. Most Administration Offices closed at five. If she did not make a decision soon her friend might not be around to allow her to risk her career. Would she be doing that? Jules had made it clear she didn't want the hierarchy to know of Ella's involvement in the discovery of the other missing wills. If their roles were reversed, Ella would not drop her friend in it. Deciding to let fate play its hand she dialled; if Jules failed to answer she would take that as a sign to go home.

"Well, well Captain Harris you really are getting more patient in your old age. I thought you would've been on the phone first thing."

"I wanted to call you then and every ten minutes after," Ella admitted.

"I'm sorry, I couldn't resist seeing how long you would last."

"Cruel."

"I know. In my defence I have been busy." Jules went on to explain she had found the link to the missing wills. Both clerks claimed to have passed the wills to a civil servant for dispatch. "Tommy was attached to us for a couple of months while he was waiting to be reassigned. We borrowed him from the Redundancy Pool." Jules explained.

When the Civil Service had been cut earlier in the year many posts were lost. Those who opted not to take redundancy were held in a pool until new slots became available. Whilst in the pool, undermanned units could request their assistance. As Jules's unit was preparing to deploy to Afghanistan she had poached a couple of civil servants to help with the increased workload.

"So what did Tommy say?" Ella asked.

"Nothing yet. He's no longer with us. He'd always worked with the Territorials and wasn't keen to go elsewhere. When they couldn't find him a job in a TA unit he decided to take his redundancy after all."

"Do you have his contact details?" The urgency in Ella's voice was not lost on Jules.

"We do, but he's not there, he's in Cancun spending his redundancy payment," Jules said dejectedly.

"When's he back?"

"Next Wednesday, but I can't wait that long. Thanks to Facebook I've managed to find out which hotel he's in. I've spoken with the receptionist, she's going to give him a message. I've also left one on his Facebook account so hopefully he'll be in touch soon."

"What sort of message? Your incompetence has left a soldier's family in turmoil and is about to cause eight others unnecessary grief?"

"Obviously not," Jules said defensively. "I've asked him to contact me at his convenience to discuss a very important matter. He's no longer duty bound to return my call so I could hardly go in all guns blazing. I must admit, I'm shocked. Tommy was an excellent clerk. If he'd been a few years younger I would have badgered him to join up. He was as good, if not better, than some of my soldiers. This cock up is completely out of character."

"Doesn't change the fact he made it. One envelope going missing could be explained but three? He couldn't have sent them. Maybe he shoved them in a drawer and forgot about them? Have you checked his desk?"

"Ripped it apart. Every orifice in his office has been probed. Nothing. They're not behind a cabinet, in a drawer or under the carpet. Think this is a mystery only Tommy can solve. I hope he calls back soon, if they're not found by this time tomorrow my neck's for the noose."

"Best I leave you in peace, in case he's trying to get through. Will you let me know what he says? You can get me on my mobile. I don't care how late it is."

"I take back what I said earlier, you're more impatient than ever." Jules laughed.

1759 hours, 03 October 2012

Larry was in a buoyant mood. Ella had made it home at a reasonable hour and not set foot anywhere near the Haddington all day. To add to his joy, Hazel had called earlier to confirm Ann had agreed not to tell his wife about Nicky's knife claim.

Having dispatched Ella to the shower, Larry turned his attention to preparing the evening's culinary delights. Unfortunately, his wife wasn't keen on oysters so he'd sourced other known aphrodisiacs. To start, Avocado salad followed by salmon as a main; rich chocolate cake with figs and whipped cream would complete the feast.

He hoped the meal, washed down with a couple of glasses of red wine and a little sexual activity might encourage his wife to sleep tonight.

1807 hours, 03 October 2012

Hoping the instigator of the call was Jules, Ella dived out of the shower and grabbed her mobile with a soapy hand.

"Sorry to bother you love. Are you busy?" Joyce asked.

'Only dripping all over the bedroom floor.'

Quickly rushing back into the ensuite, Ella pulled a towel around her whilst assuring Linda's mother she was never too busy to talk to her.

Joyce started with an apology, "I'm sorry I was short with you this morning. I've been feeling rotten all day. It's my fault I'm in this mess not yours."

"What mess?"

"I can't really go into that right now. Can you pop around tomorrow? I need to pick your brains. Our Linda keeps banging on about getting a laptop and a dangly thing so she can order all the stuff for the house online. Thing is I haven't got a clue what to buy her."

"She wouldn't need a laptop, a tablet with a SIM card would do the job."

"A what and a what? She's on enough medication at the moment last thing we need is more tablets."

"Not that sort of tablet. Something like an IPAD or…" The memory of having to sort out her own parents' Internet needs stopped Ella. "Actually, I've got an IPAD, why don't I bring it with me tomorrow? If Linda likes it we can order her one or something more economical. They're not cheap."

"Don't worry about the money love, if it stops her jabbering on about Paul coming home it'll be worth every penny. Charlie's hackles go up every time she mentions the little runt."

After locating her IPAD, Ella entered the dining room. Learning of the menu for the evening it didn't take a detective to figure out her husband's intentions. Her heart sank; cardinal pleasures were the last thing on her mind. Eating three courses washed down with red wine was also unappealing, and unheard of on a school night.

2214 hours, 03 October 2012

Sneaking the extra sleeping tablet from his tin box Dinger was plagued by the CSM's early revelation. If he was to be believed then Bradley had sealed his own fate. The discovery did nothing to dissipate Dinger's constant yearning to join his friend.

Whether at fault or not, he had no right to walk this earth if Bradley could not. He was a far better human being than Dinger could ever hope to be. So many people had relied on Bradley, loved him; needed him. Other than a quick ripple in his mother and sisters lives Dinger couldn't envisage anyone dwelling on his death for long.

Checking his drugs haul he wondered how many tablets would guarantee death. He only had one shot. If he failed, they'd probably shove him in the loony bin and watch him like a hawk so it would be impossible to replenish his stash. Like it or not, his best chance of success was at home without fear of nosy nurses or stomach pumps.

Playing nicely with his fellow patients and happily listening to his mother bleat on about Uncle Joe's Thai bride and cousin Daisy's false boobs had improved his chances of getting home. The doctors were pleased with his progress, especially when he announced his friend Beetle was visiting him on Friday and that he intended to engage the services of a shrink once he arrived in Preston. He had attributed his change of heart to the pep talk Coops had administered.

Beetle's invitation was a calculated risk. If things went to plan, Beetle would a perfect, albeit unaware, ally in Dinger's mission to convince the nurses all was well. The lad wasn't much of a talker and the last person who would push Dinger into territories he was unwilling to venture.

Firstly, Dinger intended to praise his friend's swift reaction to the gunfire. Characteristically, Beetle would play down his role. Next, he would enquire about Bradley's funeral and stress how disappointed he was that he could not attend. Being a sensitive soul, Beetle would recognise his distress at discussing the funeral and allow him to change the subject.

This would lead to the most important part of Dinger's mission, making Beetle laugh in front of the nurses. He hoped to do that by regaling the pranks of his fellow patients.

As long as Dinger could feign his own enjoyment, success was pretty much guaranteed. Beetle's appreciation of Dinger's humour was what endeared him to, the normally hardhearted, Corporal Bell; that and Bradley's obvious affection for the lad.

The only factor that could take his plan off the rails was best mate's absence. He and Brad had been as much a double act socially as they were professionally. Without his 'straight man' would Beetle find Dinger as hilarious? Without his 'straight man' would he be able to get through the performance?

2253 hours, 03 October 2012

Whilst listening to Larry's contented snoring, Ella's thoughts turned to Rick. She imagined the delectable Mr Pashley made not a murmur when sleeping, never stole the duvet or farted loud enough to wake her. As impressive as that might be, it was of no importance. Rick would never hold a candle to the slightly greying, somewhat paunchy, marginally wrinkled sex god by her side. Only her gorgeous hubby was capable of lifting her that high when she was at her lowest. He knew exactly which buttons to press and didn't mind that some of them weren't as solid as they once were. Plus his flatulence made her giggle, even in the early hours.

Accepting slumber was unobtainable; Ella grabbed her mobile and headed for her study. Switching on her phone she was disappointed to find Jules had not called. Tommy was obviously too busy washing Taco's down with Tequila. The selfish little arse.

After returning to bed it had taken her three hours to get to sleep. Her respite was short lived. Something was still niggling and after a few hours it managed to work its way to the front of her brain. *Tommy*? '*TA Tommy*?' *TA?* Could that be it? Ella resisted the urge to scream her thoughts aloud. If her memory served her right… She glanced at her alarm clock. Was five am too early? Even though the answer was obvious, Ella considered calling Jules.

Chapter 24

0812 hours, 04 October 2012

Staring at her phone, Ella willed it to ring. She had been in the office since six thirty. Larry had worried when she'd driven away so early. Having noted the time she'd spent out of their bed last night, he'd calculated she'd had a maximum of four hours sleep. Something had kept her awake and he wasn't buying it was the important breakfast meeting she failed to mention earlier.

Ella had held out until seven am before calling Jules. When her friend failed to answer she left a cryptic message telling her to check the lads personnel files. At seven-thirty she spoke to the duty clerk. Jules was yet to arrive at her office but the young soldier promised to ask her to return Ella's call as soon as she did.

As glaring at the phone bore no results, Ella scanned her computer for information on TA procedures. The more she read the more hopeful she became. Once she had scanned the relevant literature she lifted the phone again.

Jules was in a meeting she was informed. She'd instructed the clerk to tell Ella she would call her once it was over. "What meeting could be more important that this?" Ella fumed at a young Private who had no idea what 'this' was.

At nine-thirty Ella called the clerk again and huffily informed him she had to leave the office but could be contacted on her mobile if Jules could be bothered to return her calls.

0949 hours, 04 October 2012

Entering the Haddington, Ella scanned the maisonettes until she located the person calling out her name. "Wait there, I'll be down in a minute," Louise instructed.

Damn. Something else she'd avoided on her 'To Do' list was calling Louise. Since her chat with the CSM she'd had no idea what to tell the girl. She'd better make her mind up soon.

"Shall we talk in my car?" Ella asked when Louise reached her.

"Oh, we are talking then?" The girl snapped.

"I'm sorry I didn't get back to you. It's just there's nothing I can tell you. Dinger really isn't well enough for visitors."

"Really? Then how come Beetle's seeing him tomorrow?"

"I didn't know he was." Ella replied defensively. "The last I heard he wasn't allowed visitors. If that's changed I'll ask if he's happy to see Susie."

"He's not."

"Sorry?"

"He's not. Dinger's made it clear to Beetle he doesn't want to see her. Looks like she was right, he does hate her."

"Not necessarily. He's been shot and seen his best mate die. It's difficult for him. Susie's going to want to know what Bradley's last words were and Dinger probably isn't up for repeating them."

"He might not want to say them but she deserves to hear them."

"What if he breaks down? What if he says something Susie doesn't want to hear? He's in a bad place right now. He might not think before he speaks."

"Thinking before he does anything has always been tricky for Dinger. Especially if it means considering anyone's feeling but his own." Louise leaned back in her seat and closed her eyes. "I don't want her to go down there if he's going to upset her."

"Exactly. Why not speak to Beetle after he's visited. By all accounts, the three lads were pretty close so I'm sure he'll be able so suss out if seeing Dinger would help Susie."

"Maybe. It's just so frustrating. I want to do something for her but what?"

"You're there for her. If she needs anything more I'm sure she'll ask."

Louise nodded. "I hope so. Mind, I'll tell her to bugger off if she offers my services to Linda." Louise announced before opening the car door. "Better get back, I've left her on her own."

'What services?' Ella thought.

1007 hours, 04 October 2012

A pot of tea, four mugs and four generous slices of Parkin awaited Ella's arrival.

"Tea's up!" Joyce yelled up the stairs. Ella was mortified when Dave descended them.

"Come on lad. You're due a break," Joyce told him. "Especially as you provided the cake."

Dave lifted his refreshments and attempted to leave the room; Joyce halted him. "Sit down for a minute, will you? You've been at it all morning." When he did as instructed, Joyce turned her attention to Ella. "Lad's been here since back of seven. Did you know he was a painter and decorator? Susie volunteered his services when I told her about our plans for this place."

"I've taken time off work to look after Susie. I think this is her way of telling me I shouldn't have bothered," Dave told Ella. "Listen, if this is awkward, I can leave."

Joyce interjected. "Don't be daft, lad. Where's the harm. All that rubbish is done with now. No one believes you're in cahoots to rob Linda of a fortune." Even though Joyce was smiling, Ella noticed she was uncomfortable.

Dave looked to Ella for confirmation. "It's fine," she assured him. "In fact this is the best place for us to meet. We're hardly likely to conspire together whilst we're drinking tea with the enemy."

"Exactly, so drink up," Linda chipped in. "Then show me how this bloody thing works," she ordered, holding up the IPAD. "I need some new shoes, jeans and a couple of smart tops. Which is the best button to press?"

Once Linda was au fait with the IPAD and Dave had escaped back upstairs, Joyce motioned for Ella to join her in the kitchen. As soon as she had shut the door, Bradley's grandmother burst into tears. Ella quickly moved to her side. "What is it? What's happened?"

Taking a paper handkerchief from her pinny pocket Joyce wiped her eyes. "My trespasses have caught up with me. Thought I'd be begging St Peter's forgiveness not our Linda."

"I'm sorry Joyce, I've no idea what you're talking about."

"I know love, I'm burbling. If I ask Dave to keep an eye on Linda again do you think we could pop to my place?"

"Keep an eye on Linda again?"

"Yes I had to go out first thing."

On the proviso the two women were going out to price bedding for Phil's room, Joyce and Ella vacated number thirty-three. Walking to her car Ella scanned the area for Paul. If he saw the two women leave there was a possibility he might try to visit Linda sooner than planned. She need not have worried, Paul Douglas was currently up an alley enjoying a blowjob whilst imagining all the other pleasures Bradley's money would finance.

1102 hours, 04 October 2012

Now settled around Joyce's dining table, the older woman grimaced. "It's worse than I thought," she told Ella. "Well, not necessarily worse. It depends how you look at it. I'm guessing even Linda will give something to Suzanne when she knows."

"Knows what?"

"What the lawyer told me."

"You've seen the lawyer?"

"He called me this morning, I went straight round." Joyce put her head in her hands. "Linda's going to kill me. I was just so bloody angry. I meant to tell her but the time was never right."

"Tell her what?" Ella shrilled, desperate to know what the lawyer had said. "Please Joyce, calm down, you're not making any sense."

"The day she signed the contract, I…Well…" Joyce took a sip of her tea. "Oh shit. It's probably best I start from the beginning."

21 July 1996

Joyce had called Linda as soon as Monica had left. Within seconds, she realised she would have to wait until the wine wore off before discussing the Pashley's proposal with her daughter.

The following morning, as expected, Linda failed to arrive at work. Enraged, Joyce grabbed her coat. It was time to deliver a much-needed kick up the arse.

The state of Linda's living room did nothing to diffuse Joyce's anger. She surmised the empty bottles and full ashtray had contributed to her daughter's inability to answer the door. Unfortunately for Linda, her mother had her own key so there was no way she could avoid the dressing down Joyce had rehearsed on her way over.

Storming into Linda's bedroom, the sight before her made Joyce gasp. The stench of the room told her snoring was not the only activity the pair had engaged in. Her emotional compass spun around erratically. Anger – disgust – disbelief - disappointment.

Linda's eyes flew open. Joyce and her daughter stared at each other in simultaneous horror. Without a word passing between them, Joyce left the room. Linda remained in bed until her heart stopped racing. She ached everywhere and not just from the alcohol, Paul Douglas was a far from gentle lover. Looking at the lump beside her she once again questioned what had possessed her. Her mother was bound to ask the same question. How would she respond? The wine? The loneliness? The heartbreak?

Slowly descending the stairs, Linda was mortified to find her mother sat at the dining table shuffling through paperwork. Taking the seat opposite, she prepared herself for a barrage of insults. Avoiding eye contact, Joyce pushed the contract towards her daughter. "Sign that," she ordered.

"What is it?" Linda asked.

"More than you deserve," Joyce snapped.

Linda struggled to focus on the words before her. "They've drafted a new agreement?"

"Yes."

"I take it they're cutting me off without a penny now I've broken their first one?"

"Not exactly."

"Then what?"

"Read it."

"There's loads," Linda whined. "Can't you just tell me what I need to know?"

Joyce stared at her daughter. "Do you ever intend to return to work?"

Linda failed to meet her mother's eyes. "No," she answered meekly.

"No point now Rick's not up for grabs eh?" Joyce snarled.

"Something like that." It was easier to let her mother think that than admit the idea of leaving the house made her insides scream.

"And what about Bradley? If you think I'm going to bring him back here whilst you're ..." Joyce didn't get to finish the sentence.

"I don't. I think we both know he's better off with you."

"In that case it says you'll get two hundred a month as long as you never contact Rick again."

As if she could now he knew her dirty little secret. "Okay."

"You're also not to spout off about Rick being Bradley's dad. If the newspapers or anyone else asks, you've to say you don't know who the father is."

"Fine, whatever they want." Linda had no energy for taking on the Pashley's or intentions of speaking to anyone outside her four walls.

"You're not going to fight them?" Joyce was surprised her daughter was rolling over so easily.

"What's the point?"

"None, not after…" Joyce looked towards the ceiling. *"Him,"* she sneered.

"Have you got a pen?"

1141 hours, 04 October 2012

"So Linda doesn't know about Bradley owning the salon?"

Joyce rubbed her forehead. "Or that I was receiving a percentage of the profits."

"You never gave her it?"

"Not directly, she got her two hundred a month and I bought anything the lads needed out of the profits. Clothes, toys, school trips. I also paid their gas and electricity bills once the lads went home. I couldn't bear the thought of Bradley and Phil freezing in the dark. What I didn't spend on her or the lads I banked. It's in my name but I've never touched a penny," Joyce replied defensively. "When Bradley found out about the salon I tried to give it to him but he wouldn't take it. He said I should give it to Linda, but not all at once. Told me to put her money up to two fifty a month and to continue paying the bills. She thinks it comes from the Pashley's. There's still a tidy sum in there. In his letter, Bradley said to clear my conscience, I should use the money to do up Linda's place. He said if I pretended I was using the ADT money he left me she'd be none the wiser."

"In that case you're in the clear. Linda won't find out about the profits," Ella pointed out.

"No, but she'll find out Bradley owned the salon."

"But not because of the contract. Tell her Monica left it to Bradley in her will."

"That's not all she left him." Joyce grabbed Ella's hand to prepare her for the shock. "He was due to get half a million pounds when he turned twenty one."

"Half a million?" Ella was astonished. "Did Bradley know?"

"He was told on his eighteenth."

"I bet he regretted joining the Army when he found out he had that amount coming his way."

188

"Not at all. According to the lawyer he wasn't interested in Monica's guilt money. Once he and Suzanne had climbed the ranks, he intended to visit Rick's dad with a copy of his bank statement. Wanted to show him he'd succeeded without touching a penny of his wife's precious money. The lawyer suspected he'd change his mind once the money was in his account. Now we'll never know."

"I've a feeling he would've stuck to his guns," Ella answered.

"Rick's old man would've had a heart attack. He's been sat in his ivory tower for years patting himself on the back for the pittance he's paid for his son's little mistake. I'm tempted to visit him myself. I'd love to see his face when he realises our Linda's finally getting her hands on the salon. And all that money."

"Linda's getting it? You're kidding. Surely the money goes to Rick," Ella asked hopefully.

"The lawyers are looking into it. Thing is, the money belonged to Bradley whether he could spend it or not so they think it will be added to his estate. The only stumbling block would be if Monica included a clause in the event of Bradley's death. If that's the case the money will probably go to her other benefactors."

"I think the others might make a claim anyway when they realise Linda's getting it."

"And Paul," Joyce reminded Ella.

"Rick will definitely have something to say about that."

Joyce slowly rubbed her brows then run her hands down her face. "How's she going to cope when she hears she's on her way to being a millionaire? The shock alone will send her back on the ale."

Sensing Joyce's distress, Ella shuffled her seat around and placed her arm around the older woman. "Not necessarily, you'll be there to support her."

Joyce allowed her head to rest on Ella's shoulder. "And how will I do that? I don't know anything about legal stuff. Once the muck starts flying she's bound to hit the bottle again." Joyce pulled back and stared at Ella. "And what about Susie and the baby? They'll get nothing. How can that be right?"

"Don't worry about that, Rick will provide for them." Ella patted Joyce's shoulder. "Right now, I'm more concerned about you. This is a lot of baggage to carry on your own. Have you spoken to Charlie?"

At the mention of her husband's name Joyce wrung her hands. "He never read the bloody contract either. I just told him he'd succeeded in scaring Rick's dad off and Linda was going to get the extra money he'd demanded."

"Why didn't you tell him the truth?"

"He would've asked how the hell I got Linda to sign it and I didn't want to tell him about Paul. Daft now, because she ended up with the loser anyway."

Ella's heart went out to Joyce. She'd spent years lying to those closest to her and her deceit was about to catch her up in dramatic style. Or was it?

Ella smiled, "Listen, there's no reason anyone has to find out what was written in the contract. The salon and money was left to Bradley in Monica's will. The contract said the profits were in your name so technically no harm done. Linda doesn't know where the money is really coming from so don't tell her. Play dumb and pretend to be as surprised as they are."

Joyce blinked away her tears. "Do you think that will work?"

"I can't see why not. No one broke the contract so I doubt it will be mentioned. I think they'll be more interested in the amount of money at stake."

"I don't want Linda to get all that money," Joyce confessed. "It'll ruin her. She'll drink herself to death. Paul will help. It's not like he'll give a damn. If she does peg it he'll inherit the lot."

"Not necessarily. Someone in the Pashley family is bound to challenge this. Even if they fail, it could be years before the case is settled. You never know, in that time Bradley's will could turn up." Ella wished she could confide in Joyce about TA Tommy. "There's still a possibility he   wrote one."

Joyce smiled briefly. "The lawyer's got a copy of the one he drafted for Bradley."

Ella could hardly contain herself. "What did it say? Was he leaving the money to Suzanne? Why didn't he sign it?"

"I've no idea. They emailed the draft to Bradley so he could print it, sign it, then return it but they never got it back."

"Can you get a copy of the draft? Even unsigned it will come in handy if the case goes to court."

"Do you think so?"

Ella had no idea about the legality of an unsigned will but right now she wanted to give Joyce hope. "I'm sure if Susie's mentioned in it they will have to take that into account."

"And if not, Rick will give her his half," Joyce said hopefully.

Ella squirmed as a horrible thought entered her mind. Rick wasn't on the boy's birth certificate so would not be regarded as Bradley's next of kin. Would he be able to carry out the necessary DNA test to prove he was and if so would the court see him as an eligible benefactor? It was too big a gamble. The will was the key to solving this and she would be damned if she was going to pussy foot around the issue any longer.

Signed or not, there was a will out there and she was going to find it. If she couldn't locate the signed copy, she would make the law aware of the draft version. If furnished with the truth a good lawyer could easily argue the email copy should be honoured. Especially if the judge was made aware of the other eight missing wills. If those boys swore to signing and sending theirs it shouldn't be too hard to convince a jury that Bradley had done the same.

"I don't suppose you could get me the details of the company who drafted the will, could you?" Ella asked Joyce.

1143 hours, 04 October 2012

Had Linda been aware of the vast fortune being discussed in her mother's kitchen she might have been asking Dave's opinion on items from Harrods not New Look.

At first, Dave had felt uneasy when Linda had wandered into the room to enquire whether he preferred the blue or the green dress. His reply, 'She would look lovely in both' had been all the encouragement she'd required. Sitting on Phil's bed she complimented Dave on his decorating prowess then brought the subject back to her wardrobe.

More comfortable in the role of audience than performer, Dave enjoyed hearing Bradley's mother prattle on about what did and did not suit her shape. Precariously balancing a sheet of pasted paper he'd looked down to approve Linda's latest choice. His now, expected response, 'You'd look lovely in that' was rewarded with a big smile and a commentary on why she had chosen it. Linda was in her element; she'd forgotten how much she enjoyed the attention of an appreciative man.

Dave had been privy to numerous conversations about the elusive Linda Craig but no one had ever mentioned her girlish charm, warm sense of humour and gorgeous eyes.

"Think it's time I bought some new slap as well," Linda announced. "Been years since I've bothered with make-up but if I'm getting new clobber my face will need a bit of sprucing too." A quick entry in the search engine made Linda squeal, "Avon have a website."

Linda sashayed to the side of Dave's ladder, "I'll warn you now Mr Jarvis, the next time you see me, best leave your jumper at home because I am going to be smoking hot. Mind you, keep your pants on, I don't care what you've heard, I'm not that kind of girl," she chortled.

Chapter 25

1212 hours, 04 October 2012

Standing outside number thirty-three, Joyce tried to coax Ella inside. "At least stay for your lunch, I've got some lovely corned beef."

Ella shook her head, "Sorry, I'm expecting an important phone call. If you could just get me the lawyer's number I'll get off."

Whilst Joyce went to retrieve the contact details, Ella pulled out her mobile phone then labelled herself everything from an imbecile to a buffoon. How the bloody hell was Jules suppose to contact her when her battery was flat. Snatching the piece of paper from Joyce, Ella bid a hasty farewell.

"What about your IPAD, love?" Joyce called after her.

"Linda can keep hold of it until she gets her own," Ella replied rushing away.

"And you'll help me pick one for her?" Joyce shouted.

Hoping Ella's muffled reply had been a yes, Joyce yelled her thanks for both the IPAD and the chat.

1234 hours, 04 October 2012

Paul Douglas fought the urge to run over and kick Ella's interfering scraggy arse when he saw her drive into camp. For the past twenty minutes he'd listened to Linda wittering on about the bloody Internet, what she'd bought, what she intended to buy and how her mother had given her a credit card with a thousand pounds limit. "Mum's going to buy the big stuff on her card," Linda had told an unimpressed Paul.

Fucking credit cards were no good to him. Whores didn't take plastic. If Joyce was controlling the money did that mean she'd stop giving them the cash from Rick's dad? Come to think of it, now the lad was dead would they still get it? He'd been surprised the old bastard had kept paying after Bradley's eighteenth birthday and put the amount up. Now Rick had attended the lad's funeral the Pashley's secret was well and truly out so there was no requirement to pay for Linda's silence.

Fucking brilliant! Two fifty a month down and the gas and leccy to pay. Now Linda was sober and had discovered the joys of the Internet she'd probably want a larger cut of the benefit money. At this rate he'd be lucky if he could afford a hand job once a month.

'Not for long,' Paul reminded himself. Once Bradley's compensation came through he'd be loaded. His lawyer had already approached PAX and the army pensions people to stake Linda's claim. As there was no will they should receive the money soon. Annoyingly, Paul didn't know if his version of soon and the lawyers were the same. He'd tried to pin the bastard to a date but he'd refused to commit.

One thing was certain, he'd need to get Linda back on the booze before the money arrived. Her obedience faltered when not under the influence. Earlier, she'd ignored his instructions to stop spending money on the house. When he'd insisted she was wasting her time as once they got their hands on Bradley's money they would be able to afford a much nicer place, Linda had moaned, it could be years before she felt well enough to leave the maisonette. She had then added venomously that if he tried to pull the same stunt he had to get her into number thirty-three she'd put his nuts in a blender.

Once he'd assured his wife he would never go to such extremes again, Linda softened then gushed about the homecoming meal she intended to cook. Paul couldn't resist a dig at his wife's lack of culinary prowess. The smirk on his face soon disappeared when his wife told him she was not nuking anything to death, they were having chicken in a white wine sauce, sautéed potatoes and profiteroles for pudding. They would wash it down with diet coke as she had opted not to get the wine that was part of the meal deal. Once again, Linda was raving about the joys of the Internet. She'd ordered the food from Tesco's click and collect.

When Paul moaned that he would be the one who had to collect the stuff his wife's reply troubled him. Since when did Doormat Dave start running errands for Linda? The last thing he needed was Suzanne's posse hanging around the house. As soon as he got back he'd show that pillock the door, Joyce and Charlie would soon follow, as would Linda's sobriety.

Pushing Linda off the wagon without receiving his father in law's wrath was going to be tricky. With less than twenty-four hours to plan his wife's downfall, Paul decided, as appealing as the thought was, he didn't have the time to put Ella on her arse. Shame.

1311 hours, 04 October 2012

Ella glared at the red line on her mobile. Even though she had yelled at it three times it refused to charge any faster. Sod this, she thought. Jules obviously didn't think her important enough to talk to so she would contact Rick and ask him to reinstate his lawyers. Once they heard that the Army's incompetence had led to not only Bradley's, but a further eight wills being lost, surely they would demand his draft will be taken into consideration? Even if that was not a possibility, Suzanne might be able to sue the MOD.

'What are you thinking Harris? Not only are you going to stuff your employers, you want to stab your mate in the back whilst doing it? Jules is the one that'll hang for this,' Ella's inner voice scolded.

Closing her eyes, Ella leaned back and waited for her mind to stop racing. She could not let her temper get the better of her. Yes, she was frustrated but there was no way she would intentionally drop Jules in it. Picking up her office phone she called her friend whilst trying to send her a psychic message. *'Come on Jules, be in your office for God's sake.'* Sadly Jules wasn't picking up her phone or Ella's telepathy.

"Is that Captain Harris?" the young clerk enquired.

"Yes, is the RAOWO around?" Ella repeated forcefully.

"Sorry, ma'am, she's at lunch, she asked me to tell you she'd ring you as soon as she got back."

"Was that it?"

"Yes, ma'am."

Slamming down the phone, Ella looked for something unbreakable to throw. Her mobile phone's bleeping stopped her. Snatching it from her desk, she was annoyed to see she had missed three calls from Jules. She then listened intently to the two voice messages her friend had left. The first urged her to call back, the second informed her Jules had to attend a Long Service Award

195

ceremony for one of her civil servants but she would call her as soon as she could escape without seeming rude. Great. No hint of what, if anything, Jules had discovered.

This had to stop. If she spent another minute considering new, and mostly absurd, possibilities she would end up in a straight jacket. Resting her head on her desk, Ella struggled to control her emotions. She always got weepy when tired. A proper night's sleep was what she needed.

1322 hours, 04 October 2012

As the aircraft taxied along the runway, Rick contemplated his future. His resignation had received a frosty response from the hospital board so seeing out his notice was going to be testing. The estate agent had been equally aggrieved when he'd slashed the price of his property to encourage a quick sale. What she failed to realise was he didn't care about the money. All that mattered now was being there for his grandchild. His mother had left him more than enough cash to restart his life in Sheffield so if the apartment hadn't sold by the time he was due to leave he intended to donate it to one of Monica's favourite charities.

Accepting the whiskey from the flight attendant, Rick toasted his new appointment. The news he was to become a grandfather had prompted his epiphany. He'd wasted too many years in a country that held no appeal. There was no reason to stay. He avoided his father and the attention of women who sought his. He could do the job he loved anywhere. He was still a British citizen; as such he could avoid the rigmarole of immigration.

Learning of the vacancy at Sheffield's Children's Hospital, a month before Bradley's death, Rick had believed that fate had finally fortuned him. The post would become vacant in time for him to witness his son's pride at becoming a father. Yesterday, he had accepted the role of Paediatric Surgeon with a modicum of regret. Why had he waited so long to come back to his boy?

Ten years ago, after reading the letters Joyce had sent his mother, he'd believed that gaining custody of his son and taking him to Australia was his only option. Why had he never considered returning to Sheffield instead?

July 2002

Standing on Joyce's doorstep, Rick begged her to let him reconnect with the son he had abandoned six years earlier. Knowing he had recently lost his mother, Joyce thought it too cruel to deny him access to the little family he had left. Had she known his real agenda was to convince his child to return to Australia with him, she would not have been so accommodating.

The knowledge that Bradley had only recently returned to his mother's care pleased Rick. Linda obviously wasn't that bothered about their son so, if the money was right, she might allow Rick to improve Bradley's lifestyle as well as her bank balance. Six years ago it hadn't been financially viable for Rick to make such an offer but now money was no object. Linda could have the lot if it meant he got his son, especially now Rick had discovered the boy shared a home with the man of his nightmares.

He was not naive enough to think he could just buy the child and hop on a plane. The process was going to take time and unless Bradley wanted to go there was little chance of him gaining custody. Before going down the legal road, Rick would need to win his son over.

Rick was encouraged by how quickly they bonded. The boy obviously preferred to be with his real father than at home with Paul Douglas. At the end of their first week together Rick had tentatively broached the subject of Bradley visiting him in Australia. His son's excitement at the prospect was contagious.

Rick's joy soon evaporated when Bradley asked if Phil could accompany him. His negative response resulted in his son declaring he would never leave his sibling home alone. He'd promised Phil he would look after him and he couldn't do that from the other side of the world. No matter how much Rick attempted to reverse his son's decision, Bradley could not be tempted by the sun, sea and sand his father promised. As much as it pained Rick, he admired his boy's devotion to his younger brother.

Accepting he would have to wait until Phil was older, Rick put the custody battle on hold. Suzanne's appearance in his son's life resulted in him dropping the case completely. He had no intention, or chance, of separating Bradley from his first love.

The noise caused Ella's head to part company with her desk. Blinking the sleep away, she searched for the offending item. In her haste to retrieve it she knocked the phone into the waste paper basket. Quickly peeling away the yogurt lid, she stared at the smeared screen. Seeing the 'missed call' was from Jules she hit the call back button.

The euphoria in Jules's voice was contagious. "You're a bloody lifesaver, Ella Harris. You were right. The wills were in the personnel files."

"Thank God!" Ella squealed. "You have no idea how badly I needed to hear that." As annoyed as she was that she'd fallen asleep at least it had stopped her taking the drastic action she had earlier contemplated. "How long will it take to get Bradley's will to the legal team?" Silence. "Jules, can you hear me? If you can I'll call you back in two…"

"Ella, I'm here. Listen, before you go ballistic there's still a chance Bradley's will could be found."

"What do you mean could be found?"

"The others are here but not Bradley's."

Although Jules had never heard her friend utter such expletives she understood her need to vent. "For fuck sake Jules you've got to be kidding me. You have no idea how important this is. If that will isn't found." That was it, the dam finally broke and Ella's tears flowed.

"Please Ella, calm down. I'm sure we'll have it soon. You were right about the TA filing wills in the soldier's personal documents until they deploy. Tommy couldn't have known regular soldiers are sent straight to APC. I'm guessing he thought we'd send them once the lads left for Afghan."

"So if he filed them in their personnel files why isn't Bradley's there?" Ella screamed.

"I'm not saying it isn't. The problem is we don't have Bradley's file. His documents were dispatched to APC."

"So they have them?"

"'Not yet, but they will soon. They left here yesterday afternoon."

"So how do we get them back?"

"We don't. It would be pointless. We're not allowed to open his will so we'd only delay things. Best wait until it gets to Glasgow. I've spoken to someone there, they're going to let us know the minute it arrives."

"How long will that take?" Ella was bordering on collapse.

"Hopefully, we'll all sleep easier by the weekend. Monday at the latest."

God give her strength. When was something going to go Bradley Craig's way? '*Er. Never. He's dead remember?* Her inner voice replied unhelpfully.

Jules interrupted her internal conversation. "I'm going to call my boss now and give him the good news. I really wish I could let you take the credit but I think that could land us both in it."

"Don't worry, I'm not looking for any accolades. Right now, I'm more concerned about what to tell Bradley's grandmother."

"Nothing. You can't tell anyone. Remember you're not supposed to know."

"I need to tell her something, she's worried sick."

"No, you can't. Not until it's found. Even then, you'll have to wait until you're told officially. If my bosses find out you knew before them I'd be in more trouble than I already am."

"Okay. I'll keep quiet but please call Pete Waller as soon as you hear anything. I'll do my best to sound surprised when he tells me."

1613 hours, 04 October 2012

It was no good, even though Ella had managed to complete her staff's annual appraisals she had not given the task the attention it deserved. She would need to revisit their reports when her mind wasn't full of unsolvable problems. Shutting down her computer,

Ella concluded starting any new projects would be equally unproductive. She may as well go home.

Steve Wright's radio broadcast being cut off alerted Ella she had an incoming call. Hitting the receive button on her steering wheel, Joyce's voice filled the car.

"Sorry to bother you, love but Linda's insisting. The I-wossit won't let her on the Internet. Dave thinks its run out of credit and she wants to know how to get some more."

"I think it probably needs a top up. I don't have the details with me." Larry always dealt with increasing credit on her IPAD SIM card but Ella had no wish to inform him the expensive gadget was residing at the Haddington. "How about I bring around my dongle that's on a rolling contract."

"Are you sure you're not too busy? I've already dragged you away from your office once today. It's just the thing keeps her happy and I'd rather her be addicted to that than her other vices."

"It's no trouble. I'm on my way home so I can pop in on route."

Chapter 26
1653 hours, 04 October 2012

Charlie ushered Ella inside. "Perfect timing. We've just finished eating."

Seeing Dave and Suzanne sitting around the dining table, Ella froze.

Suzanne put down her cutlery. "If this is awkward I can leave," she offered.

"No, not at all. As long as you're okay with me being here." Ella replied.

Charlie groaned, "Stop pussy footing around you two. What harm is there in you being in the same room?"

Ella smiled. "None." The CO had said that if she bumped into Suzanne she should be polite so she wasn't breaking any rules. "How are you?" She asked the girl.

"Getting there. Some days are better than others. Still finding it hard to believe Brad's not coming back." Suzanne said as her smile faded.

"We all are, love," Joyce replied placing a cup of tea on the table and inviting Ella to take the seat next to Suzanne.

"I only came over to bring Linda some make-up and ended up staying for dinner," Suzanne told Ella.

Linda jumped up to retrieve the IPAD from the sideboard. "So do you think you can get this thing working again? I want Susie to help me pick out some eye shadow. Dave said he'll fetch it from Boots for me tonight. I've ordered some clothes, next day delivery, so with a bit of luck I'll be all tarted up when Paul arrives." With the exception of Linda everyone grimaced at the mention of her husband.

Once reconnected with the Internet, Suzanne sat patiently writing down Linda's choices as Charlie kept them amused with his story of a thief who attempted to pass himself off as a woman in order to turn over a beauty parlour.

The sound of Suzanne's laughter eased Ella's earlier tension. It was the first time she had witnessed the girl genuinely belly laugh. It brought the room alive and everyone was pleased to hear it. It was also endearing to see Bradley's mother and fiancée interact. Suzanne's gentle teasing at Linda's choice of blue eye shadow was received with mock anger and then acceptance. It was true, wearing the makeup of her youth would not return Linda to her teens.

Charlie's suggestion that Dave join him for a pint, while the ladies talked makeovers, was met with resistance. He wasn't much of a drinker and didn't think it fitting to discuss such activities in front of a recovering alcoholic. It was only when Linda insisted he deserved a drink after all his hard work that he relented.

"Only half mind," he told Charlie. "I'm fetching Linda's orders later."

Joyce signalled for Ella to join her in the kitchen. Carefully closing the door she asked if the officer had contacted the lawyer.

"Not yet. I don't want to bother him until I'm absolutely sure Bradley hasn't left a signed copy somewhere. There are still a few possibilities."

"Like what?"

"There's a chance it's in the system somewhere."

"I thought you said they couldn't find it."

"Not yet but there's still hope." Ella couldn't afford to reveal what that hope was, so racked her brain to come up with a suitable alternative. "He may have left it in his room on camp. I've asked someone to check."

"The Sergeant Major said he'd boxed all his stuff up before he left for Afghan. They are going to send the boxes here."

"All the lads have to box up their kit before deploying but the guys on camp will go through it to take out any military kit before sending it here." Ella knew they would also remove anything that might cause the family further distress. "I've asked them to look out for the will," Ella lied.

Thankfully, Joyce accepted her explanation. "Well, I pray to God it's there because having read Linda and Phil's letters it obvious he meant them to benefit from it."

Ella was pleased. "You've given them their letters?"

Joyce looked sheepish. "No, I steamed them open." Before Ella could respond, Joyce jumped to her own defence. "I had to know what he'd said. I felt bad not handing them over. If they didn't contain anything about the salon then there was no reason not to."

"But they do?"

202

"Yes. They're a bit vague but he definitely wants Phil to take over ownership for five years and then give it to his mum if she's sober enough to run it."

Ella was stumped. "Sorry Joyce, but I still don't think that justifies not handing them over. They are going to find out Bradley owned the salon at some point. It will be nice for them to hear he wanted them to benefit."

"I suppose so but what if she starts asking questions. I'll have to tell her I knew all along."

"Did he mention you were aware?"

"No."

"Then you're in the clear. Give them the letters. It could be a good thing. If the will isn't found the salon will go to Linda but this way she might let Phil have five years at the helm first."

"I doubt that. Paul will sell it as soon as they get ownership."

"Maybe you could use the letters to stop him."

"I'll think about it."

"Well don't think too long. Linda and Phil have a right to read them."

"I know. I'll deal with it, I promise. Let's get Paul's return out of the way first. What time are you bringing him round tomorrow?' Joyce asked unenthusiastically.

"I'm not sure. Shall we ask Linda?"

Walking back into the living room both women froze when they saw Linda and Suzanne embracing whilst they sobbed. Noticing her mother's return, Linda kissed Suzanne's forehead then pushed her gently away. Giving each other a knowing smile they both wiped their eyes. "Just having a moment," Linda explained then held up the IPAD. "Look what Suzanne just pulled up. Gorgeous isn't it?"

Bradley's face filled the screen.

Suzanne turned to face the women, "I just wanted to show Linda his Facebook page. There are some lovely messages on there. I haven't got round to answering them yet. I want to but it's so hard to write about him in the past tense." With that Suzanne's tears resurfaced. Linda gently pulled the girl back into her arms.

Ella wondered what Bradley would have made of the scene before her. Witnessing his mother comforting his fiancée, albeit heart-warming, was a huge surprise.

Once everyone had regained their composure, Linda told Ella to deliver Paul after twelve the following day. "That will give me time to make myself presentable," she added.

Heading for the door, Ella was irked when Suzanne followed her. She didn't want to be seen with the girl but couldn't think of a polite way of declining her company.

Once outside Suzanne spoke, "Have you got time for a quick coffee at ours?"

A cold shiver ran down Ella's spine. "I need to get home."

"Really or are you afraid someone will see us?"

Ella smiled, "A bit of both actually."

"Listen, I don't blame you for not wanting to look after me anymore."

"It's not that I don't want to," Ella protested.

"I know. Jess has explained everything. Still I don't think a quick coffee is breaking any rules. I've dropped the legal case and Paul's your new best friend so who's going to object?"

"Your mother?"

"You're wrong. The last thing she wants is you getting into bother because of us."

Reaching the place where they should part company, Suzanne tried again, "Please, just one coffee." Ella looked doubtful. "Mum said you were a scaredy cat, I thought the army would have toughened you up."

"Your mum should've also told you I don't react to taunts."

Suzanne grabbed her stomach and took a deep breath. "I think I'm having a contraction, you're going to have to help me up the stairs."

"Shouldn't I be taking you to the hospital instead?" Ella smirked.

Suzanne grinned, "I suppose we could talk on the way."

"Okay, I give in. One coffee then I really will have to get going." In order to keep up the pretence Ella took Suzanne's arm and guided her up the stairs. "May as well play to the crowd," she said placing her other arm around Suzanne's shoulder.

Once indoors, Suzanne removed her hand from her stomach and stood upright. "See that wasn't so hard was it?"

"Get the kettle on, you're on a timer," Ella laughed.

Placing their beverages on the coffee table Suzanne began. "I was thinking, would it help if you and mum made up?" Ella struggled not to spray her coffee all over the girl. "Surely your boss couldn't have a problem with you visiting an old friend now all the money business is finished with?"

"It's not that easy, Suzanne. For more reasons than I care to go into, your mum and I will never be able to reconnect. It's too late, too much has happened."

"It's never too late. Look at Linda she spent the best part of sixteen years in lala land but today she was lovely. If a couple of weeks off the booze can do that for her, what could a quick chat with mum do for you two?"

"That's different. The booze changed Linda. Your mum and I are still the same people."

"After nearly twenty years?" Suzanne asked sceptically. "I'm not asking you to become bosom buddies again but wouldn't it be nice to clear the air? You were best friends. I know she missed you, especially when all that shit went down."

Ella was unsure which 'shit' Suzanne was referring to. Her father's violence, the fight between Ella and Nicky or just the years of her mother taking Ella for granted. "As you say that was years ago, I'm sure she doesn't miss me anymore." Ella considered her statement. She no longer missed Nicky but that didn't stop her thinking of her. At least meeting Suzanne had answered some of the burning questions she had over the years; sadly new ones had replaced them.

As if reading her thoughts Suzanne continued, "I still think she'd like a chance to explain a few things. Especially about what happened in Skegness and her leaving Dave."

It was no good, Ella could no longer feign disinterest; that was one story she would kill to hear. "What makes you think she'd tell me?"

"Because when she finally came clean about all this, she kept moaning that you never got to hear her side of things."

Remembering her promise to Larry, Ella resisted being drawn into a place she'd sworn never to venture. It was bad enough she was currently sitting with Nicky's daughter. "I'm sorry but I think it's best to let sleeping dogs lie."

"I think you're wrong. If losing Bradley's taught me anything it's not to avoid important issues and this is important to me. Aunty Tray says you used to be like family. I could do with some of that around me right now."

"You've got Dave and Louise."

"Yes and they're great but they know diddly squat about childbirth. Mum's miles away and Aunty Tray has her own grandkids to contend with. The rest of the family are all down south. Nan and Gramps went to live near Uncle Steve and Aunty Mel's in London living the dream."

"What about Joyce and Linda?"

"They've enough on their plate without worrying about me. Don't get me wrong, I enjoyed spending time with them today but I can't add to their burden."

"I was surprised to see you there."

"Dave volunteered me to be Linda's interior designer. Not that she needs one. It's just a ruse to get me out of the house. When he said I hadn't left here since the funeral, Linda insisted he brought me over straight away. According to her, the longer you leave it, the harder it is to step outside. I sort of get what she means. It's difficult facing people. They're all so bloody sympathetic. Today, I only had to look at Mrs Malone and we were both in tears. Then The Mouth collared me on the stairs. Usually you can't shut her up but all she wanted to do was hug me. When I finally broke free she kept harping on about how everyone on the estate was going to look out for me and the baby. I know she means well but it's not them I need."

"It's me?" Ella knew the negative response she hoped for was not likely to be forthcoming.

"I think so. We made a connection, don't you think?"

Ella didn't trust herself to respond. If she told the girl how much she cared for her there would be no turning back.

"I'm scared," Suzanne admitted stroking her stomach. "It's my first baby and I haven't got a clue. I know mum will be up here as soon as my waters break but what about the rest of the time."

"I'm hardly an expert. I haven't got any kids."

"No, but you were with mum during her last few months of pregnancy and for Louise's birth. According to her you more or less brought Lou up in the first few months. She said she never got a look in when you were around."

"That was a long time ago."

"Still, mum reckons if it wasn't for you she wouldn't have coped. She says you were brilliant. Don't you see, I'm in the same boat? My fella isn't here either. I don't want to do this on my own."

"Suzanne you are not on your own. You have an army of people looking out for you."

Suzanne's shoulders sagged in defeat. The sight was too painful for Ella to bear. "Still, if you think I can help, then I want to. I'll need to speak to a few people first though. Please don't get your hopes up, I've a feeling some of them will say no."

"What about if I speak to Jess? Tell her mum doesn't mind you popping round. You could get Paul to say the same. If they speak to your bosses surely they'll listen."

"I don't want to step on Jess's toes. I'd hate her to think I thought she wasn't up to the job."

"I'd make sure she didn't. I still want her as my CVO, she's been brilliant about me joining the army."

"So you still intend to do that?"

"Don't have much choice. Bradley was adamant his death shouldn't ruin my life. He said I wasn't to worry about the baby he'd make sure we were taken care of. Not sure how he intends to do that." Ella suspected she did. "I'm still not a hundred percent sure I'll join," Suzanne said rubbing her stomach. "Think I'll have to see how I feel once this one makes an appearance. Still, it was nice of Jess to get me all the info. I didn't think the army would take single mothers."

"Oh, we're very much an equal opportunities employer these days."

2145 hours, 04 October 2012

Deciding to come clean about her conversation with Suzanne had been a mistake. Larry was furious that the girl had put his wife in such an awkward position. "She's just like her mother, all take and sod the consequences for anyone else."

Ella's pleas fell on deaf ears; even promising not to visit when Nicky was in town bought her no favour, Larry was not for turning.

Now lying in bed, Ella cuddled into her husband whilst obediently listening to his plans for their weekend. Saturday, weather permitting, they would take a long walk around Ladybower Reservoir then pop into the Plough for a light lunch. He had invited Ann and Hazel over for dinner that evening so when they returned, Ella could have a soak in the bath while he prepared Hazel's favourite meal.

On Sunday, he would serve breakfast in bed then whisk her off to the cycle shop so she could order the bike she'd been eyeing up the weekend before Bradley's death. After that they would head to Mrs Malone's maisonette. The old lady had insisted on returning the Johnstone's hospitality. That was the only item on his itinerary that Larry did not enthuse about. He loved Mrs M but not the location of her dining table.

Of course, somewhere in the middle of all that, Ella would be expected to show her appreciation for his total dedication to ensuring her happiness. Maybe once her breakfast had settled on Sunday morning he would join her in bed.

Ella quickly pointed out she would rather that particular activity did not have to abide to his timetable. "Personally, I am a fan of spontaneous love making," she laughed jumping up then sitting astride her husband. "What about you Mr Harris?" She asked seductively.

Larry's physical response was all the encouragement she needed. Gently licking her husband's lips she informed him of what duties she expected him to complete before lights out.

2157 hours, 04 October 2012

Dinger couldn't believe it. Coops had stuck his oar in again. Now, instead of going home, he was being sent to the Personnel Recovery Centre in Catterick.

According to Coops, it was the perfect solution to his mother's accommodation problem. At the PRC, Dinger would have his own room and access to exercise equipment. There was also transport on standby to ferry him to his physiotherapy and psychiatric appointments.

The Centre's close proximity to camp meant Coops could visit daily, as could the lads when they returned from Afghan. Not that Coops expected Dinger to still be there by then, hopefully be he would be fit to return to light duties in a month or so.

Transport to the Centre had been booked for seven am on Monday morning. As residents were expected to wear green during working hours, Coops had arranged to have his boxes delivered that afternoon. Along with his uniform, they contained his television, stereo, X box and other essential items. Hopefully, being surrounded by his personal belongings and living in a military environment would give him a much needed sense of normality.

Dinger didn't want normality nor did he want to welcome his comrades back from Afghan. The only positive thing to arise from the CSM's interference was he no longer needed to worry about his nephews discovering their uncle's dead body.

Chapter 27
1113 hours, 05 October 2012

"Not yet but there's still hope," an exasperated Jules told Ella for the third time that morning. "The afternoon post arrives at APC around three. They've promised to call as soon as they receive Bradley's documents. Fingers crossed our weekends won't be totally ruined."

Sitting at her desk, Ella's feelings of frustration were replaced by self-pity. Why was she always forced to choose? In the past it was between her husband and Nicky now it was between Larry and his nemesis' daughter.

Was she being selfish? Was Suzanne playing her? When she had asked Larry what possible motives the girl could have to do so, he had readily supplied a list. Free child care, free transport to and from hospital, the money Ella wouldn't be able to resist spending on the child, someone to be at her beck and call to fetch nappies, milk and anything else she required. Although he assured her he could carry on all night, Ella had silenced him.

It didn't matter what Larry said, her gut told her Suzanne was incapable of being so sly. Even if she was, what did it matter? If Ella was happy to be mugged off why should it bother Larry? The question was irrelevant; Larry had said no and that was an end to it.

1138 hours, 05 October 2012

Louise was livid. "Dinger strikes again!" she raged at Beetle. It had taken all her powers of persuasion to convince the lad to let her accompany him to the hospital and now that selfish arsehole had cancelled. Dinger had said there was no point in Beetle travelling all the way to Birmingham when he'd be in Catterick by lunchtime on Monday. That might suit Beetle but Louise had had to take the day off work and she couldn't see Mr Gray being happy about her asking for Monday off as well. All of a sudden Louise started to cough. She might be getting a cold. Maybe flu. She suspected that by the time she had coughed and sniffled her way through her Sunday evening shift it would be obvious she would be unfit for work on Monday.

Finding Paul Douglas leaning against her car, hopefully for the last time, Ella clicked open the doors and smiled. "Shall we get off?"

Lifting his small case, Paul returned the gesture. "Yes please. I can't wait to see Linda."

As soon as Paul opened the living room door, Linda threw the IPAD at Suzanne and stood to greet him. Dave glanced down from his ladder as Joyce rushed into the kitchen. Paul's smile momentarily faded when he saw the intruders.

After quickly fluffing her hair, Linda hugged her husband, "Welcome home sexy," she cooed.

Paul pulled his wife closer. "I'd thought we'd be alone," he whispered huffily.

"We will soon, I promise." Linda replied releasing her grip then twirling around. "So what do you think?"

His one word response 'Nice,' was disappointing. When she had entered the room earlier, Dave had been a lot more appreciative of her efforts. He'd said she looked stunning. Red was definitely her colour and Paul was a very lucky man. 'Nice' just didn't compare. She comforted herself with the knowledge Paul was opposed to public displays of affection. Once they were alone she was sure she'd hear the compliments she longed for.

"Susie did my makeup," Linda told Paul. "She's got good taste hasn't she? She's going to help us do this place up for us. We've just decided on the dining table. Do you want to see?"

"Not really," Paul replied flatly. The glare Joyce threw made him reconsider. For the time being he needed to keep the old bitch sweet. "I'm sure whatever you two have picked will be perfect. If Susie can make this place look half as good as you, I'll be a happy man," he soothed kissing his wife full on the lips.

Linda giggled. "Dave finished our room yesterday. The bedroom furniture is being delivered today and mum went and got new bedding. It's going to look stunning."

Placing his arm around his wife's waist he pulled her close. "Not as stunning as you. I can't wait to christen the new bed," Paul leered causing everyone else in the room the level of discomfort he'd aimed for.

Suzanne could stand it no longer. "I'll get off now," she announced turning to Dave. "What time do you want to go into town to look at the table?"

"Why don't you go now?" Paul suggested.

Linda playfully slapped her husband's arm. "Don't be silly, he's halfway through papering."

Dave was as keen to leave as Susie. "I'll finish this wall and then we can get off. I'll do the other two later."

"Not before you've had your lunch," Joyce ordered. "You too Susie, and Ella." The thought of being left alone with the reunited couple was obviously not a pleasant one for Linda's mother.

As usual, Joyce ignored all protestations to her offer of food, so Susie turned her attention back to the IPAD, Dave rushed to finish the wall and Ella joined Joyce in the kitchen. To everyone's relief Paul went upstairs to unpack, Linda followed like a lost puppy.

Once out of earshot of the meddling masses Paul let rip, "I didn't expect a fucking welcoming committee." He snapped. "What are they all doing here? Get rid will you?"

"It's not for long. Dave's worried about Susie so he brought her over to give her something to do."

"Fuck Susie, it's us that matters. Me and you against the world, remember? They don't give a shit about you."

"Dave's been great and he's made a good job of this place, don't you think? Billy put the carpet down yesterday. Only charged me seventy quid. Apparently it was end of line."

"He won't have paid for it. He's a bloody thief. I don't want him in here again."

"He's a right scream. He was telling us about Ella in her youth. She wasn't so much of a goody two shoes then."

His wife getting friendly with the neighbours was not an option. Paul had always led her to believe they slagged her off, if she learned otherwise she might just be able to step outside one day. Surveying the room, Paul was annoyed he was unable to find fault in Dave's work. "I don't see why you want to waste money on this shithole. It's not like we're going to stay."

"I'm not leaving until I'm well enough to walk out of my own accord," Linda snapped. She then eyed Paul suspiciously. "And don't even think about drugging me again."

"It wasn't drugs, it was cider." Paul said in his defence.

Casting her mind back to her arrival on the Haddington, Linda's thoughts turned to alcohol. The memory, or lack of it, was far too painful to handle without a drink.

August 2002

Paul had decided they needed to get away from the backstabbing and curtain twitching of Kemmel Street. Mrs Nosey Parker rightly suspected that Paul was claiming Child Benefit and other allowances even though the boys were living with their grandparents. On learning that the interferring old bat was threatening to alert Social Services, Paul reluctantly brought the boys home for, what he hoped would be, a temporary visit.

After reviewing their options, Paul decided a move to the Haddington would be advantageous. Everyone on that estate was playing the system so they wouldn't report them for fear of reprisal. After a short time, the boys could return to their grandparents and Social Services would be none the wiser.

When selling his plan to Linda, Paul failed to mention his intention to dispatch the boys back to their grandparents after a short residency in the Haddington. To convince her the move was in their best interest he laboured on the fact that her sons would have their own rooms and the residents of Kemmel Street would no longer plague her. Whilst under the influence, Linda would agree it was the best thing for the family. However, as soon as she started to envisage the move it brought about one of her episodes. Once recovered, Linda refused to engage in further discussion. For her the matter was closed. Not so for Paul.

He marched into the council offices daily demanding to be rehoused. Being told they were not considered a priority infuriated Paul. His complaints that single mothers and foreigners were taking away homes from hardworking British people like himself received amused sniggers. When he resorted to insulting the staff, the manager was summoned.

Paul was estatic when Mr Barrow threatened to ban him from the establishment if he continued to refer to his staff as the

Rug muncher, Salad Dodger and Quasimodo. It was obvious the toffee nosed cretin had a short fuse and he intended to ignite it.

One carefully delivered sentence was all the encouragement Mr Barrow needed. Yelling, "I am not a fucking faggot, you worthless piece of shit!" the manager physically dispatched Paul from the building. Landing on the tarmac outside, Paul lessened his screams of pain just to in time for everyone to catch his aggressor instructing him to 'go fuck himself.' As most of the inhabitants of the waiting room shared Paul's view of the staff, none recalled his declaration that 'it was no wonder the fucking lesbo, fat slag and raspberry ripple couldn't organise a piss up in a brewery with a faggot like him for a boss'. They all, however, were able to repeat verbatim the insults the manager had directed at the poor man who had badly sprained his wrist when he'd been attacked.

A compromise was made. Paul would not make a formal complaint if his family were rehoused within the month. The Salad Dodger came up with the solution. Some old fart on the Haddington had been complaining he couldn't manage the stairs up to his maisonette. As his kids and wife had run off with the guy from the chippy he no longer needed three bedrooms. Although Crooks wasn't his preferred destination, Fatty Arbuckle thought he could be persuaded to exchange to the two bedroomed semi in the quiet cul-de-sac. After some crafty negotiating by the old man it was agreed the two families would exchange their furniture as well as their homes. This arrangement suited Paul; not having to pack up their possessions meant Linda would remain oblivious right up to the last minute.

The week before the move, Paul took Bradley into his confidence. It was risky but necessary. Bradley would have to pack the boys belongings without raising Linda's suspicions. The prospect of his own bedroom and a sober mother encouraged Bradley's co-operation. Naively, he believed if his mother got away from the backstabbing she would no longer need lager to function.

Hearing the van pull up outside, Bradley ran downstairs to let the driver in. Although the sight of the wheelchair horrified him he understood its necessity. Leaving the device in the hall, their visitor joined the party in the living room.

Linda was thrilled with the full strength cider Paul had brought home that evening. Much better than that pissy lager he insisted was all they could afford. To add to her exuberance, Paul didn't like the stuff so she had his share too. Her mood dampened slightly when Paul's cousin turned up though after a couple more drinks she'd found herself enjoying Andy's company. He was a lively one, insisting she dance with him and constantly topping up her glass. When he returned Linda to her seat, after an energetic jive, she failed to notice the wheels on the bottom of her chair.

Whilst Andy was entertaining their mother, Bradley and Phil quickly loaded their belongings into the van. Lastly, trying not to inhale the vile smell emanating from his mother's bed sheets, Bradley had stuffed the bedding and threadbare towels into three black bin liners.

Once Linda was comatose and Paul was sure all the neighbours were asleep he and Andy laboured to push the wheelchair up a makeshift ramp into the van. Wrapping a couple of blankets around his wife Paul hit the side of the van to signal they were ready to go.

The Douglas family entered the Haddington at four am. By the time the rest of the estate awoke, the two men had carried Linda and the family's meagre belongings up three flights of stairs. Linda had stirred only once. Paul's grip had slipped and she'd ended up in a pile on the floor, it had taken five minutes to coax her back into the chair. She was vaguely aware of the unfamiliar surroundings but too drunk to comprehend their meaning. Once re-seated she had dutifully passed out.

The next morning when Paul, Bradley and even little Phil insisted she had sung 'Always look on the bright side of life' when she had happily walked from the car park to their new home, Linda struggled to breathe. Even though she had no memory of the event, learning she had been outdoors terrified her.

It was her bruises that had led Linda to discover the truth. Phil's confirmation they had been caused when daddy dropped the wheelchair compounded her humiliation.

1232 hours, 05 October 2012

Paul turned to his wife, "I don't know why you're complaining, it was me and Andy who had to carry you up the fucking stairs. We did you a favour. You wanted to move."

"I wanted my boys back."

"The money more like."

"What's that supposed to mean?"

"If the neighbours hadn't threatened to report us to the social we wouldn't have needed to bring them home."

"That's not why I did it."

"I didn't realise you'd done anything. You were permanently pissed whilst I was negotiating with the old bastard that used to live here." Linda's shaking curbed Paul's assault. He knew the signs. Those parasites downstairs would love it if she had a full-blown attack within minutes of his return. He couldn't afford to stir up trouble with them until Linda was back on the bevy. Placing his arm around his wife he softened his tone, "I'm sorry love, I didn't mean that. I've missed you so much. You're the last person I should take it out on. So what if I didn't have a penny to my name, or a bed to sleep on, that wasn't your fault. Knowing you wanted me back was all that kept me going. I love you so much."

Linda stroked her husband's face, "It must have been awful."

"It was, but not as bad as being kept away from you. Come here and give me a kiss, sexy."

1237 hours, 05 October 2012

Joyce cranked up the radio to drown out the squeaking of the floorboards above. She could kill her daughter. What was she thinking with a house full of people downstairs?

Linda was thinking she wanted Paul to stop. She wasn't enjoying their fumble on the floor. Had he always been this rough? How would she know? On the rare occasions he touched her she was always semi-conscious. She had tried to say no but pointing out they would be heard had only fuelled her husband's ardour. In the end it was easier to give in. He never took long and she didn't want to argue anymore. Biting her bottom lip she stifled her screams. Not of pleasure but of pain.

Ten minutes later a sheepish Linda and a triumphant Paul joined the crowd around the dining table. They all ate quickly and quietly. As soon as Suzanne had swallowed her last bite she thanked Joyce and left with Dave. Ella waited until she was sure she wouldn't be accosted by Suzanne then followed. Paul polished off the remaining sandwiches then parked himself on the couch whilst Linda and Joyce cleared the table.

The dressing down Linda received in the kitchen came as no surprise. She was as mortified as her mother that their guests had heard what was going on above them.

1542 hours, 05 October 2012

So that was that, no matter how much effort Larry put in to planning their perfect weekend it was already ruined. Bradley's documents had not been in the afternoon mail.

1555 hours, 05 October 2012

Walking to the bus stop, Joyce questioned her decision to leave her daughter and son-in-law alone. Not that it had really been her decision. The welcome home meal her daughter had planned only fed two and Linda had neither the inclination nor ability to stretch it to three. Insisting Joyce should go home to feed her own husband, she had dispatched her mother with strict instructions not to return before nine o'clock. She wasn't due her meds until then so what harm could Paul do in five hours? Joyce dreaded to think.

1702 hours, 05 October 2012

Paul's mood was not enhanced by his wife's insistence he turned off the television as she lit the candles. It was bad enough he couldn't have a beer with his dinner without having to sit at the bloody table. The food was okay but the diet coke and conversation less appetising. So what if Ella used to live five doors down and got sacked from her job for turning up pissed? Who cared that she used to smoke? Why his wife was so fascinated with the stuck up bitch was beyond him.

Dinner over, Paul grabbed his coke and switched on the television. Linda's heart sank. Her husband had not shown the slightest interest in her plans for the house, nor had he complimented her on the food or new dress. Washing the dishes a familiar feeling came over her. She'd hoped Paul's return would subdue her cravings but it was having the opposite effect. What she wouldn't give for a can of lager.

After returning the crockery to the cupboard, Linda headed for the stairs. Pulling the box from under her bed she selected her favourite letter. The words instantly soothed her.

It was an hour before Paul noticed his wife's absence. The relief of being back in his old seat had dissuaded him from his mission. In order to succeed he had to keep Linda sweet, maybe it was time to try out the new mattress.

Linda had beaten him to it. Holding a sheet of paper in her hand she was fast asleep. Observing his wife, Paul conceded she was still in good nick. Even though her face was stained with mascara, her tits were still awesome. Walking over to the bedside he helped himself to a handful. Linda stirred.

"Thought it was time we christened the mattress," Paul suggested. Pulling Linda to her feet he spun her around and unzipped her dress to reveal her other new purchase. When selecting the basque Linda had looked forward to Paul's reaction but now seeing it disturbed her. Pushing her to the bed Paul quickly removed his trousers. After releasing her bust from the top of the garment he pulled down her pants. Minutes later he let out a loud wail then collapsed on top of her. Rolling off, Paul pick up his trousers and searched the pockets. Removing his cigarettes he sat on the edge of the bed and raised his lighter.

"Don't smoke in here." Linda choked out.

"Why the fuck not? We always do."

Fighting back her tears Linda pulled up the straps on her basque and retrieved her knickers from her ankles. "Not anymore. It's too nice. I think once the downstairs is done you should smoke on the balcony."

"Only if you join me." Paul sneered.

"I'm hoping I'll be able to soon. That will be the first step to my recovery."

Paul's look of disbelief wounded Linda. "You think it's going to be that easy?" He asked.

"Anything but, that's why I'm going to need your help. If you can't give it me, I don't see any point in you staying."

Fear replaced Paul's disdain. "Don't say that love. You know I'll do whatever it takes to make you happy. Nobody wants you to get better more than I do."

Linda stood then headed for the bathroom. "I hope so, because this time I'm going to stay sober. It's what Bradley wanted."

On hearing the shower fire up, Paul wandered into Bradley's old room. Dave had been busy in there too. The décor was neutral, the floor tiled and a huge wall mirror fitted. So this was where Linda intended to restart her career? He'd need to put a stop to that. Having all and sundry parading through his home was unacceptable.

Linda intimating she would rather he left than her fail irked Paul. He had imagined she would come to heel the minute he returned but even though she appeared needy, sober Linda was determined. These traits were unusual for his wife so he had no idea how to handle her. It the past, a packet of cigarettes and a bottle of wine had been enough to keep her in line.

Remembering their first encounter, Paul decided a charm offensive was his best course of action. Linda always responded well to flattery so he would compliment her at every opportunity until her return to alcoholism. He had intended to wait a few weeks before reintroducing her best friend to the house. Now he concluded Mr Pinot Grigio needed to pay a visit much sooner. The longer he left it the more resistant she would be. Plus, there was no way he could sustain his Mr Nice Guy persona indefinitely. It was hell smiling through her constant chatter. The content bothered him more than the sound. In the past, their conversations had always been to the detriment of others. He'd enjoyed bemoaning Linda's parents and sons, along with the neighbours she had never met. Now, instead of joining in, Linda loved everyone. They were all funny, sweet and helpful. Especially that bitch Ella. They all fawned over her. Thankfully, now he was home he no longer needed to. Once he regained his rightful status at number thirty-three he would resume his mission to destroy the stuck up cow.

He was already collecting ammunition. According to The Mouth, Ella had been ordered not to go near Suzanne's family. Given Dave and Suzanne's reaction when the officer had delivered him home it was clear it wasn't the first time Ella had ignored her superiors' instructions. They were all a little too cosy for his liking. He'd also caught her conspiring with Louise. What would Ella's bosses make of that?

Chapter 28
0915 hours, 06 October 2012

Dave's eight am arrival at number thirty-three had infuriated Paul. His complaint that he liked to lay in at the weekend garnered little sympathy from Joyce. "Why? Because you work so hard in the week," she had retorted.

His mother-in-law's scorn and Dave's presence had prompted Paul's departure. Claiming it was best not to max out her credit card too soon, Paul had volunteered to collect the bedding and bathroom accessories Linda had selected from the Argos catalogue.

With one hundred pounds of his mother-in-law's money, Paul headed for Twenty-One Garvey Close: The address of the most prolific shoplifter on the Haddington. Though unimpressed by the hour of Paul's visit, Mac was soon appeased by the offer of sixty quid for a morning's work.

Annoyingly Argos was one of the few stores Mac could not ply his trade but he promised to do his best to source similar items from Dunelm Mill. An hour later, Paul took ownership of a single duvet set, valance sheet, bath mat, toilet cover, bog brush and a pile of towels. Not an exact match to Linda's requirements but Paul was sure she'd be appeased by the superior quality.

With the remainder of Joyce's money, Paul replenished his vodka stash. He had hit it quite hard last night. Thankfully, Linda hadn't noticed how many times he had visited Phil's room to top up his diet coke from the bottle he'd hidden in his case. He still had a tenner left so decided, if he was going to have to witness his wife being so personable with Doormat Dave all afternoon, a few pints might make the task more bearable.

1220 hours, 06 October 2012

Concerned his lengthy absence might encourage awkward questions from his mother-in-law, Paul downed his third pint then headed for the bus. Once home, he ran upstairs whilst announcing he was desperate for a slash. Before leaving the bathroom, Paul glugged a quarter of a bottle of vodka then brushed his teeth.

The sound of laughter coming from the living room caused Paul to pause before entering. Plastering on a fake smile he attempted to join in with the hilarity. "What's so funny?" he asked.

Linda responded. "Billy's just been telling us about when he first met Ella and his missus. Joy spotted him shoplifting in Tesco's and dared him to get her some tampons. Cheeky beggar got her them supersized ones. Can't believe she went out with you after that," Linda told Billy. "I would've given you a right slap."

"Oh, I got a slap all right but it was soon followed by a tickle." Billy winked.

Paul forced himself to laugh along. "Good for you," he said looking around the room. "You guys have been busy. It looks great in here. Where have you hidden the furniture though?"

Linda answered. "Amir and Ben took it to the tip. Wasn't fit for owt else. Joy and Billy's going to lend us a bed settee and a bean bag until the new one gets here."

"You can bin them once it comes. They're well past their sell by date," Billy added.

"When do we get the new couch?" Paul asked.

"In two weeks. The coffee table, fire place and units arrive on Monday though, along with a forty-two inch flat screen telly." Linda enthused. "You've always wanted one of them haven't you, love?"

Paul worried he'd overdone his whoops of joy when everyone turned to stare. "Sorry, I'm a bit excited," he lied. Yes he'd always fancied a flat screen but why did they have to get rid of everything else before it was replaced. He'd miss his old chair. The thought of squeezing on a bed settee with Linda whilst Joyce sunk into a beanbag did nothing to appease his sense of loss.

1734 hours, 06 October 2012

Under the guise of ironing the bedding and making the bed up in Phil's room, Paul had carried the iron and ironing board upstairs. Downstairs, everyone believed his tardiness in completing the task was due to his lack of acquaintance with the domestic appliance. This however was not the case, Paul had spent the majority of his time swigging the vodka hidden under Phil's bed whilst perusing 'Readers Wives'. With the help of the voddie and the time he'd extricated himself from the group he'd managed to stay amiable until the last of the invaders had left.

Once again, Joyce had been ordered home to feed Charlie so Paul parked himself on the bed settee whilst Linda prepared dinner. Picking up Ella's IPAD he quickly added a few items to the

Tesco order Linda had prepared. His plan was risky but he was confident once his wife had succumbed to temptation he could convince her of his innocence.

"Do you want to give me the credit card love and I'll send this order off for you?" He offered.

"I need to add a few bits first."

"Tell me what and I'll do it. Best you get it sent off now if you still want Dave to pick it up in the morning."

"There's plenty of time. Come and get your dinner, I'll do it after we've eaten."

Paul deleted his purchases then joined his wife at the table. In hindsight it was probably for the best. There was a chance Doormat would notice the bottles when he collected the order. If he did, the snivelling little turd was bound to inform Joyce of his discovery. Paul's impatience was clouding his judgement. Failure was not an option so he would need to box clever if he was going to get Linda back on the bevy without getting the blame for her lapse.

Of course, getting booze in the house did not guarantee success. There was always the possibility of Linda not succumbing to temptation. Fortunately, Paul had a sure fire way of weakening her resolve. Over dinner he nonchalantly mentioned bumping into the The Mouth. "As usual, the woman couldn't hold her own water," he told Linda. "Not that I wanted to listen. It really pissed me off when she said Dave and Billy were taking the piss out of your makeover. Only so much you can polish a turd. What is that supposed to mean?"

Seeing his wife's distress, Paul added, "They're only jealous because neither of them could pull a bird as fit as you. Have you seen Billy's missus?" Linda shook her head. "As for Dave, he couldn't pull a muscle. Too busy scheming with his ex's brats. Do you know Susie told The Mouth no matter how much you tart this place up she's never gonna bring her child in here? What's all that about? She sits with you picking furniture then tells people she has no intentions of sitting on it? I might just have to have a word with the two faced little madam. Find out what her motive is for buttering up to you." Linda was staring at Paul in disbelief. "It's probably the money. She knows she isn't getting it now, so she'll probably try and fleece you for it before the kids born."

"She'll not get a penny off me," Linda replied vehemently. "Not unless I see that child. She can't keep it from me. It's not fair." Linda started to blubber.

"I'll make sure she doesn't, love. We might have to pay her to bring it over but if that's what it takes, I'll do it. You're going to be a cracking Gran and I'll not let a little tart like her spoil it for the kid."

Linda smiled. "Thanks love. I can't believe I fell for her bullshit."

"Whilst we're on the subject, you need to be wary of Ella. She's only playing nicely because I caught her out. That's why she helped me back. Knew I'd sussed her. She's been sneaking around behind your back again. I saw her with Louise. Not sure what they were cooking up. Plus she's thick as thieves with your mum. Caught them bitching in the kitchen yesterday. Cheeky cow was talking about us going upstairs after she brought me back. Said something about a tart in a nice frock still being a tart. Your mother's as bad. Said she'd give you a month before you were back on the bottle and in your shitty leggings."

Linda looked horrified. "She wouldn't say that. She's been trying to help. She's really looked after me."

Maybe convincing his wife her mother wasn't onside was a step too far, Paul noted. "I know, love. She probably didn't mean it. Bet she was just trying to impress her new best mate. I don't get why she's always creeping up to her. Ella love this, Ella love that. It's pathetic."

"Dad's just as bad. Thinks the sun shines out of her arse."

"Well we know better eh, love? Billy was right she aint no saint that's for sure."

"Hearing that just made me like her more. I thought we were getting on."

"Listen love, she only cares about her career. I dropped her in it when I told them about her and Nicky. Why did she lie about that if she wasn't up to something?"

Linda shrugged. "So you think they're all taking the piss?"

"I'm sorry love, but yes. They're taking advantage of you while you're battling your demons. As if you haven't got enough on your plate without them slagging you off to the likes of The Mouth."

As his wife crumbled before him Paul assured her he was only telling her for her own good. If there was one thing he couldn't stand it was people being two faced. He promised they would have the last laugh. When she walked sober through the estate on the way to her beautiful new home she would do so with her head held high. "They'll have to eat their words then," he promised. Linda's confidence about leaving number thirty-three faded with every word her husband uttered. At that moment, she would give anything for a sip of cider.

Joyce returned to a subdued Linda. After obediently taking her meds she slouched off to bed. Afraid his mother-in-law might notice the affect the voddie was having on him, Paul followed to find his wife reading those blasted letters again.

2215 hours, 06 October 2012

Tonight Dinger happily depleted his suicide stash. Having considered his pending move to Catterick, he saw it as the divine intervention he had been praying for. Residents of the PRC were free to come and go as they pleased in the evenings so once there he would be able to purchase a couple of packets of paracetamol daily. There was a huge Tesco in the Garrison so he would also be able to pick up a bottle of vodka to wash them down.

Adding the paracetamol to the stash of sleeping tablets and pain relief the doctors had prescribed should guarantee success. He had decided Friday was the best night to leave the world. There was no reveille in the Centre at the weekends so the earliest he was likely to be discovered was Saturday afternoon. No chance of resuscitation by then.

Having a time line calmed Dinger. The next week would be bearable in the knowledge it would be his last.

Chapter 29
0921 hours, 07 October 2012

Joyce had no choice but to agree to Paul administering Linda's afternoon medication. He had offered to do so under the pretence of confronting his wife about her abhorrent behaviour towards her mother. He claimed ignorance regarding Linda's recent mood change. Joyce's bullshit detector was off the radar but what choice did she have? Linda had been frosty with her all morning. When Joyce had brightly enquired what the matter was, her daughter had responded 'You' then informed her she didn't see why she insisted on hanging around. She and Paul were fine on their own.

Paul had suggested Joyce go to church then spend some time with Charlie. He promised by the time she returned he would have convinced Linda she still needed her mother's support. His congeniality act wasn't fooling Joyce. She'd been watching him like a hawk and had seen his fake smile falter on more than one occasion. Even so, it was time to face the inevitable, she would be sleeping in her own bed very soon.

Was that so bad? Charlie's refusal to spend a minute in Paul's company was making her life difficult. Having to tolerate Paul herself was testing. For a brief time, Joyce had believed her daughter was as unimpressed with Paul's presence as she was. Sadly, Linda's distaste had been short-lived; now he was the only person she had a good word for. Dave, Suzanne and Ella had all received a tongue lashing from the ungrateful mare that morning.

Joyce had no desire to hear her daughter berate those she cared for further or spend another night under the same roof as Paul Douglas. When she returned at five pm she would give them the news they wished for, then pack her bags. The only solace she could take was Ella had been right about Paul's drinking. He had not touched a drop.

0927 hours, 07 October 2012

Once satisfied Joyce was off the estate Paul shoved the IPAD in his wife's hand and promised not to be long. When Linda protested, Paul claimed he wanted to prove to those meddling berks his wife was a lot tougher than they gave her credit for. Their insistence on babysitting her was a show of no confidence. He, on the other hand, had total faith in her; after all she'd always been okay in the past. '*And pissed.*' Linda thought.

Seeing the suitcase in Paul's hand, Linda's stress levels threatened an attack. Opening the empty case, Paul laughed. "For God's sake woman you've spoilt the surprise. I want to pick up a present for you. It will be easier to carry in this."

Having calmed his wife sufficiently, Paul kissed her goodbye before instructing her not to open the door to any of those nosey twats.

0929 hours, 07 October 2012

Dave resisted the urge to jump for joy when he saw Paul leaving the house with his suitcase. Two nights with the idiot had been enough for Linda to see sense. She was far too good for the likes of Paul Douglas.

1022 hours, 07 October 2012

Neither the IPAD nor television had been able to stop Linda dwelling on the awful things people were saying about her so she was overjoyed when Paul ran through the door announcing he needed a crap. If he had abandoned her too what would she have to live for? The thought of joining Bradley was becoming more attractive by the day. The chance to tell him how sorry she was and how much she loved him would be worth it. Not that she had any hope of seeing him. He was bound to be in the good place whereas she was definitely heading for the bad.

Ten minutes later, Paul descended the stairs carrying a wilting bunch of flowers and an out of date box of Diary Milk. He apologised profusely for the poor quality of his gifts but explained, as they hadn't received Mr Pashley's money, he had to be careful with the cash. If he had the pin number for the credit card that would be different, then he would be able to buy his wife the luxuries she deserved. When Linda suggested asking Joyce, Paul said his wife shouldn't have to go cap in hand to her mother nor did she need to. As the credit card was in Linda's name she could order a replacement pin number.

Dave was due to collect the Tesco order at one o'clock so it was time for Paul to sow the seed for the next stage of his plan. "I bumped into Mac when I was out, he said they're taking people on at my old firm. Thought I might apply."

Linda was mortified. "I don't want to be left on my own all day while you're at work."

"Your mum'll visit." Paul placed his arm around his wife. "We need the money, love. That old bastard's not going to pay us anymore and your mother's credit card won't last forever. Plus, I don't like sponging off her, I want to be the one to provide for you." Paul kissed his wife's cheek. "Mac said my old foreman drinks in the Jockey, I thought I might pop up there, see if I can find him. He might put in a good word for me."

"Have you got another woman?" Linda blurted out.

Paul laughed, "Don't be daft, you know you're the only girl for me. I wouldn't have come back otherwise, would I?"

"You've never wanted to work before."

"I wanted to, but I couldn't. You needed me at home. Now you're sober it'll be fine."

"I'm not sure."

"I am love, it'll be good for us both. Having a normal life, like other couples. I'll wait until Dave's delivered the shopping then I'll pop to the Jockey. I'll just have a chat with the bloke. Don't look so worried, it might not come to anything."

1322 hours, 07 October 2012

Dave was gutted when Paul took the bags then closed the door in his face without so much as a thank you. How had he won Linda back so soon?

Paul had revelled in Dave's look of dejection. What did he expect? To be invited in for a cup of tea? That would never happen again. When he turned up tomorrow Paul would see him off. If he was owed any money he could go to Joyce for it.

After receiving the shopping bags, Paul ran upstairs. Two minutes later he stuck his head through the living room door. "I'm off now love. I won't be long. The food's in the hall."

1325 hours, 07 October 2012

Linda had no idea what Paul was up to but was sure it wasn't getting a job. Was he meeting that bitch, The Mouth? He certainly talked about her a lot. Reckoned he'd seen her when he'd bought the flowers. She'd teased him he didn't need to buy his wife presents to get her into bed; she'd heard Linda was happy enough on a creaky floor. That snippet of info could only have come from Suzanne or Dave; the backstabbing bastards.

Shuffling into the hall, Linda grabbed two of the six shopping bags and headed for the kitchen. Unpacking the

227

vegetables she thought about the roast dinner she intended to cook; anything to take her mind off the gossip.

Returning for the rest of the shopping, she heard the bottles clink as soon as she lifted the bag. Strange she couldn't remember ordering anything in glass containers.

1622 hours, 07 October 2012

Confident Linda would be nearing the end of the second bottle of Pinot, Paul entered the Haddington. He would need time to convince his wife the others had planned her downfall before his mother-in-law tipped up. Not that she should take much convincing. If she was as far gone as he expected she would believe anything as long as he fetched her more booze. He'd stashed another bottle upstairs to encourage her obedience.

What if she hadn't succumbed to temptation? It was unlikely but possible. He'd upped the ante by hiding her medication and her other comfort blanket but there was still a slim chance she hadn't bitten. Not to worry, whether she drank or not his defence would be the same. Under Suzanne's instruction, Dave had added a bag of booze to the shopping hoping to tempt Linda off the wagon. The girl was obviously still bitter they had thwarted her attempt to steal Bradley's money. He might even be able to implicate Joyce. He could say Linda's mother agreed not to come home until five because she was in on it.

The house was silent when he entered the hall. Maybe Linda had passed out and pissed all over the bed settee. Not to worry they were getting a new one soon Paul laughed to himself. "Hi Honey, I'm home!" he shouted jovially.

The hand around his throat wiped the smile from his face. "You evil bastard!" Dave screamed. "How could you do that to her?"

"What? I haven't done anything." Paul's mind was racing he had to get to his wife. "Linda? If you've hurt her..."

"Me? I'm the one who found her you bastard. You knew she'd drink it."

Inwardly, Paul congratulated himself, Linda was back on the bevy. "Drink what? She hasn't has she? Where did she get it from?"

"You know where. Where you left it, you arsehole."

"You were the one who brought the shopping in not me." Shit, Freudian slip, Dave hadn't said it was with the shopping. "If that's where it was I mean… It could have been somewhere else… I'm just guessing."

Dave tightened his grip on Paul's throat. "Stop with your lies. No ones falling for your bullshit."

"I wasn't even here."

"And why was that I wonder? Because you bought three bottle of Pinot, smuggled them back in your suitcase then hid them amongst the shopping before you pissed off?"

"How did you…" Paul stopped himself.

"Know? How did I know? The Mouth saw you in Tesco!" Dave yelled, dragging Paul to the door and opening it. "Now get out and don't come back!"

Paul attempted to pull away. "This is my house. I'm not going anywhere until I've spoken to my wife."

Linda stumbled into the hall. "Where are my letters you bastard?"

"Ask him," Paul said trying to free his throat from Dave's grip.

"He didn't even know about them!" Linda screamed.

"He must've found them when he was decorating."

Dave launched Paul out of the door. "Stop with your lies, they're not going to work."

Paul attempted to re-enter the house. "Please love, he's the one lying. I'd never hurt you."

Linda fell to her knees. "Please just tell me where they are." She started to sob.

Dave grabbed Paul and forced him into a headlock. "Tell her where her letters are you bastard, can't you see she's in bits?"

"I haven't got them. You're not pinning this on me. You've got to believe me, Linda."

"What the hells going on?" Joyce yelled running up the veranda. Arriving at the door she peered in to see her daughter gasping for breath. "Oh my God, Linda what's happened?" she screamed running through the door.

"Can't breathe," Linda gasped.

The smell of alcohol brought tears to Joyce's eyes. "Close the door," she yelled to Dave.

When Dave loosened his grip, Paul kicked his captor's shin then struggled free. Keeping his eye on Dave as he fled, Paul failed to notice Ella heading up the veranda and crashed straight into her. "What the fuck are you doing here?" he yelled scrambling to push past her.

"What the hell's going on?" Ella yelled.

Dave was heading towards them so Paul slammed Ella into the wall then ran straight into Larry's fist. "Don't ever touch my wife again," he warned.

Paul scrambled to his feet. "Let me go," he demanded.

"With pleasure," Larry said moving out of his way.

"Are you all right, babes?" Larry asked.

Ella turned to Dave, "What the hell happened here?"

As most of the doors on the veranda had faces peering out of them, Dave suggested they talk inside.

In the hall, Joyce rocked Linda as tears fell down both women's cheeks. "Deep breaths sweetheart, that's right. He's gone now. We'll look after you," Joyce soothed.

"He's got my letters," Linda kept repeating between sobs.

Chapter 30

1704 hours, 07 October 2012

"I need a drink," Linda told Dave as he carried her to the couch. "Where did you put the rest of the wine?"

"I poured it away."

Linda sprung up. "What the fuck did you do that for? I need it."

Joyce ran to her daughter's side. "No you don't sweetheart. You can do without, you've proved that."

"Well I've fucked up now, so I might as well finish what I've started. Get me the other fucking bottle," she screamed throwing herself back on the couch and curling up into a ball.

Larry's look of disgust pained Ella. "Do you want to go and tell mum and dad what's going on?" she asked him.

"That'd be difficult as I haven't got a clue." Larry replied sarcastically.

"Just tell them I'm okay and I'll be down in a minute."

"And what if that moron comes back?"

Dave spoke up. "I can deal with him."

"Please Larry, I need you to go." Right now, Linda was too highly strung to realise a stranger was amongst them but Ella worried once she did it would trigger another attack.

"Fine, I'll take them back to Mrs Malone's. Don't be long." He replied, storming out.

"Mrs M's?" Joyce asked.

"We were having Sunday lunch at hers. I heard the commotion as we were leaving. I'm sorry about Larry, I asked him not to follow me."

"He's only looking out for you love." Joyce replied. "God knows what he'll think of us lot." Ella had a fair idea. "I'm going to call the doctor, I think that little runt has stolen her tablets."

"I don't need fucking tablets, I need a drink," Linda snarled.

Dave pulled Linda into his arms. "You don't love, you're better than this. Don't let that bastard win."

Looking up at Dave, Linda blinked. "He took my letters," she sobbed.

"I know, I know," Dave soothed gently wiping the tears from her eyes.

Joyce picked up her mobile and retired to the kitchen. Ella was still clueless as to what had happened and desperate to know. "I take it Paul gave her the booze?" She asked Dave.

"Not directly."

"It was in the bags," Linda mumbled.

Joyce returned to the room. "The doctor's on his way. Why don't you go for a lie down love until he gets here?"

Linda looked up. "I need a drink mum, please."

"I'm sorry Sweetheart, that's not going to happen."

"Then my letters. Find my letters. They help. Not the ones that are there now. The nice ones."

Joyce looked confused. "I'm sorry love, I don't know where they are."

Linda's breathing started to get erratic so Joyce grabbed a paper bag and scrunched it up. "Get her to breathe into that," she told Dave before running in the hall to collect her handbag.

Retrieving the envelope, she quickly made a sign of the cross then looked upwards in silent prayer. Ella wasn't sure now was the right time but understood why Joyce might think so. "Here love, read this. It's from Bradley, better than all them others put together."

Linda glared at her mother, "How sick are you? That's not even funny, you spiteful cow!" she raged.

"Seriously love, he left it for you. We all got one."

Dave chipped in, "Susie got hers the other day."

Fortunately, Linda was too shocked to question why she hadn't received hers earlier. Holding out her hand tentatively she took the envelope then stroked the word mum.

"Go on love, open it." Joyce encouraged.

Remembering Suzanne's reaction, Dave suggested Linda might want to read it alone.

"I'm not sure I should've done that," Joyce told Ella as Linda climbed the stairs. "Do you think it'll help?"

Ella shrugged. "I guess we'll find out soon enough. Should one of us listen out, just in case?"

"I'll go," Joyce insisted then crept to the top of the stairs and sat outside Linda's bedroom door.

Ella turned to Dave. "So what did you mean not directly?"

"He mixed the wine in with the Tesco order. I think he was planning on blaming me for bringing it in the house."

"How did you find out?"

Dave raised his eyebrows. "Cath the Mouth. She heard Paul showing off in Tesco because they wouldn't sell him alcohol before ten o'clock. Apparently, he'd yelled if he hadn't needed to buy their brand he'd have fucked off elsewhere. Cath told me she suspected Linda wasn't the only alcoholic in the house. If Paul was hiding booze in a suitcase he obviously had a problem too. That's when I twigged."

"Twigged what?"

"I'd seen him with the case first thing this morning. I thought Linda had kicked him out but when I dropped off the shopping he answered the door. On my way home I saw him heading for the bus stop. I thought maybe I'd forgotten something but alarm bells started ringing when Cath told me what she'd seen. Unfortunately, that was over an hour after the bastard left."

"So Linda had already started drinking?"

"Luckily, she was still on her first bottle. It could have been worse. He'd left two."

"I can't believe he'd do that." What Ella really wanted to say was 'I can't believe I helped him get back here, so he could do that.'

"Well I think there's enough evidence, though he's trying to pin it on me."

"That's crazy. What did Linda say?"

"Not much. I ran up here as soon as Cath told me. When she didn't answer the door I let myself in. She was just sat sobbing and drinking. I took the wine from her poured it down the sink then hid the other bottle. She didn't half put up a fight." Dave said tilting his head to show angry scratch marks on his neck. "Once

233

she realised I wasn't going to give in, she had a fit? I was trying to calm her down when he turned up."

"And you kicked him out?"

"Not before he'd told Linda it was me. You don't think she'll believe him do you?"

"Not once she's sober. Right now she's not thinking straight. All she wants is a drink."

"Do you think that's it then? She'll go back on the booze."

"I don't see how. No one here is going to fetch it for her. It's going to be hell for Joyce though getting her back off it."

1724 hours, 07 October 2012

Upstairs, Joyce sneaked into Linda's bedroom. Her daughter was on her side, clutching Bradley's letter to her chest and staring vacantly at the wall, fresh tears on her cheeks.

"Are you okay, love?"

Linda turned slowly. Her pained expression tore at her mother's heart. "Bradley wants me to stop drinking and go back to work in the salon. If I do that, he says I can have it."

Joyce sat on the edge of the bed and took her daughter's hand. "That would be nice, wouldn't it? You in charge, it's what you always wanted."

Linda's bottom lip trembled, "I did, but not like this. Sometime I wish I'd never set eyes on the bloody salon. Then again if I hadn't I wouldn't have had him at all.

"Then I'm glad you did. We might have only had him for twenty years but I'll cherish every moment."

"Me too. Especially the sober ones. It's shit. If I'd have known…" Linda sat up. "I didn't want him to go out there but I didn't tell him. Didn't even warn him to stay safe. I can't remember what he said the last time he rang." Linda placed her head in her hands. "What I wouldn't give to have that conversation again."

"I know, love. I was sober when he rang me and I can only remember snippets. Still what he wanted to tell us he wrote in his letters."

"Did you get one?"

Joyce had been dreading this since she had impulsively handed Bradley's over. "Yes, on Sunday. It was lovely. He was the one who asked me to do this place up for you."

"So I read it right? Wasn't sure if I had. Thought the alcohol was playing tricks. He really thought it through didn't he? Set me a goal to get me off the ale. If only he knew I tried before he asked me to."

"He does love," Joyce said looking up. "Who do you think sent Dave up here to rescue you?"

Linda smiled. "Would be nice to think that but I doubt your God would let Bradley look after the likes of me."

"Oh I think you would be his top priority. You're trying so hard to make things right and you've been doing so well. Please love, don't let Paul drag you down again."

"I didn't even drink the full bottle." Linda grinned, "Mind you, I would've if it hadn't been for Dave." She put her hand to her mouth. "I didn't half wallop him when he took it off me."

When her daughter started to giggle Joyce was horrified, "I don't think that's anything to laugh about young lady."

"I know but I can't help it. I only met the guy this week. You bring him in to sort this place out and he ends up having to sort me out as well, poor sod. Still I hear his ex was a bit of a brawler so maybe that's what turns him on." Linda winked at her mother. "I do hope so." Even in her dazed state the thought of arousing Dave was a pleasant one.

Joyce tried to stifle a giggle of her own. "Enough of your dirty talk young lady. The doctor will be here soon. I think until then you should try and sleep it off."

"I'll read this one more time," Linda replied holding up Bradley's letter. "While I think about it can you bin the ones over there?" She pointed to four envelopes in the middle of the floor. "Sick bastards. Some of the things they wrote. If I could leave this place I'd hunt them down and chop their balls off."

"What are they, love?"

"Hate mail. Tossers saying Bradley deserved to die and that he's burning in hell. To be honest I only read two then I hit the bottle. My nice letters had been replaced by those. Not hard to guess who did that," Linda said dejectedly.

"Yes, well we've seen the last of him, I promise."

"But I want my letters back. He must have hidden them somewhere."

"Don't you worry about that now. Get some sleep and I'll search the house. On a scale of one to ten how badly do you want a drink?"

At the mention of alcohol Linda tensed. "About a hundred and ninety nine. If I thought Dave would part with the wine he took I'd offer him my body right now," Linda admitted.

"Well he won't, so don't," Joyce snapped. "Read Bradley's letter. I'll bring you up a cuppa."

"Thanks, mum. I don't deserve you."

Linda rolled on to her back and looked up at the ceiling. 'And I never deserved you' she told Bradley, 'but thank you so much for loving me, even though I was the world's worst mum.' Clutching his letter, Linda broke into a huge grin, 'I'm going to be an awesome Granny though. That kid's going to love his Nanna Linda but not as much as I'll love him.'

1749 hours, 07 October 2012

"How is she?" Ella asked when Joyce returned.

"Not too bad. How much did she drink?"

"About three quarters of a bottle." Dave answered.

"Enough to put me on my back but just a taster for her. The downside is she wants more but I think she's ready to fight that again."

"What about Bradley's letter?" Ella asked.

"It seems to have helped. Thankfully she's not asking too many questions though I'm sure when she's thinking straight I'll have a lot of explaining to do."

Larry's arrival at the door stopped the conversation. "It's nice to meet you at last," Joyce said ushering him inside. "I just wish the circumstances were different."

Ignoring Joyce, Larry stormed into the living room. "Are you ready?" He asked his wife. "I think it's time to look after your own family. Your mum and dad are worried sick," he sneered.

Joyce looked sympathetically at Ella. "You get off love. There's nothing you can do here. I'll call you later."

Ella stood and put her arms around Joyce. "I'll pop in tomorrow," she said gently hugging the older woman. Turning to

Dave, she thanked him for his intervention then headed for the door glaring at Larry as she passed.

Once outside she let rip. "How dare you treat Joyce like that? They're going through hell in there and all you can do is stand in judgement."

"It's a hell they've created for themselves. I've no sympathy."

Ella swung around. "And don't I know it you self righteous prat." When Larry started to protest Ella held up her hand. "Not here. I think the neighbours have had enough entertainment for one day."

1833 hours, 07 October 2012

The journey to Ella's parents' house was excruciating. After a few stilted words everyone fell silent giving Ella time to brood over her husband's behaviour.

Whilst waving the Johnstone's goodbye, Larry went on the offensive. "I don't see why you're angry with me. I was the one who put that bastard on his arse."

"For your own pleasure. He wasn't a threat to me, he just wanted to get away from Dave."

"He hit you."

"Pushed me actually, but that's neither here nor there. You were rude to Joyce."

"I'm sure she's heard worse. Water off a duck's back to the likes of her."

"The likes of her? Who do you think you are talking about? She is one of the nicest people I've ever met."

"Then you need to get out more. They're scum Ella, can't you see that? They're dragging you down to their level."

"I started at their level, Larry. We didn't all grow up in suburbia with rich parents and a top-notch education. I had to work to get where I am today."

"Unlike me who had it all?" Larry snapped.

"Not quite. There is an abundance of love in the house you just left, unlike the one you grew up in."

"My parents did a damn sight more for me than they have for that drunken hoe."

"If you say so, but I'm not so sure they'd rush to help if you had similar problems."

"But I never would and that's the point. She got herself in that state and now you're supposed to help her out of it?"

"Her life got her there. She was a single parent, abandoned by the father and trapped by a control freak."

"For God's sake, stop making excuses for her. She's not worth the effort. She got herself knocked up by choice. She could've escaped that shithole if she'd wanted to, you did."

"There but for the grace of God go I, eh? If my womb wasn't so messed up I could have easily ended up in the same situation. I was hardly a parody of virtue in my teens. You know how pissed I used to get back then, and I smoked."

Larry hated being reminded of his wife's sordid past. "You sorted yourself out though."

"After one monumental cock up and with the intervention of my friends and family, yes. Still if I'd have had a baby in tow it would have been different."

Pulling up outside their house Larry turned to Ella. "I don't know what you want from me. I can't feel sorry for those people."

Ella snapped, "Stop calling them those people. They're human beings just like us except their lives are shittier. That drunken hoe, as you call her, has just lost her son. To add to her pain her pillock of a husband tried to get her back on the booze and he seems to have stolen the one thing that was helping her through all this. She was served up one hell of a shit sandwich at the buffet and if I can get her a piece of cake to take away the taste I intend to."

"So you're going to keep helping them?"

"I never said otherwise did I?"

"I think you've done enough."

"I don't give a damn what you think. In fact I might as well tell you now, I intend to help Suzanne too. If she needs me, I'll be there."

"No you will not!" Larry raged.

"Yes, I bloody well will. It's my decision. Seeing what a controlling husband can do to a woman opens ones eyes. I will not let you stop me!"

"So you're prepared to lose me in order to see her?"

"If you're prepared to lose me by stopping me, yes." Ella opened her car door. "Your choice Larry, if you do decide to piss off again just remember you left me. I didn't ask you to go." Ella went to close her door. When Larry failed to move, she reopened it. "Oh and if you do bugger off go to your loving parents this time instead of bothering MY friends."

1917 hours, 07 October 2012

Throwing her bag in the hall Ella stormed into the kitchen and flicked on the kettle. She was too angry to worry about her husband disappearing again. He was a snob; she hated snobs. How had she ended up marrying one? He was also manipulative and overbearing. From day one he had made it his mission to remove her from her old life.

Nicky had been right all along, a girl from the Haddington was not good enough for Larry so he had recreated her. Walking past the mirror Ella winced. Larry preferred her hair long and brunette. Years ago she'd experimented with shorter cuts and different colours but his constant whingeing had resulted in her having the same hairstyle for the last seven years. The clothes she wore were also his choice. Though, unlike Paul, he would never dare buy them without his wife present, he always insisted on accompanying her on shopping trips and had the last say on what made it to the check out.

Larry referred to her look as classy elegance but was it actually her look? Her husband had supplied all the expensive jewellery. 'Only the best for his little lady.' His little lady? Is that how he saw her? She'd always believed herself to be the stronger force in their relationship but had Larry played her as Paul had Linda?

Looking around the kitchen, Ella thought it more a show house than a home. She was as proud as Larry of their achievements but deep down suspected he was more driven by bettering his brother than creating a comfortable home. His sibling and parents had only visited once. She had taken as much pleasure as Larry at their envious reaction. Was that the whole point, Larry wanting to upstage the favoured child? Was she a means to that end? She had thought it her idea for Larry to give up work so she could further her career but had it been his agenda all along? He'd never been much of a soldier, whereas she had shone from the beginning. Was she his cash cow as Linda was Paul's?

Sipping her tea she shook her head. As usual, she was being overdramatic. Trust her to go off at a tangent. Larry was nothing like Paul. He had always tended to her every whim and she could never doubt his love. Everyone said he spoilt her rotten. What women wouldn't want expensive jewels and their dinner on the table every night?

He'd stood by her when she couldn't give him kids and when she cheated. His behaviour today was irreproachable but she had to believe it was borne from love. He worried about her, as a husband should his wife. Was it controlling to point out what was best for the person you loved? She had never liked any of her experimental hairstyles as much as her present one. Larry was right, it suited her, as did the clothes he helped her choose.

His issues with Nicky had been the hardest to accept but her friend had started the hostilities. Larry had put up with years of abuse and his wife putting her friend's needs before his, no wonder Ella taking a beating was the last straw.

All that said, Suzanne should not have to suffer for her mother's failings. It was unreasonable of him to expect Ella to freeze the girl out. Maybe she should have handled that disclosure differently. Was Suzanne worth losing her husband over?

Seeing the white handkerchief being waved through the doorway Ella was relieved. "Is it safe to come in?" Larry asked. Ella hope this meant, for once, she wouldn't have to choose.

Chapter 31
0820 hours, 08 October 2012

Thoughts of the previous evening's debate with Larry had dissipated as soon as Ella arrived at her desk. The will was now the only thing on her mind. Having convinced Larry the decision as to whether or not she should re-enter Suzanne's life should be left to her bosses, she was praying they would agree soon. She desperately wanted to be present when the girl was told Bradley's will had been discovered.

Not that it had, but hopefully it would be within the hour. The morning mail arrived at APC around nine am. Jules had promised to call Ella and Pete Waller as soon as she knew if Bradley's will was in his documents. Ella prayed Pete would call her as soon as he had spoken to Jules. She would need to be told officially before giving Joyce the good news. The next forty minutes were going to be the longest of Captain Harris's career.

0917 hours, 08 October 2012

Paul had no intention of spending another night in a shop doorway. Number thirty-three was his home; he had rights. He'd thought about enlisting the help of the police but wasn't sure they would be sympathetic to his plight. His sister certainly hadn't been.

Cindy had happily absorbed every gory detail of his eviction but once she'd surmised he'd lost his claim to Linda's future fortune she'd shown him the door. In an attempt to encourage her sympathy he had asked for a couple of blankets and a pillow. Annoyingly, his sister's ability to show compassion matched his own. Cindy had happily handed him a couple of her dog's old blankets and a travel pillow before closing the door in his face.

Well bollocks to Cindy. She had just made a monumental mistake. Even if Linda didn't take him back he could still lay claim to her money. The courts were bound to be suspicious of a spouse who threw her husband out when on the brink of inheriting a small fortune. Unfortunately, there was a slight technicality that could trip him up if he went down the legal route so he'd rather avoid that.

During his sleepless night he'd reviewed other options. There was a slim possibility he could convince Linda that Dave had orchestrated the whole event in order to appear her saviour.

However, there wasn't a hope in hell of his witch of a mother-in-law letting him close enough to regale that untruth.

Blackmail was another tool at his disposal. He was yet to figure out the finer details but was sure he could come up with something his wife would want to keep under wraps for a price or Joyce might make a better target for extortion. How much would she pay him to stay away? No, he was after a bigger pot than Joyce could provide, especially as Linda had reduced the twelve grand her mother had been gifted by buying unnecessary crap for the house.

He could use the letters. Linda would pay good money for those. That would definitely be a last resort. Once he'd admitting taking them all hope of returning home would be scuppered. Unfortunately, there was a snag with that option, technically he needed them in his possession to be able to sell them.

Looking out on to the estate, Paul quickly jumped out of the bush he'd been hiding in, stretched off his legs then returned to his vantage point. He had a perfect view of number thirty-three and the surrounding maisonettes. The few residents that worked had already left, Charlie and Dave included. Now he just had to wait for the stragglers returning from dropping their kids off at school. Most went back to bed so hopefully he would make it to number thirty-three without incident. It was a little risky; everyone on the estate would be aware of yesterday's shenanigans and probably relish the chance of warning Linda he was heading her way or telling him what a twat he was. If he was spotted, he could cope with the verbal attacks, it was unlikely any of the neighbours would try to physically stop him. As Charlie and Dave weren't around, the only person who might put up resistance could easily be removed.

0959 hours, 08 October 2012

Finding herself on the veranda floor, Joyce cursed herself for not checking the identity of the caller before opening the door. Rushing inside, Paul yelled he'd let her back in once he'd spoken to his wife. Jumping to her feet, Joyce pounded the door.

Linda ran from the kitchen. "What the bloody hell are you doing here?"

"We need to talk."

"No we don't. Get out!" she screamed.

"Not until you've heard me out. It wasn't me. They set me up. Honest, sexy I would never do anything to hurt you."

"Bollocks. I've spoken to Cath. She never said any of that shit you fed me and she saw you buying the booze."

"She's lying."

"Why would she do that?"

"She must be on their payroll."

"Don't be so stupid they haven't got any money to give her." Linda attempted to push past her husband. "I'm letting my mother in."

Paul held up the door key. "Not without this."

"Give it me."

Joyce opened the letterbox. "We've called the police. They're on their way."

Paul grabbed Linda's arm and dragged her upstairs. "Come with me," he demanded. "I need to get my stuff."

Pushing Linda into their bedroom he threw her onto the bed then grabbed a pile of carrier bags containing her latest purchases. Emptying the contents on the floor he started to fill the bags with his clothes. "Listen, I'll go now but we need to talk. I swear to you, sweetheart you can't trust any of them. You're not thinking straight because of the drugs but deep down you know I'm the only one that has ever looked out for you. They never gave a shit about you until Bradley's money came into play."

Linda was confused. Last night she had been sure of Paul's guilt but if he was telling the truth she'd be left to rot once they had Bradley's cash. "I don't know who to believe anymore," she wailed.

Sensing possible victory, Paul grabbed the bags and headed for Phil's room. "Me, that's who. I've never lied to you. They're just taking advantage while you're poorly."

Linda followed her husband. "I just don't understand, why?"

"I've told you, the money," Paul said, pulling his case from under Phil's bed.

1008 hours, 08 October 2012

Ella heard the commotion as soon as she left her car. Seeing Joyce banging on the door, she sprinted across the path then took the stairs two at a time. Spotting Ella hurtling up the veranda Joyce yelled out, "He's got her locked in. I didn't know it was him. He pulled me out of the house then locked the door."

Cath ran out of her maisonette. "The police are on their way. Not long now, love."

Reaching Joyce, Ella computed all she had heard then looked upwards. In her youth she had been a dab hand at using her parent's bedroom window as a means of entry when she'd forgotten her house keys. All the kids had. Fortunately, Linda had opted not to have the new double-glazing fitted and her window was currently on the latch. Ella turned to Cath, "Do you think you can take my weight?"

Cath smiled knowingly. "Of course I can, there's nothing on you, you skinny bitch."

Car keys in hand Ella placed her foot in the hand cradle Cath provided and allowed herself to be pushed upwards. Grabbing the ledge she pulled herself up. When she had first tackled the six-foot wall at Guildford she was pleased she'd mastered swinging her leg upon the sill beneath the window before starting her training. Scrambling on to the ledge, Ella listened. She could hear Linda yelling but thankfully the noise was not coming from her bedroom. Sliding her key against the latch the window swung open. Joyce quickly put her hand over Cath's mouth when she started to whoop.

Once inside, Ella edged towards Phil's room. Fortunately, Linda yelling was loud enough to drown out the sound of the creaking floorboard. Pushing the door ajar she saw Linda holding a bottle of wine. Ella's fear that Paul had managed to get Linda to drink again was dispelled by the abuse flying from his wife's mouth, "I'm guessing Dave put this in your case to frame you as well. You lying piece of shit."

Paul cowered as he snatched his case from the floor, unsuccessfully trying to close it. "I can't talk to you when you're like this," he whimpered. "Put the bottle down."

"Oh, you'd love that wouldn't you? If I poured it down my neck? Sorry but that's not going to happen." Linda unscrewed the bottle's lid and poured its contents all over Paul's bags of clothes.

"Don't do that you stupid bitch." He lurched towards her grabbing the bottle from her hand -for a split second Linda thought he would hit her with it. Thinking the same, Ella ran into the room, grabbed Paul's arm and hit it against the wall. As the bottle fell to the floor she placed a well-aimed knee in his groin, hitting her target with millimetre precision. As Paul fell to his knees, Ella pulled his arm behind his back.

"Get off me, you fucking bitch," Paul yelled.

"Not a hope. Where's the key tosspot?"

Linda bent down. "It's in his pocket, I'll get it."

Exerting pressure on Paul's arm, Ella pulled him to the left so Linda could retrieve the key.

"This isn't over," Paul told his wife. "I'm entitled to that money. I'm your husband."

"No you're not," Linda answered flippantly then looked at Ella, "I changed my name by deed poll. Only good thing to come out of this bloody illness is I couldn't get to the registry office."

"That doesn't matter, I'm your legal partner, and we've been together years. I'm still due my cut."

It was Ella's turn to smile. "I'm not sure that will be much. The reason I'm here is to tell you Bradley's will has been found. I've no idea who he has left his money to but I'm damn sure it won't be you."

"You're lying," Paul accused desperately.

"Of course I am, after all that's what everybody except you does isn't it?"

The police's announcement they were at the front door prompted Linda's departure. "Best let them in before they break it down," she squealed.

Yanking his arm further up his back, Ella pulled Paul to his feet. "You don't smell too great Mr Douglas. Rough night?"

"Slept in a fucking doorway because of you," Paul snarled.

"Now isn't that a shame? Still, hopefully you'll be more comfortable in the cells tonight."

"They've nothing on me. I'm entitled to enter my own house."

"Possibly, but assaulting a pensioner in order to do so and threatening your wife with a wine bottle are pretty serious charges, don't you think?"

Downstairs, Linda took a deep breath. "I'm trying," she whined. The police were getting agitated. She'd managed to place the key in the door but was struggling to turn it. Joyce's called to her, "It's okay love you can do this. Just turn the key then go back in the room. We won't open the door until you have."

Linda called on her son to give her strength. Opening the door she invited the police inside. Joyce quickly grabbed her arm and led a shaky but exuberant Linda into the living room.

Paul protested when the police cuffed him and led him downstairs, "Why the cuffs? I've done nothing wrong. It's a set up, I only came for my fucking suitcase."

"We can discuss that at the station." Paul was told.

"I need my case. At least let me take that," he begged.

"We don't do luggage," the officer informed him. "Maybe someone could drop it off at the station later?" he asked.

"Certainly. As long as everything in it belongs to him." Ella replied then turned to Paul and raised her eyebrow.

"You keep your fucking hands off it bitch. It's nothing to do with you!" Paul screamed.

As Paul Douglas protested all the way to the car the officer struggled to suppress their laughter. The things the man was calling the army officer would make Frankie Boyle blush.

1342 hours, 08 October 2012

Entering his new accommodation, Dinger took in his surroundings. He decided it was as good a place as any to die. Seven large cardboard boxes sat in the middle of the room. He only intended to open the one containing his uniform. The rest would be forwarded to his mother once the deed was done.

The envelope on his bed stopped Dinger in his tracks. It was definitely from Bradley, no one else would have the balls to refer to him as 'The Lancashire Lothario'.

Epilogue
27 May 2012

Promising his Company clerk that he would complete his will by the end of the day, Bradley rushed to his room and turned on his computer. As he had done many times since its receipt, he reviewed the document his lawyer had drafted on his behalf. As tempting as it was, signing it was not an option.

Before discovering he was about to become a father, Bradley had known exactly how he wished to distribute his assets. Suzanne was to receive the PAX insurance and compensation payments. To his family, he would leave the salon, any profits he had received since taking ownership and the ten years of interest that had been accrued on the money he had inherited from Monica. Given the hell the Pashley's had put the Craig's through, Bradley thought it fitting they were the ones to reap the rewards from his paternal grandmother's guilt money. The half a million she had bequeathed him would be returned to Richard Pashley. With luck, learning his wife had left the sum to his bastard grandchild would send his paternal grandfather to an early grave.

Suzanne's pregnancy had changed everything. If she decided a career in green was no longer an option, two hundred thousand pounds would not afford his child the life he hoped it to lead but how could he increase her inheritance without penalising his mother, brother and grandparents?

That wasn't his only concern. The prospect of having to redraft farewell letters was also playing on his mind. Impending fatherhood had already prompted the rewriting of Rick and Suzanne's letters plus the creation of two new ones for 'The Bump' and Dinger'.

Bradley had been compelled to write Dinger's letter the previous evening when he had decided, in his absence, he would want his offspring to have a strong male influence. Although he hoped Phil, Dave and Beetle would teach his child the compassion Dinger lacked, they were not ideal role models. All three were quiet, unassuming characters. Dinger on the other hand was confident, funny and feisty, traits he dreamed his son or daughter would emulate.

Bradley suspected few people would entrust their child's welfare to Dinger but for him he was the obvious choice. In many ways, Dinger was as much his soulmate as Suzanne. They shared the same humour, professionalism and zest for life so he was the perfect stand in. He was also fiercely loyal. Bradley took comfort knowing Dinger would give his own life to protect his child.

He was not only making Dinger Godfather, and leaving strict instructions about how he expected his friend to carry out the role, to benefit his child. Contemplating how he would feel had their roles been reversed he was aware, once Dinger returned from Afghanistan, he would need something to focus on other than Bradley's death.

Considering Dinger would have enough to contend with in the aftermath of his death, Bradley had decided not to pass his letter to the Padre. Instead he planned to sneak back into the accommodation on the day they deployed to push it under his friend's door so he could read it when he returned.

All his other farewell letters had been passed to the Padre. If he decided to amend any he would need to retrieve them.

In his grandparents' letter he had spoken of his desire for Charlie to retire early and to take Joyce on her dream holiday. He'd listed a few wine bars near the Vatican where his granddad could hang out whilst his grandma carried out her pilgrimage. The information had only been added to encourage the old man's laughter; he knew Charlie would hold his wife's hand throughout. The twelve thousand pounds ADT money would easily cover the cost of their trip but not Charlie's early retirement: To cover that he had set aside forty percent of the salon profits and inheritance interest. His confidence his grandparents would approve of the sum being redirected to their great grandchild would ease the pain of deleting that bequest. At their time of life a large sum of money would not make a huge difference, regrettably the same could not be said for Phil.

Of all his family, contemplating his brother's future caused the most anguish. Getting Lucy pregnant at fifteen had put an end to Phil's dreams of becoming a mechanic. Lucy's father was adamant Phil would join the family firm of carpet fitters. As his future father-in-law provided the roof over his head, Phil could not refuse.

Bradley had thought long and hard about how he might provide a better future for his brother's young family. Lucy had made no secret of her desire to become a hairdresser. Gifting the salon to Phil for five years would allow her to carry out her apprenticeship, guarantee her a job and provide childcare for Poppy. Bradley, Phil and their mother had all been brought up in the salon, the thought of Poppy continuing this family tradition was comforting. Lucy's income from the salon and Phil receiving all future profits should fund his apprenticeship as a mechanic. As for Lucy's dad's threat to make the lad homeless, Bradley had made provision for that. Phil's fifty percent cut of the salon's previous profits and interest on his inheritance should provide a decent deposit for a small house. The remaining ten percent would be set aside for Poppy to receive on her twenty first birthday.

In Phil's letter, he had mentioned the salon's ownership but not the deposit for the house. That meant, if he let Phil keep the salon, he could redirect the money to Suzanne without having to amend his correspondence. Bradley's hand hovered over the delete button reluctantly. If he pressed it what would become of the boy he had sworn to protect? Being controlled by an overbearing father-in-law whilst lugging around carpets that were heavier than him was not the life Bradley wanted for Phil. Maybe if he deleted the line about handing the salon to Linda in five years time that would ease his conscious.

That would mean changing his mother's letter in its entirety. Everything he had written related to her taking over ownership of the salon. Instead of money Bradley had left her an incentive. In five years time, on the proviso she was teetotal and had worked in the salon for a year, Hair Perfection would become hers, if not Phil would remain the proprietor.

The five years time line had been an educated guess. If his suspicions regarding his mother's panic attacks were correct, she needed to stop worrying about what others thought, stop drinking and stop Paul Douglas from dictating her every move. Recalling his mother's 'episodes' Bradley was convinced her fear of facing the gossips were their trigger. Paul obviously believed that too because whenever Bradley had attempted to coax his mother from their home his step father had repeated some cruel comment made by a neighbour then offer Linda a drink.

Although he had never breathed a word to anyone, Bradley suspected the cause of his mother's attacks was agoraphobia. He had researched the condition. Heartbreak, low self-esteem, alcohol and controlling husbands could all play their part. Though he could pinpoint his mother's downward spiral to his father's departure he fervently believed Paul had provided all the other contributing factors. His plan therefore was to get his mother sober enough to realise what an insignificant little man, Paul was. In order to do that he had to set her a goal, the salon seemed the perfect prize.

In his letter, Bradley claimed people often remarked about his mother's hairdressing skills and commented on how she had been the best stylist in town. They remembered him from the salon and what a good mother Linda had been. Lastly, and purely to play to his mother's vanity, he stated that they often said how nice it would be to see her pretty face again.

Without alluding to his suspicions regarding her condition he'd stressed he believed if she gave up the alcohol she would return to the beautiful, confident, capable woman he remembered from his childhood and to the place they were both happiest.

He prayed his words would give his mother the incentive she needed to rid herself of her demons. Including Paul Douglas. Fortunately, she would not need a divorce to finalise his dismissal. During one of his mother's more lucid moments, and without the ever-present Paul hovering, Linda had confirmed Bradley's suspicion that they had never married.

The thought of his family's grief made Bradley feel extremely guilty. When signing on the dotted line he had accepted by doing so he might reduce the time he spent in their lives but they had signed up to no such thing. His desire to be a soldier would cause them irreparable damage but hopefully having his child around would soften the blow his death would deliver.

He guessed of all his family members his father would suffer the most. Since their reunion, on his tenth birthday, Rick had overcompensated for his absence. His constant appeals for forgiveness troubled Bradley, especially as he considered his father blameless regarding the events that had taken him away.

In his letter to Rick, Bradley had asked him to look after Suzanne and the baby and to play an active part in the child's life. He was not to feel guilty if he could only manage annual visits as long as the child knew it was loved, that would be enough. Bradley then begged Rick to stop punishing himself for his father's trespasses. Richard Pashley was to blame for the distance between them.

It occurred to Bradley that the only person he had ever truly hated was a man he'd never met. Even the thought of Paul Douglas didn't evoke the hatred he felt towards his paternal grandfather. The arrogant arsehole had brought about the downfall of his mother, bullied his father, belittled his beloved grandparents and broken his other grandmother's heart by not allowing her access to her grandson. He was evil personified. Even so, would returning Monica's money satisfy his need for revenge? Telling the old bastard he'd happily survived without the Pashley's intervention might have stung the belligerent old fart but informing him that the money had been gifted to the people he had been determined to keep it from would surely be a better way of exacting his need for revenge.

His decision finally made, Bradley was pleased he had requested an electronic copy of his will. Given the tight timeframe, he would make the necessary amendments then pass it to the clerks to dispatch to APC, it was as safe there as anywhere.

Now all he had to do was redistribute Monica's fortune. His grandparents and brother would receive one hundred thousand pounds each. His niece, Poppy, would get thirty thousand pounds on her twenty-first birthday.

In a moment of madness Bradley decided his best friends, Mr Howard Jackson and Mr Jason Bell, should each receive ten thousands pounds. His reason for this gesture was the knowledge they always had more days than money left at the end of the month.

Changing Richard Pashley's bequest to a bottle of Bunnahabhain 25 whiskey and a copy of his will caused Bradley to laugh out loud. 'Stick that in your pipe Grandpappa' he thought.

His unborn child would receive the remaining two and fifty hundred thousand pounds on his or her twenty-first birthday. Rick would be the trustee and could, if he felt it necessary, release the funds earlier. He felt this clause necessary in case Suzanne struggled. Not that she should, she would receive the interest on his inheritance, the salon's last two years profits, the PAX insurance and compensation payment.

The thought of Suzanne killed his earlier euphoria. No amount of money or career options would heal her wounds. His gorgeous, fragile yet feisty girl had already suffered enough without having to bring up his baby alone. His baby? She was the only one tortured by that question. When she had first raised the

251

possibility that her one night stand could have resulted in her pregnancy, Bradley had quickly rejected her notion. The thought wasn't implausible but it was unnecessary. The biology of the child's creation was of no concern. Bradley would be its father even if they did not carry the same genes. As the identity of the baby's mother was not in doubt how could he not adore it?

Suzanne's protestations, he could not be expected to bring up another man's child, had been quelled by Bradley's observation that the father he hoped to emulate was Dave and not Sid. As always the mention of Suzanne's biological father silenced her.

One last read through and Bradley was satisfied. He wondered why he hadn't thought of this sooner. He didn't need to be dead to share his wealth or get his mother back on track. As soon as he turned twenty-one he would put a large deposit on a house for Phil then sign the salon over to him. He would tell Linda what she needed to do if she wanted to take it over and give his grandparents the money they were long overdue. He would also make it his mission to extract Paul Douglas from their lives. He should've kick the lout out years ago. As for his Richard Senior's whiskey, he might just deliver that in person.

Bradley was grateful he had needed to rewrite his will. Not that it would ever be read. Nothing was going to happen to him. He had too much to live for.

Acknowledgements

Firstly I would like to thank my friends and family for their never ending support, especially my husband Ian who has accepted it is unlikely I will ever return to the ranks of the employed and my mother Carole Drummond who embraced my instructions to be as critical as possible when test reading this book.

Credit must also go to the wonderful lionesses of the WRAC/ATS who supported my first novel 'Too Good to be Forgotten' and demanded a sequel. Many I had not met through my Army career but that did not stop them rallying around. A special mention must go to the following ladies:

 - Cathy Munro MBE who created the book's website, test read the sequel and gave me a severe talking to when I suffered with self-doubt.

- Alison Slater who promoted the book at every opportunity and would make an excellent PR guru.

- Lisa Barnes who carried out the final proofread of this novel. For any new authors in need of help, guidance and an expert eye I suggest you contact her at lisa.barnes@outlook.com.

- My dearest friend, Deb McEwan who once again read, critiqued and offered sound advice throughout the writing process.

Once again I must thank my neighbour and friend Brian Cullion for his photographical prowess and patience when creating the front cover.

Lastly an extra-special thanks must go to Alison and Stewart Fleming who graciously agreed to their son, Lance Corporal Jamie Fleming's photograph being featured on the cover of this book.

Writing this book has brought so many new and special people into my life and for that I am truly grateful.

Final Note:

Thank you for reading my book. If you'd like to be notified when the third book in the Lest we Forget series is published, please email me at rachelcrawford100@gmail.com and I'll inform you when it is available or visit the Too Good to Be Forgotten Facebook site for regular updates. I would also appreciate it if you could take the time to review the book on Amazon or Goodreads.

Made in the USA
Charleston, SC
24 September 2015